It was Pete who found Annabel Bates lying on the floor of the porch.

She lay on her side, clutching her purse to her chest as if to ward off the pain. . . . There was something so frozen-looking about her that Pete knew before he touched her. Annabel was dead.

Connie knew, too. Pete could tell by the way she stopped in her tracks behind him, by the way she shouted Annabel's name, but even Connie couldn't wake the dead. "I knew it!" she said. "I *knew* it! Clara said she was worse, she said she'd had two attacks this week, she . . ."

Only after Connie had spoken her name did they remember about Clara.

"I'll check on her."

They went inside, Connie to check on Clara, Pete to phone Hardy Rogers, but Pete was soon in Clara's room.

Connie had again pulled the straight-backed chair next to the bed and sat in her usual pose, holding Clara's hand.

"Clara, I'm—" Clara didn't move. Pete turned around and looked at Connie. Connie didn't move either. The only difference between the two women was that Connie still breathed. . . .

Books by Sally Gunning

Hot Water
Under Water
Ice Water
Troubled Water

Published by POCKET BOOKS

A PETER BARTHOLOMEW MYSTERY

TROUBLED WATER

SALLY GUNNING

POCKET BOOKS

New York   London   Toronto   Sydney   Tokyo   Singapore

This book is a work of fiction. Names, characters, places and incidents are either products of the author's imagination or are used fictitiously. Any resemblance to actual events or locales or persons, living or dead, is entirely coincidental.

An *Original* Publication of POCKET BOOKS

 POCKET BOOKS, a division of Simon & Schuster Inc.
1230 Avenue of the Americas, New York, NY 10020

ISBN: 0-671-76006-8

First Pocket Books printing December 1993

10 9 8 7 6 5 4 3 2 1

POCKET and colophon are registered trademarks of Simon & Schuster Inc.

Cover art by Jeffrey Adams

Printed in the U.S.A.

Dedication

For my favorite gardener, my mother,
whose loving care of her family
inspired much of this book

Acknowledgments

Many thanks to Dr. William Whitelaw for allowing me to pick his brains and tap his imagination wherever it's been medically necessary. Thanks also to Marilyn Whitelaw for reminding me I'd locked all the doors, and to attorney Richard Perry for guiding me through the legalities, with my apologies if I've created any errors from his facts.

To my sister, Jan Carlson, my heartfelt gratitude for continuing to buy my books as fast as her dog eats them, and for all those other tidbits of support and encouragement that have kept me going from the start. And for Tom, as always, love and thanks for wading through this with me once again, *without* waders.

TROUBLED WATER

Chapter

1

Peter Bartholomew stood in the middle of the Bates sisters'
dilapidated flower garden and looked down at the old
woman as she struggled with a recalcitrant root.

"I don't know, Annabel. The attic I can handle. The
mowing and the raking, and the trips to the dump. But
this—" Pete felt momentarily guilty of false advertising. He
did, after all, name his odd-job company Factotum—
person employed to do *all* kinds of work. And how was the
eighty-two-year-old Annabel, who suffered from angina and
arthritis and God only knew what else, going to do all this
shoveling and edging and digging up of plants? But in
addition to these chores, Annabel also wanted Pete to do
things like prune winterkill and transplant delphiniums.
Pete didn't even know what a delphinium *was*.

Annabel straightened up and sighed. "I know," she said.
"It seems quite the task, doesn't it? And I honestly don't
know that I'd bother if it weren't for Clara, but she's been so

down of late. She's confined to her bed completely now, but she can see the garden from her bedroom window, and it must depress her so. This really was *her* garden, you know."

Yes, Pete knew. In the days when Annabel's sister Clara had been up and running, Factotum had been there, too. Pete had done his share of grunt work in the garden but it had been his employee and then wife, Connie, who had worked with Clara in making the garden the true showplace it had been.

But a lot had changed since then, thought Pete, as he looked out over the brown stems, ragged edges, and cracked earth that had once been Clara's glorious flower beds. Now the ornamental pool was full of scummy water and sodden black leaves, the gazing globe was fogged with dirt, Clara was an invalid, Annabel was three years older, and Connie had run away with another man.

"If only Connie were here," sighed Annabel, as if she'd read Pete's mind, but then she seemed to recollect herself. "Pete. Forgive me." She placed a gentle hand on his arm. "I was only thinking that Connie could set this garden to rights in no time. And we all worked so well together here, didn't we? We were happy out in this garden, weren't we, you and Connie, Clara and I . . ."

It was like the moment in the cartoon when the light bulb appears over the character's head. The leathery crinkles at the corners of Annabel's eyes deepened, and the pale gray eyes began to glow, to scheme.

Because, after all, Connie *was* here. No matter that Pete had divorced her, no matter that she'd had to run a gauntlet of eight hundred or so raised island eyebrows, a year after she'd left—Connie had come back to the island of Nashtoba, alone.

"Now, Pete, I wouldn't for one minute want you to think that I'm suggesting—"

"No. Oh no." As if the whole island hadn't been *suggesting* for a whole year now.

"Or that I for one single little minute would attempt to *butt in—*"

"Of course not, Annabel. You? Butt in?"

"But the thought did occur to me, since she *is* here—"

"Annabel—"

"And you *are* short of help, as you were saying earlier—"

"Annabel. Wait a minute here."

"And Connie worked at Factotum before. She worked in this *garden* before. It certainly does seem fortuitous that—"

"Annabel. I'm not crazy enough to hire my ex-*wife.*"

Annabel stopped walking and peered up at him. "Why, of *course* you are, Pete."

Yes, thought Pete, two days later, back in Clara's garden. Annabel was right. Connie *is* happy here. *We* were happy here. But even if I'm crazy enough to offer Connie a job, she's not crazy enough to take it. It had been hard enough getting her to the Bates house at all, but finally she'd agreed to visit the sisters and offer a consult, at least. Pete watched her long legs straddle a mess of dry leaves so she could peer more closely at some green shoots underneath.

"Here come the Siberian iris!" she called to Annabel as if she'd found an old friend. "And a tulip the rabbits missed! And the daffodils, Annabel—they don't mind a little neglect, do they?"

Apparently not. The slope was covered with them.

"And no matter what happens to the rest of the garden, wait till that field of daylilies blooms!" Connie straightened up and beamed.

At Pete.

It was like some ancient kind of earth magic. Suddenly Pete saw not this May day with its indistinguishable green spears and brown rot and gray chill, but a July from years ago. There were flowers everywhere: tall blue pyramids, waving white lace, splashy pinks and purples and yellows, neat red and white borders along the ground, and that field full of orange lilies. There was hot sun, and Pete and Connie leaning comfortably against each other as they took turns drinking from the hose.

Would they ever be that comfortable, that companionable, again? Although some confusion remained in Pete's mind about what had gone wrong *before* Connie left, he had a pretty good idea what had gone wrong since she'd come back. You couldn't jump back into things in the middle of the lust stage—not when you still had a whole lot of anger on board. Of course somewhere in the back of Pete's common sense he knew that *hiring* your ex-wife wasn't the way to do things either, but for the moment it was the best he could do.

They went inside to talk to Clara.

Annabel had moved Clara downstairs into the dining room once she could no longer manage climbing the stairs. The bed sat facing the window in the middle of the room, an antique rolltop desk immediately at hand to the left of it, a bedside table with a book, a lamp, and an old windup alarm clock to the right.

Clara Bates was the older sister. Where Annabel was tall, tan, and sinewy Clara was pale, small, soft. At least, she seemed so among all the pillows and white sheets. Connie had pulled her straight-backed chair close to the bed and held Clara's hand in hers. Several years ago this had been a familiar sight—the two heads together, one silver, one gold, the two pairs of eyes alight.

"Blue ageratum," Clara said now. "Wouldn't you suppose? With the white impatiens and the red nasturtiums?"

"Blue ageratum, of course! And in the perennial bed? The asters again?"

Clara Bates shook her head. "They take over everything. And those iris are sadly in need of dividing."

Connie waved a hand behind her. "Oh, Pete can take care of that."

Clara Bates beamed at Pete as if Connie's taking him for granted this way was a major step forward, which, actually, it probably was. Pete should have been used to this by now, the whole island scheming behind his back, *and* in front of his face, to reunite them, but he couldn't help wondering why they seemed so convinced of their own success. Weren't there plenty of relationships that were unfixable? Weren't there plenty of marriages that just plain weren't worth the work?

Pete looked at Connie again, this time with a more dispassionate eye. She was perched on the very edge of her chair, her body and face in motion along with her words, as if with her own vitality she could will Clara back to life. If Connie returned to Pete, she'd either bring *him* back to life or kill him. It was a fifty-fifty shot. What the hell, thought Pete. Either way, it would be worth it.

"So do you want the job?" he asked her. "Weekends and what afternoons you can while you're still teaching, full-time once summer is here?"

Connie bent down to pick something up from the floor. When she righted herself her face was bright red, either from being upside down or from the absurdity of the proposition. "I'm not that crazy," she said.

"Why, of *course* you are, dear," said Annabel from the door.

Pete showed up at the Bates house every spare minute he could find, but it was clearly now Connie's, and Clara's, garden. Almost every day after school Connie managed to find an hour or two to spend there—if not actually in the garden, then at least scheming and planning for it with Clara. Annabel tried to help, of course, but she got chest pain with very little exertion now, and they tried to keep her out of it. When Pete showed up on the weekend there was a list of chores waiting for him, but no matter how much sweat and grime he applied, Connie and Clara seemed to add to the list faster than he could detract from it. But Pete didn't mind. There was an old twinkle back in Clara's eyes, and a pleased-to-bursting look to Annabel. And Connie? Pete had to admit it was awkward at first. They sidled around each other, constantly on the lookout for those old landmines of trouble, but maybe they had finally learned, or grown, or grown *up*. Or maybe it *was* some kind of ancient earth magic in the garden, reminding them that they could be happy, that they *had* been happy once before.

It was the second Saturday in June. Pete walked along the beach on his way from Factotum to the Bates house, listening to Connie add page two to a long page one of chores. Or at least he tried to listen. Pete was feeling lazy. He could feel the sun on his neck, and on Nashtoba, sunshine in June was not something to take for granted. Sunshine in June was something to soak up, something to play hookie over, something to blow off work about.

Unfortunately, Connie didn't seem to be getting the point.

"Come on," she called from three paces ahead. "We're late. We've got to stake the delphiniums today, and we've still got a load of annuals to get into the ground."

"Delphiniums *again?*" It seemed to Pete that these delphiniums were a lot more trouble than they were worth. "What do you say we stake up the delphiniums tomorrow? I could go back for a blanket, a couple of beers, some cheese—"

"And what's Clara going to say? I told her we'd be there bright and early this morning and here it is almost noon. Besides, Annabel is counting on you to go to the dump. She's been spring cleaning. The trash barrels are full."

Pete looked out to sea and sighed. The ocean was pond still and whisper quiet. Even the water was lazy today, but not Connie. Not Annabel. So maybe Connie was right, maybe this was no time for a picnic, but if Pete had learned anything over the past year or two it was that sometimes being right was not the last word on the subject.

"Tonight, then. We could quit a little early, before it gets too cold."

"Sure," said Connie, but Pete didn't fall for it. He knew that if he couldn't divert Connie *before* they arrived, he'd never succeed at dragging her away from the garden once they got there.

He gave the water a last lingering look as they left the beach for the path to the Bates house, and turned his mind to the prospect ahead. "Let's try to keep Annabel away from

6

the wheelbarrow, all right? She's not supposed to lift heavy things."

"I keep telling her that. She shouldn't do half the things she does! I don't know how she handles Clara all alone. I know it worries Clara. She said Annabel had two attacks of angina just this week."

"What about that great-niece? What's her name?"

Connie snorted. "Paula Steigler. Don't hold your breath waiting for *her*."

"So maybe it's time Annabel gave up."

"Gave up taking care of Clara?" Connie's face clouded and her step slowed.

Nursing home, thought Pete. She's thinking nursing home. But if she was, she thought it only briefly. Soon she was back in stride and talking about, yes, delphiniums.

"Maybe we should cut the delphiniums right back. They'd go again in August that way. The painted daisies, too. We need things that will come up later on, like the daylilies. It gives Clara something to look forward to, you know?"

Something to look forward to. Yes, along with the first sun, there was that in the day as well. Suddenly Pete felt like they *might* have something to look forward to, and just as suddenly, he didn't feel lazy anymore.

"Race you." He sprinted ahead of her up the path.

Connie ran fast, but Pete's legs were a hair longer and a lot stronger. Besides, he'd cheated off the start.

He won.

Or lost.

It was Pete who found Annabel Bates's body on the porch.

She lay on her side, clutching her purse to her chest as if to ward off the pain. An unopened bottle of pills seemed to have rolled just out of her reach, and there was something so frozen-looking about her that Pete knew before he touched her. Annabel was dead.

Connie knew, too. Pete could tell by the way she stopped in her tracks behind him, by the way she shouted Annabel's name, but even Connie couldn't wake the dead. "I knew it!"

she said. "I *knew* it! Clara said she was worse, she said she'd had two attacks of angina this week, she . . ."

Clara.

Only after Connie had spoken her name did they remember about Clara.

They went inside, Connie to check on Clara, Pete to phone Hardy Rogers.

Hardiman Rogers was Nashtoba's only doctor and therefore the man to call if you were sick or injured. He was also the medical examiner, which made him the man to call if you were dead. Pete supposed there might be the occasional gray area where it would prove handy to have both functions provided by one man, but he didn't think Annabel Bates was one of those gray areas. Still, Pete pretended that the call to Hardy was urgent. It allowed him to postpone the realization that Annabel was dead, it allowed Connie time to break the news to Clara. If Clara had to hear the news, Pete knew Connie was the one she'd want to hear it from. But Hardy Rogers came on the line fast and left it faster, and no matter how slowly he walked, Pete was soon in Clara's room.

Connie had again pulled the straight-backed chair next to the bed and sat in her usual pose, holding Clara's hand. Clara's face was pale, her eyes closed. Pete moved two steps closer to the bed and leaned over.

"Clara, I'm—" Clara didn't move. Pete turned around and looked at Connie. Connie didn't move, either. Pete leaned closer. The only difference between the two women was that Connie still breathed.

Pete stepped back, stunned. "Not Clara, too?"

Connie didn't speak. Pete gently removed Clara's hand from Connie's and felt for a pulse, but he didn't find one. He laid Clara's hand on the bed cover, but Connie picked it up again.

"She's dead," said Pete. As hard as it was for *him* to believe, there was something about Connie that made him feel he had to explain it to *her*.

Still Connie said nothing.

There were footsteps on the porch. Pete went out to meet the doctor.

Hardiman Rogers had a physique as impressive as his name. Tall and bony, with a head of wild white Mark Twain hair and eyebrows that clashed like thunderclouds over burning blue eyes, he caused a tremor of terror in those who didn't know him and great waves of relief in those who did. For the latter group, "Hardiman Rogers" had become just plain "Hardy" long ago.

"Thank God you're here," said Pete.

"I'd like to know what God's got to do with it," Hardy snapped back. He was always cranky when one of his patients died, almost as if they'd done it to spite him, or done it *in* spite of him. He kneeled on one knee beside Annabel, looking at her without touching her, and said "heart."

"I found these pills." Pete pointed to the bottle on the floor.

Hardy picked it up. "Nitroglycerin. One under the tongue would have stopped the chest pain, saved her life." He tossed the bottle down. "Damned childproof caps." He set about examining Annabel. "Died of a coronary. Rigor's just retreating in the face. Been dead at least since yesterday, I'd say. When'd you see her last?"

"Last weekend. But Connie saw her on—" Pete thought. This was Saturday. It was the last week of school and Connie had had two days of teachers' meetings Thursday and Friday, but he knew she'd been out here the day before that. "Connie saw her Wednesday afternoon."

Hardy nodded. "How's Clara holding up?"

"Not so hot."

Hardy looked up. Pete pointed through Clara's open door to where Connie still sat, leaning over the bed.

"She's dead, too."

Hardy's eyebrows flew high and wide. He scrambled off the porch floor and strode into the bedroom, brushing Connie aside. When he finished examining Clara he sat down on the foot of the bed and glared at the dead woman.

9

"Pulmonary edema. She hasn't been dead long, not nearly as long as Annabel."

"Pulmonary what?"

"Edema. Heart failure. When Annabel didn't come back she probably missed a few doses of her furosemide, her digoxin. Her lungs filled with fluid and she died."

Connie made a strange noise beside Pete. "Her lungs . . . filled? You mean she . . . she drowned?"

Hardy gave Connie a good long scrutiny. He cut back a decibel or two when he answered.

"You might say that. Drowned from inside. But it's not such a bad way to go. You don't have to be sorry for Clara."

Connie looked back at the bed.

Hardy sat at the kitchen table and filled out the death certificates in silence. When he stood up to go Pete walked out with him, but when they hit the porch Pete wasn't able to walk past Annabel as if she weren't there. He looked down. It was too hard to face up to the whole, Annabel, dead, so Pete found himself concentrating on the parts.

"Those marks—" Pete pointed at bruiselike blotches on Annabel's upper arm and leg.

Hardy ignored him. "You can handle the rest of this? Call the funeral home? Get hold of that niece?"

But Pete was still concentrating on the blotches. He'd seen them before. And several years ago Factotum had been hired by a medical student to do some research, and in the course of the job Pete had learned a few things that had stuck with him. Sort of. "Hypostasis, isn't it? The blood pools after death and leaves blotches like that?"

"So you've learned a new word. Here." Hardy handed Pete the two death certificates. "Call the funeral home. Give these to Blackout Bernie when he comes." Blackout Bernie was the funeral director, so called because of his habit of showing up everywhere, even at the beach, completely in black. "And call that niece."

Hardy left.

Pete went back inside. Connie was still sitting in Clara's

room, once again holding Clara's hand. She was starting to make Pete nervous.

"Why don't you go home? I'll get hold of Paula Steigler."

"I can't go home. I have to plant those flowers."

Pete couldn't see any point in telling her that nobody would care if the flowers went in now or not.

Connie went outside.

Pete looked through the Bateses' personal phone and address book on the table by the phone. Paula Steigler's number wasn't entered under S. It wasn't listed under P. Pete thought of his mother's filing system and checked under N for niece, even G for great-niece, but it was in neither of those places. Odd. He'd have to call Directory Assistance. But where did Paula live? Pete didn't have a clue, and he didn't think Directory Assistance was much help in those circumstances. He went outside to find Connie, who was sitting cross-legged on the ground with a trowel in one hand and a small green plant in the other, jabbing at the dirt.

"Do you know where Paula Steigler lives?"

"No," said Connie, without looking up. She continued her digging—a hole the size of a cesspool for a plant the size of a corsage.

Pete went back inside. The desk. Maybe the sisters never phoned Paula, but wrote to her instead. Maybe a return letter from Paula would be in that desk. Pete went back into Clara's room and over to the desk.

It felt pretty strange to be in the same room with the dead Clara. Actually, it felt pretty horrible. "Excuse me, Clara," Pete said to the bed, and then he sat down at the desk and began to rifle the drawers.

Everything in the desk was dust free and neatly arranged, and Pete suspected Annabel had included this desk in her spring cleaning chores. He found bills, receipts, check registers, insurance policies, all neatly grouped, but few pieces of personal mail, and none from Paula. The bottom right-hand drawer was locked, but in typical Nashtoba fashion the key to it was in the unlocked center drawer. Pete

11

unlocked the bottom drawer and withdrew a sheaf of envelopes. One was longer and stiffer than the others. He fished it out. It was labeled WILLS, in Annabel's own no-nonsense hand. It wasn't what Pete had been looking for, but if he couldn't find Paula Steigler, the wills might include instructions for the funeral home, at least.

Pete opened the envelope. The wills were dated a month ago. Annabel's will left everything to her sister, but named their next-door neighbor, Simon Cole, as executor, with complete powers over the property. If Clara predeceased Annabel, the great-niece Paula would inherit and serve as executrix. There were no instructions about funerals.

Not expecting to find anything much different in Clara's, Pete read it anyway.

Then he read it again.

As with Annabel's will, Clara's left everything to her sister, but if her sister predeceased her, which, according to Hardy, was indeed the case, it was not Paula Steigler who benefited.

Pete returned to the garden and handed the will to Connie.

"What." She tried to wave the paper away, deep into her second cesspool now. Pete straightened it out in front of her and pointed to the last sentence. "In the event that my sister does not survive me I leave all my property to Connie Bartholomew, the keeper of the gardens, with thanks for the help with the definitions."

Connie stopped digging and stared at Pete, her face full of things she didn't let people see too often, things that Pete had to struggle to put in place. What was this? Shock? Pain? *Fear?*

Suddenly something seemed to have happened to the sun. It felt sticky on his skin, and out of place.

12

Chapter

2

"Baloney," said Connie finally. She batted the paper aside and jammed a plant that looked too fragile to withstand her feelings, let alone her fingers, into the dirt.

"It's probably not baloney. What does this mean—'with thanks for the help with the definitions'?"

"You're asking me? I have no idea. It's all baloney. You call Paula Steigler. She'll tell you it's baloney."

"I can't *find* Paula Steigler. All evidence seems to indicate that Paula Steigler did not figure prominently in the lives of her aunts."

"All *what* evidence? And how do you know that thing's even legal?"

Pete looked over the paper in his hand. "It looks legal to me. There are two witnesses. One of them is Sarah Abrew." Sarah Abrew was an old friend, old in both senses. She had signed her name slightly querulously but in heavy black ink. The other witness was the mailman, Warren Johnson.

Warren the Worrier. He was a small, quiet, middle-aged
bachelor who was compulsively efficient, but no matter how
well he did his job he seemed bent on worrying over how it
might have been done better. His forehead was constantly
crumpled in a frown. Anyone who worried as much as
Warren was certainly a credible witness. "I wouldn't brush
this off so lightly," Pete told Connie, and backed up in
surprise when she jumped to her feet, hollering. Pete was
used to Connie hollering—he just hadn't expected her to do
it right *then*.

"Baloney! I told you it's baloney! Clara has a *relation*. A
niece. Why would she leave *me* anything? I don't want to
talk about this anymore."

Pete stared at Connie. What was going on here? "It isn't
the end of the world to have someone leave you a house."

"You don't leave houses to total strangers."

"Wait a minute, here. You're not a total stranger. You
spent *years* here. You were *friends* with Clara."

Connie didn't seem to know what to say to that. She
changed the subject. "If you don't have anything better to do
than stand here, you can fix that outside faucet. It leaks. I
have to turn it off from inside the basement every time. Now
stop bothering me. I have to finish this." She bent down to
pick up a plant, but stopped halfway up. "I don't though, do
I? I don't have to finish this."

"Why not? It's yours."

Connie stared at Pete. She scooped up Clara's tools and
carried them to the bulkhead door. She disappeared inside,
then reappeared empty-handed. She closed the doors and
snapped the rusty padlock shut. It was probably the first
time that lock had been locked in twenty years. There was
something ominous about it. Connie about-faced for the
beach path.

"Hey!" Pete hollered after her, but there wasn't much he
could do. He couldn't leave without first reaching Paula,
contacting the funeral home. He didn't exactly want to ask
Connie to hang around with two dead women still inside.

"I'll be by later!" he called after her, but either she didn't hear him or she just plain didn't want to answer him.

Pete went back inside.

After about a hundred phone calls he finally tracked down Paula Steigler on Cape Hook, the mainland peninsula from which the island of Nashtoba had sprung. Nowadays a long wooden causeway connected the two—at least, it connected the two unless there was a good northeaster or a moon tide. Pete had always suspected Nashtoba's telephone cables were wound around the causeway's unstable pilings—when Paula Steigler finally came on the long-distance line she sounded froggy and faint, and that was before he told her about her aunts.

After that, she sounded much better.

Paula lived in Bradford, the "capital" of the Hook, forty-five minutes away. Pete felt it only right that he offer to wait there for her, that he offer to call the funeral home, and both offers were accepted. Pete made his call and then decided to wait outside for the hearse, away from the peaceful-looking Clara, the bruised-looking Annabel. He stayed out in the garden until Blackout Bernie's hearse had pulled away with its double load inside.

Pete was still in the garden when Paula Steigler drove up to the house in a plum-colored Saab. She looked like one of the up-and-coming generation who had migrated to Bradford to make a fortune: stiff clothes, stiff smile, stiff dark hair. Pete had been looked over by a few women in his day, but he had never had the faintest idea what they meant when they did it. With Paula Steigler he didn't have that problem. She started at the rubber caps on his basketball sneakers and traveled up the jeans and over the T-shirt to his face, stopping at the cowlick that usually sprung up about this time of day. She pursed her lips as she pondered what use she was going to be able to make of him. Pete didn't much like getting the once-over as if he were a piece of meat. He also didn't much like being made use of. Still, he held out his hand.

"Peter Bartholomew. Factotum. We were hired by your aunts to do some gardening, make some trips to the dump. When we got here today they were dead. I'm sorry I had to break this news by phone."

"Factotum. Yes. I'll be able to use you, I'm sure. I imagine there will be quite a *few* trips to the dump."

Pete figured there were more appropriate things Paula could have said than that.

She began to circle the living room the way the vultures circle the dead cows in the movies. "Although I suppose there are a few things here it might be worth my time to sell." She fingered an antique whatnot in the corner. She began to fiddle with the custard cup full of paper clips and rubber bands and neat bits of string that Annabel had so carefully saved. She smiled at Pete. It was a smile that she might have used on a hotel bellboy just as well.

"Gee," said Pete. "Sorry. My schedule's full up this spring. I gave the death certificates to the funeral home when they picked up Clara and Annabel. Let me know if you need any other information."

Paula Steigler tipped out the custard cup, pawing through and dismissing its contents. "Very well. I'm sure the contractors can arrange these little details."

"Contractors?"

"Contractors. This house will be coming down. I'm putting a road through the gardens. That field out back holds six house lots and I plan to develop them." She turned her back on Pete, dismissing him much the same way she had dismissed the custard cup.

Pete went out to the truck. He stood there a minute, looking at the neat Victorian house, the revitalized gardens.

This house will be coming down. I'm putting a road through the gardens.

Poor Connie, thought Pete.

Then he remembered.

He went back inside.

"Gee," he apologized. "I almost forgot." He unfolded the long envelope from his back jeans pocket. "I found this in

16

that desk. According to the medical examiner, Annabel died first."

Paula Steigler ripped the envelope open. The stylish eyebrows drew together as the eyes beneath them darted back and forth over the first page. Annabel's. They moved on to the second page. Clara's. Pete could tell when her eyes reached the last line by the fury that filled them. It was the first real emotion he'd seen in those eyes all day.

"Connie Bartholomew? *Bartholomew?* I take it this is some relative of *yours?*"

"Not anymore." The minute Pete said it he was sorry, it sounded so disloyal, but Paula Steigler didn't seem to notice.

"And what's this garden business? This definition?"

"She took care of the garden."

"She took care of the garden. That's *it?*"

"No, that wasn't it."

"I'm asking you what this . . . this Connie Bartholomew . . . ever did for my aunts."

Pete mulled that over. "She liked them," he said.

"She *liked* them!"

He had been wrong about Paula's face before. This was fury.

"She *liked* them? And this is goods received? This *liking?* For this she gets *what? My* house? *My* land? You think this *liking* will stand up in court? *Don't bet on it!*" She threw the wills on the floor and blew out the door.

Pete picked up the wills. Then he returned to Annabel's desk, scooped the paper clips, rubber bands, and odds and ends into the custard cup, and carried them with him. It wasn't until he was closing the front door that Pete noticed the ring of keys dangling from the lock. Like the rest of Nashtoba the Bates sisters never locked their house, and the lock was stiff when Pete turned it. He wasn't even sure why he turned it, but he continued around to the back of the house and locked that door, too, taking the keys with him.

Pete returned to his truck, carrying the custard cup. He looked once more at the Bates sisters' house, remembering what he had just attempted to explain to Paula Steigler about Connie. *She liked them.*

Well, Pete had liked them, too, and if there was one thing Factotum had taught him it was that sometimes the simplest chores were the most meaningful after all.

Pete walked around to the back of the house, collected the full trash barrels, loaded them into the truck, and took them to the dump, his last gift to Clara and Annabel.

Connie lived in two rooms that were once the Coolidges' garage. Actually, she lived in two rooms that were once the *top* of the Coolidges' garage—the garage was still there, underneath. Connie met Pete at the bottom of the flight of stairs leading to her rooms, and Pete knew after one look at her that she'd been crying; the bones and planes of her face, usually so clearly defined, seemed smudged, dissolved. Connie seldom cried and the sight of her rattled him into bluntness.

"I spoke with Paula Steigler. She says she's going to fight you for the place."

Connie led Pete upstairs. "Why shouldn't she? By rights it's hers."

"By what rights? There aren't any rights. The house was Clara's—she could do what she wanted with it."

"Paula Steigler is their only relative. Annabel left it to her."

"And Clara didn't."

At the top of the stairs Connie whirled around. "And Clara didn't! Why? That's what I want to know. She didn't know what the hell she was doing. What was all that about the definitions? It makes no sense!"

"Are you sure? Maybe if you think about it—"

"Think about *what,* for chrissake? Definitions!"

"Whatever she meant by 'the definitions,' it's clear she didn't mean for Paula to have her house, and I can see why. Paula walked in there today acting like she already owned the place. She's taking everything to the dump. She—"

"So take it to the dump. Who's left to care?"

"You are. You've worked hard on that place. Annabel and Clara loved that place. Do you know what Paula's plans are? To tear down the house, put a road through the gardens, and build six houses out back."

Connie reached behind her, as if she were feeling for an anchor. She found the kitchen counter and held on. "A . . . road?"

"Yes, a road. Even if you don't want it, you don't have to let all your hard work go down the—"

Connie stumbled out of her "kitchen," entered her general living space, and slumped into the rocking chair. "I didn't work hard on that place thinking Clara was going to leave it to me."

Pete sat across from her on the lobster trap she was using for a coffee table, the only other piece of furniture in the room. "I know that. Everyone knows that." He didn't know what else to say. Connie had looked away and he was afraid she was crying again.

It was evening now, and a damp draft whispered in from the leaky windows. If this is what it's like in June she must have frozen in here all winter, Pete thought. So what was it with her? Why didn't she just accept this gift and go live someplace *warm?*

Connie scrubbed at her face, and suddenly Pete felt like a jerk. He was forgetting what was really going on—that Clara and Annabel had died. What was the matter with him? Was he so angry at Paula Steigler that he had come charging over here to make Connie angry, too? No, that wasn't why he had come over here. He had come over here to see if Connie was all right, to be with her if she felt the need.

"Do you want to get something to eat?"

Connie shook her head. "I'm all right. Go home."

Pete peered at her, trying to figure out if she meant it. Connie usually meant what she said. It was what she *didn't* say that was the problem.

"Go home," she said again.

Pete went.

When Pete got home the first thing he did was to set Annabel's custard cup full of odds and ends on his bureau, safe from Paula's prying hands. He put the Bates keys, together with his own, next to the custard cup, but while he did these things he wasn't thinking about the Bates sisters at all. He was thinking about Connie. It wasn't until later, when Pete lay in bed, that the Bates sisters came crashing back to mind.

Clara.

Annabel.

He struggled to rid his mind of the images of the dead sisters. Clara, lying at peace in her own bed, looking like she was asleep, this didn't bother him so much as the ugliness of those "bruises" on Annabel. He knew they weren't really bruises. He knew she had probably not suffered long herself, but still, there they were, those discolored patches of flesh along her upper arm and leg and—

Pete shot up out of the covers.

He knew it. There had been, all along, something about those marks that haunted him.

Marks of hypostasis were made by blood pooling after death, but blood, just like everything else on earth, had to act in accordance with the laws of gravity. Hypostasis was found on a body at the lowest gravitational point. A body like Annabel's that had lain on its side for twenty-four hours after death would have marks of hypostasis on the side closest to the ground. Annabel Bates's marks of hypostasis were on her uppermost arm and leg.

Pete turned on the light.

Sometime after she had died and before Pete and Connie found her Annabel Bates's body had been moved.

Who did it?

Why?

20

Chapter

3

As seemed to be the case more often of late, when Pete struggled out that Monday morning from the two rooms of his cottage in which he lived to the three that housed the business of Factotum, his partner, Rita Peck, was already at her desk, bright-eyed and bushy-tailed, not a silky hair out of place.

On Nashtoba news always seemed to fly faster than Pete did. Not only did Rita know all about the Bates sisters, but somehow she knew all about the quirks of the wills, too. Pete knew that Paula Steigler had to be the original source on the wills, but he had a sneaking suspicion that Evan Spender, a telephone repairman who divided his time between Beston's, the local hardware store cum rumor mill and Rita's desk, had to be the conduit.

"Clara *and* Annabel," sighed Rita, her large brown eyes full, but shortly afterward they narrowed. "Paula Steigler plans to contest. She's moved into the Whiteaker Hotel and says she's not moving out till she gets her due. How's Connie taking it?"

"If you mean about the sisters, not so hot. If you mean about the house, she doesn't want it."

Rita's eyes went round again. "Doesn't *want* it? Why on earth not, when she's stuck in that silly garage? Is it because of the sisters dying? She'll get over that in time. She may not want to move in right away, but she'll think differently later on."

Pete wasn't so sure, but he didn't want to think about Connie in that garage. He changed the subject. "I have to see Hardy Rogers today."

That was all it took to set off Rita's mother alarm. "Hardy Rogers? What's the matter? Are you sick? I told you you'd get sick if you didn't—"

"I'm not sick. I just need to ask some questions about the Bateses. I'd better call and see if I can worm myself in." He reached for the phone, but Rita's long red nails fenced him off. Pete had originally hired Rita just to answer Factotum's phone, and she still treated the telephone as her personal sphere of influence. Before Pete could say much about it Rita had dialed the doctor's office and booked Pete in at ten.

Pete's first job of the morning, traditionally, was to read the paper to Sarah Abrew, whose eyesight was failing. Reading to Sarah was usually far more of a pleasure than it had ever been a chore, give or take an argument here and there, but today Pete wasn't looking forward to it. Not only had Sarah been a witness to Clara's controversial will, but she had been a good friend of the Bateses' as well. Still, Pete wanted to tell Sarah himself, before somebody like the milkman did it. But before Pete could leave for Sarah's he was delayed by the arrival of Factotum's other employee, Andy Oatley.

The twenty-one-year-old Andy wasn't too good at those overrated skills of chewing gum and walking at the same time, nor had he mastered the more necessary little trick of turning the doorknob *before* slamming the full weight of his rippling shoulder into it. The hinges screamed. Pete turned the knob from his side, the door opened, and Andy came hurtling through it. Into Pete.

They picked themselves up, Andy quickly, Pete more slowly, and Pete made a second try for the door, a little more cautiously this time.

But the delay had been just long enough for the milkman to do his dirty deed.

Sarah Abrew was perched in her favorite high-backed chair, waiting for Pete when he arrived. Thanks to the milkman, her short white hair was rumpled, her cardigan was misbuttoned, one tiny foot, crossed over the other, pumped frenetically up and down.

"Clara *and* Annabel? Both?"

"Yes, both." It seemed to Pete that both sisters dying at once didn't double the shock and pain, it quadrupled it. If Clara were alive she would have forced them all to rally around her. If Annabel had lived she was down-to-earth enough to have picked up and gone on, carrying her friends along.

But both sisters were gone. All at once there was nothing left but an empty house and garden.

"What happened?" asked Sarah.

"Annabel had a heart attack. We found her on the porch. Hardy says Clara probably died soon after she missed her medication."

And that made it all the harder to fathom. Both the Bates sisters had had serious medical problems, and either of them dying wasn't very surprising; the fact that they had done it almost at the same time was.

"At least they had good timing," said Sarah. Her voice, her words were light, but Pete wasn't fooled. He let her look out the window at the scrub pine and bull briars until she was ready to speak.

"What happens to the place now? The sisters had different ideas on that, I believe."

"Since Annabel died first, it all goes to Connie. There's only one little snag. Connie doesn't want it. Paula Steigler does."

Sarah snorted. "And Connie wouldn't need it if the two of you'd stop being so foolish and she moved back in."

It was an old argument, but Pete was getting better at ignoring it. Sort of. "When you witnessed Clara's will, did she say anything about why she wanted Connie to have the place?"

"Seems obvious, I'd say."

"To you and me, maybe, but not to Connie. You didn't ask Clara about it?"

Sarah's chin lifted. "No, I didn't. It's none of my business what she leaves and to whom. Andy had dropped me off for a visit, and I don't mind telling you the way that young man drives I'd as soon have walked home. Shortly after I arrived, Warren Johnson came by with the mail and the sisters called him in. They'd written up new wills, they asked us to witness, and we witnessed. But all Clara talked about was that garden. Connie was the one who took care of it. Paula Steigler didn't give it a look. Or her aunts, for that matter."

"That part in the will about the definitions. What did Clara mean by that?"

Sarah frowned. "What part about what definitions?"

"You didn't read it?"

Sarah further straightened her four feet, ten-and-some inches that she continued to insist was still five feet. "I did not. Clara told me what she wanted to about what was in it. It was not my job to read the will, it was my job to witness Clara's signing it. Why are you fussing on about the wills?"

Pete sighed. "Since Connie doesn't think she has any right to have the house, and since Paula Steigler is going to contest the will, I'm worried Connie's just going to let her have it."

"But you have other plans in mind? Why? You think Connie's having a house will settle her down where you couldn't?"

Sarah had a way of narrowing things down to the point. What concern of Pete's was it if Connie wanted to give away a house? *Was* he trying to keep her on the island with property entanglements? *Did* he think Clara's house would be the insurance against her running away again? No. Pete wasn't that dumb, was he? What was wrong between them had driven her away before. Only something right between them would keep her here now. So why was he so upset about Paula Steigler contesting the will?

Because of Paula Steigler.

Because Pete didn't like her, and because Pete didn't react well to change. Not on his island. Not in his life.

"Paula Steigler's going to bulldoze the house and gardens and put in a road to the six back lots."

Sarah was silent for a second, but then the chin rose again. "So be it. If she gets it. That's her right."

What was wrong with these people? Didn't they have any sense of history? Or any sense, period?

"I remember that day of the wills," Sarah went on. "I was visiting, and Warren came by with the mail. Annabel and Clara had just written up these new wills and were in a hurry to get them signed. Once we put ink to paper they burned the old ones in the fireplace. Of course, Annabel changed hers because she was worried about Clara. She needed someone she could count on to take care of . . . things. She gave the job to Simon Cole. You know Simon Cole?"

Pete nodded, but Sarah didn't see it. She was looking out the window again.

"Annabel's health was worsening. More angina. I think for the first time it occurred to her she might be the first to go, and who knew what state Clara would be in when that happened. So she left all the decisions, all the work, to Simon. Clara's will was a surprise to Annabel, I know that, but she didn't really mind. They neither of them had married—it wasn't like one of their own children was being pushed out of place. I'm not sure what prompted Clara to change her will. Connie back on the garden job, maybe you two being split and Connie living in that drafty old attic." Sarah peered at Pete to see how he took that last remark.

Pete just peered back, used to it by now.

"Clara must have realized what Connie was to her, what her own niece Paula wasn't. She saw a place where she could do some good for someone else and feel better about dying at the same time. I'm sure Clara liked the idea of Connie moving in, keeping the gardens up. She knew her niece would never move to Nashtoba, and who knew if the person who bought it would be a gardener or not."

"That's what I mean," said Pete. "I think it would be awful if Clara's gardens were destroyed. Those gardens are like a . . . like a memorial. I don't see how you can—"

"Hogwash," said Sarah. "I hope I won't be so daft as to think a couple of plants will make anyone remember *me*. When you're gone, you're gone. If people remember you, they do. If they don't, they don't. That's it."

Sarah's mouth was grim. Too grim.

"I'll remember you by the black-and-blue marks where you've thumped me with your cane," said Pete, and as he had hoped, Sarah chuckled. It was one of Pete's favorite sounds. Today, however, it faded out faster than usual, and she gazed out the window even longer this time.

"I'll get the newspaper." Pete rose, but Sarah stopped him.

"No paper today, Pete, please."

"No paper?"

Sarah shook her head. "I think I'll just sit here and think for a while. Go home."

Everyone was sending him home lately, it seemed.

For some reason, though, Pete was a lot more comfortable leaving Sarah with *her* thoughts then he had been to leave Connie with hers.

He kissed Sarah's papery cheek and left.

Pete had a few minutes before he had to be at Hardy's, so he stopped by Beston's Store first. The usual scene greeted him—the fat, alcoholic Ed Healey to one side of the bench on the store's porch, Evan Spender and that snake-in-the-grass Bert Barker on the other.

"Well, look who's in the money now!" Bert sang out.

Pete gave a second's thought to the possible ramifications of finally popping Bert one.

"Leastways you will be if you ever get your butt in gear and marry your wife again! Right, Ev? Sell off the Bates place and sit back nice and pretty for a while, right, Ev?"

Evan Spender said nothing, which was not unusual for Evan. Thank God. Pete bought a Coke in a tall green bottle from the rusty machine on the porch, sat down next to Ed Healey, and took a long swig.

"Annabel *and* Clara," said Ed. He shook his head, which also shook his many chins, as well as his several bellies. "And you had to find them."

"Oh, what the Christ does it matter who found 'em?" said Bert. "A couple of old spinsters croaked, Connie's efforts paid off. Now what's important is what she's going to do with the place. If I were her I'd—"

"If I were you I'd shut up," said Evan Spender. "How is she?"

"As a matter of fact," said Pete, "Connie doesn't want the house. Paula Steigler's going to fight the will in court, and Connie's going to let her." It was not his place to say any of this, of course, but it was either that or let Bert's cloud of crud infect the whole island. *That* was all Connie needed to hear—Bert Barker sounding off on the steps of Beston's Store about how all her efforts paid off in getting her the house.

Bert's eyebrows went up. "Is she ready for the funny farm? Or is she planning on moving back in with you?"

It suddenly seemed clear to Pete why Connie had wanted to leave this island. He finished his Coke and stood up. "She's not as desperate as you are, Bert—*she* doesn't have to start living off *me.*"

Bert Barker deserved that. He'd been living off his wife's property for years. But saying it only served to make Pete feel as mean as Bert. It wasn't a good way to feel.

Still, as Pete left Beston's he thought that maybe Bert had something there after all. Maybe that was what was bothering Connie—that people would think she was freeloading off the Bates sisters, that people would think she'd spent all those years in Clara's garden just on the off chance she'd get left the house. But Connie had never cared what people thought before—why should she all of a sudden start to care about it now?

Pete was still puzzling over Connie's behavior as he swung off Main Street and down the unnamed side road that led to Hardy Rogers's unmarked office. Hardy didn't need to advertise—besides being the island's only doctor, he'd delivered most of the population. People were born knowing where he was.

Pete didn't as a rule care much for doctors' offices, but for some reason Hardy's wasn't as bad as most. It was low on stark white linoleum and high on mellowed wood; the magazines in the rack were magazines most normal people, and all the marketing surveys, had never heard of. Pete was deep into *Gorilla News* when Hardy waved him down the hall. Pete followed him into the deep, dark recesses of his private office.

"What?" said Hardy.

Pete also liked a doctor who got to the point. He explained his problem with Annabel's marks of hypostasis.

Hardy pulled at an eyebrow. "Gravity. Right." He didn't say anything else, so finally Pete spoke again.

"I mean somebody must have moved her. Those marks were on top."

Hardy pulled his eyebrow some more. "You didn't?"

"I didn't."

"So maybe I did."

"Not until later. When you got there the marks were on the top."

"Your wife didn't touch her?"

Pete had long ago given up correcting people with an "ex-wife" response. "No, she didn't."

"So Clara moved her."

"Clara?"

28

"Clara. Annabel didn't come. She waited. She got worried. She went to find her. She found her. She rolled her over, discovered she was dead, overstrained her congestive heart, went back to bed, and died."

"I didn't think Clara could get out of bed. I'm sure Connie said that she hadn't been able to get out of bed for a while now. I think—"

Hardy shook his head. When Hardy shook his head it didn't leave room for discussion. "You'd be surprised what adrenaline will do for you in a crisis. Clara wasn't that weak that she couldn't move around, but she was weak enough that exertion like that could kill her. What else do you think happened?"

What else. Yes. What was Pete supposing? That someone stole in and moved Annabel after she had died, but told no one she was dead, and left poor Clara there alone? There had been no signs of foul play. There had been no obvious sign of theft.

Hardy stood up from behind the desk, looming over Pete like Zeus. "Enough. Out. I've got an office full of people waiting for me to explain things a hell of a lot stranger than this."

Pete stood, too.

He would have been hard-pressed to explain just what took him to Willy McOwat's office next.

Despite a recently elevated homicide rate, Nashtoba Island didn't run to much in the way of crime. That had made it surprising when the selectmen had hired a hotshot out-of-towner, Will McOwat, to run the police force, but not at all surprising that as Pete walked into the station he found nothing much going on. The dispatcher, Jean Martell, was talking to her daughter on the phone and Ted Ball, the one remaining police officer, was watching her do it. Even the chief was idle, sitting at his desk counting the bullets in his gun.

"Now let me get this straight," he said, once Pete had explained why he was there. The chief leaned back in his chair so that his considerable weight was all on the back two legs, and the chair groaned.

"You have a medical examiner who has certified two deaths by natural causes and has explained exactly how they probably occurred to boot. One sudden death by coronary, and a second, slower death by congestive heart failure. The first party was found and moved by the second party, which in turn explains very neatly the death of that second party. Now what's your problem?"

"My problem," said Pete, "is that I remember Connie telling me that Clara couldn't get out of bed."

"At all?"

"I think so. I'm almost sure."

"Haven't you talked to Connie about this?"

"No. She's pretty upset."

"What did Hardy Rogers say when you told him Connie said Clara couldn't get out of bed?"

"Adrenaline," said Pete, feeling a little foolish. "He mentioned adrenaline."

Willy McOwat didn't say anything. He rubbed his long jaw with a ham-sized hand and raised an eyebrow at Pete. Pete started to feel a little less foolish and a little more like I-hope-the-damned-chair-breaks.

"Come on, Pete. You've raised some good questions, you've gotten some good answers. What's the matter? What are you trying to say happened?"

And there they were again. What *was* he trying to say happened? Two nice old ladies. What kind of crimes could they inspire? What kind of secrets could they hold? Pete sighed and stood up. "Nothing. You're right. I guess I'm just . . ." Just what? Sick of everybody dying?

"Cheer up, Pete. This makes as much sense as anything else around here, doesn't it?"

Pete didn't answer.

It was a mistake.

Willy McOwat entertained himself for the next forty-five minutes by reminding Pete of thirty or forty other Episodes of Island Life That Made No Sense.

Chapter

4

Connie shook her sopping hair out of the towel and pulled open her dresser drawer. She had to get moving. She had to get on over to Factotum.

School was out. Today, according to her agreement with Pete, she was supposed to start working at Factotum full time. It was a crazy setup—so crazy that sometimes she couldn't believe she was doing it. She'd been waiting around for him to stop being mad at her. She *hadn't* been waiting around for him to hire her, but afterward, once she'd had a chance to think for a minute, she'd decided it was more or less the same thing.

Well, wasn't it?

The odd part of it was that all the time Pete was so angry with *her*, Connie had been angry back. The more Pete blamed her, the stronger her defenses got, and the more it seemed to her that even though she was the one who had cheated and run, *Pete* had done his share to cause it. It was only recently, when Pete seemed to have finally buried his hatchet somewhere out there in that garden, that Connie began to wonder if she really deserved it at as much as she'd once thought. She began to get . . . well . . . *scared*. Did she have the guts to give this thing another shot? What if she screwed it up? Again. Whatever *she* did and didn't deserve, she knew *Pete* didn't deserve to be messed up by the same idiot *twice*.

Connie lifted out underwear, a T-shirt that was probably Pete's, and an old pair of jeans, then put them back down. She couldn't go to Factotum. Pete had hired her for the Bates job. The Bates job was the only job Pete had given her all spring. She couldn't go back to Clara's garden. Not now. And besides, who'd want her to? Connie sat down on the bed and stared at the floor.

Connie was a person of action. She responded to everything with action of some sort, and in truth it was this particular part of her nature that had gotten her into trouble in the past. She was either charging off or mouthing off, no matter how hard she'd tried to change lately. Therefore, she was much surprised to realize, when Pete's old truck announced itself outside her apartment with a series of trademark groans and squeaks, that she had been sitting on the bed for an hour without moving.

She jumped up off the bed and had just gotten her second leg into the jeans when Pete knocked.

Connie ran down the stairs and opened the door.

Pete stared at the shirt first, at her bare feet second, and at his watch third, but said nothing. Or at least he didn't say anything *else*. Pete had the kind of eyes that said everything for him a long time before his mouth ever did. Once Connie had run away with a total stranger rather than face those eyes. Today she looked away from them.

"I'm running late." She led the way back upstairs.

Pete sat down in the rocking chair and put his feet up on the lobster trap. "That's okay. I'll wait."

"Actually, I can't see that you need me. All I was doing was the garden."

"So let's do your garden."

"It's not *my* garden."

Pete's feet snapped off the lobster trap onto the floor. "It's not Paula Steigler's garden. If it were, the last thing she'd do is work in it. She's going to put a *road* through it."

A road through the gardens.

Connie felt her spine wilting. She struggled to draw herself up straight, chin first, a trick Sarah Abrew had taught her. "Paula Steigler can do what she wants. She's Clara's niece. She's *supposed* to have that property."

"Who says? A person can leave his or her property to whomever he or she wants. An inheritance is not a God-given—"

Why was Pete so worked up about this? wondered Connie. Why did he care? Or maybe more to the point, what was terrifying Connie about this? She didn't know, but she did know that her inability to explain her feelings to this man had cost her dearly in the past. She took a deep breath. "Even if I went to court I'd lose. Paula's Clara's niece."

"You don't know you'd lose. Why don't you at least talk to Roberta Ballantine?"

Roberta Ballantine was Nashtoba's resident lawyer. Pete wanted Connie to see a lawyer, over something that didn't belong to her in the first place? "I'm not going to see Roberta Ballantine. I'm not going to work in the garden."

"Okay." Pete got up and walked toward the stairs, but he spent a long time hanging around them without actually going down them, looking at Connie a lot. "I can see why you might not want to work in the garden right now," he finally said. "I can see why you might think you don't want to have anything to do with Clara's house. I can see that. But you may not feel this way in another month, or maybe in another year. I just don't want you to do something now that you'll be sorry for later."

Why not? thought Connie. It's what I'm best at. Pete should know that.

"And about Factotum. There's plenty to do, even if you want to hold off on the garden."

Yes, he'd have plenty for her to do, even if he didn't, and there wasn't much that would be harder for Connie to take than that, unless maybe it was inheriting a house she didn't deserve, out from under a blood relative. "I think I'll take a few days off. There's some stuff I have to do."

Pete looked at her closely.

Connie looked away.

"Okay. Whatever you want." Still Pete stayed. The brown eyes were not happy. "About Clara," he said finally. "You said she couldn't get out of bed at all?"

Connie shook her head.

"At *all?*"

"At all."

"Not even to—"

"Her legs stopped working. They just gave out. She had one bad fall a couple of months ago and she never got up again. Not even when Annabel burned her hand in the kitchen. According to Clara, Annabel really hollered when she did it and it scared Clara to death. She tried to get out of bed to help her, but she just rolled onto the floor in a heap. She'd never try again. I tried to encourage her not to give up, but she—" Connie's voice cracked. She could see Pete's eyes fill with pain. *Her* pain. Suddenly Connie wanted Pete to leave. Or at least she wanted his *eyes* to. "Good-bye," she said.

"Connie."

"Stop looking at me, will you? I'm all right. Or at least I will be once you leave."

"All right. All right, I'll go now. Will you please call me if—"

"I'll call you."

Pete left.

Connie sat back down on the bed and didn't move for even longer this time.

She's just upset, Pete told himself. She's just overtired. She's probably not sleeping right. This has thrown her.

She'll get a couple days' rest, she'll get some sleep, she'll be all right.

But when?

Should he have insisted she come in to work? Pete shook his head. You didn't insist on things with Connie. You didn't get her to do things she didn't want to do. She'd be all right.

But when?

Pete drove aimlessly along Shore Road, the road that circled the little island in a cracked and sandy loop. If Pete knew Connie, she would take a day or two off and resurface raring to go. Connie was not a moper. The odds were also that once she got over the shock of Annabel and Clara she'd think again about their house, think again about Paula Steigler and the road and the six back lots. Would it be too late by then? Would Connie already have knuckled under, given up, said good-bye to everything there was that was left of the Bateses, everything that was, by rights, hers? Maybe. So maybe it was up to Pete to cover a few bases while Connie was temporarily not thinking straight. He put some purpose behind his driving and had soon pulled off Shore Road into Roberta Ballantine's drive.

Roberta Ballantine was a local who had gone away, become professional, come back home twenty-five years ago, and never left again. Pete, who had left Nashtoba only long enough for a college education and a cross-country tour, had to like her for that. He was a little afraid to like her for much else. There was an alertness about Roberta Ballantine that made the rest of Nashtoba seem asleep, an alertness that tended to put Pete on his guard at the same time that it drove him to her office looking for help.

The parking lot was empty and Roberta Ballantine was alone. Business wasn't booming, but then again, on Nashtoba, what was?

Even though the lawyer appeared to have had plenty of time on her hands, she didn't seem to want to waste any of it.

"Sit down, what's the trouble?" she said in her first breath.

Pete handed over copies of the wills. Roberta unfolded a pair of Ben Franklin glasses, angled her salted and peppered head the proper distance from the two papers, and read them through.

"The great-niece, Paula Steigler," explained Pete, "the only legal relative, announced plans to contest Clara's will. What are the odds of her succeeding?"

"Problem number one. Clara Bates never mentions a great-niece or Paula Steigler by name in the will at all. She never makes it clear that she's purposely intending to disinherit her niece. The 'heir-at-law' can then attempt to prove this omission was the result of oversight or incompetence."

"Oversight or incompetence?"

"One of the most common grounds on which to contest a will. The other is duress." Roberta looked over the tops of her glasses and shrugged, then looked again at the will. "What's the meaning of this reference to the gardens and the definitions?"

"Connie took care of Clara's gardens. She doesn't know what that means about the definitions."

"So. Problem number two. If this meaning is not made clear, Clara Bates's competence could be called into question. I see Annabel Bates names someone else as executor. This might also indicate a lack of faith in her sister's mental capabilities."

"She seemed okay to me."

"It doesn't matter how she seemed to you. If the language is such that a question can be raised, it will be raised. You should try to clarify this business of the definitions."

"What else should we do?"

"Connie might have to defend herself against charges that Clara changed her will under duress. She took care of the gardens for Clara Bates. She was paid for this work?"

Pete shifted in his seat. "Yes and no. She worked for Factotum, Factotum was paid, but there was a lot more to Connie's effort than that. She spent a lot of time with Clara that was strictly on a personal basis."

"Yes. I see. So a question might be raised about undue influence."

"So what should Connie do?"

"Retain a lawyer. Neat advice, isn't it?" Roberta Ballantine smiled, and Pete felt a little less afraid of liking her. He smiled back.

"To best meet an attack on this will, you would have to provide evidence that Clara Bates was indeed competent when she made the will, that she didn't just forget about the niece, that she had valid reason to leave her property to Connie, as well as valid reason for disinheriting her niece. I would certainly also come up with some explanation regarding the definitions. The question of duress—"

"There was no duress. Connie doesn't even *want* the place. She thinks Paula Steigler should have it."

Roberta Ballantine peered at Pete as if *his* competence were in question. He supposed it did sound odd, one party who wants it, one who doesn't, and a third party, whose business it isn't, sitting in the lawyer's office.

Roberta took off her glasses and folded them up with two brisk snaps. "Is there anything else?"

Pete hesitated. "Maybe one other thing."

Roberta Ballantine popped him a look that clearly told him to get on with it.

Pete cleared his throat. "Annabel Bates died prior to Clara. There appeared to be no question of the order of death. But if by chance Annabel had died second, Annabel would have inherited Clara's property, and therefore the great-niece would have inherited it all."

"Has the niece ordered autopsies? She should."

"I don't know," said Pete. "But my question is really this. If there were a doubt of any kind regarding *how* the sisters died, would it make any difference—legally, I mean? In regard to the wills? Annabel died first. No matter how. It wouldn't make any difference if it turned out that—"

Roberta Ballantine's eyes looked simultaneously less alert and more remote, but Pete didn't really believe she was either of those things. As a matter of fact, the look brought him back to reality. What in the world was he saying? And to whom?

He stopped talking.

"It would depend on what you mean," said Roberta cautiously. "Any number of things can tie up a will for months, even years."

"I see. Thank you." Pete stood up.

Roberta Ballantine rose with him. "The police, of course, should be notified of any—"

"Yes. I did. They feel it's nothing. Thank you." He held out his hand. Roberta Ballantine shook it and hurried him out in a rush not to waste more of all that time.

Idiot! Pete said to himself once he was back in his truck. Clara Bates moved Annabel's body, with a little help from a whole lot of adrenaline. But all Pete could think about was Clara lying in bed, hearing Annabel cry out when she burned her hand. If that hadn't gotten her adrenaline flowing, nothing would, and how far had Clara's adrenaline gotten her then? As far as the floor.

But if Clara didn't move Annabel's body, who did? Didn't Sherlock Holmes always say that if you eliminated the impossible, whatever was left was it?

If Pete eliminated what he was starting to believe was the impossible, there was nothing else left at all.

Chapter

5

Rita Peck jumped out of her chair the minute Pete came through the door. "Paula Steigler's asked for *autopsies*."

"Yes. Roberta Ballantine hinted she might."

Rita, always annoyed when she failed to excite Pete with one of her scoops, plopped back down in her chair. "Well, I'd like to know what she's trying to *prove*."

"That Clara died first, leaving her half of the house to Annabel as she did so. That Annabel died second, thereby leaving both halves to the niece."

"Oh, for heaven's *sake*." Rita picked up the phone and began dialing with such single-mindedness that for a minute Pete was sure she was putting in a call to the governor. "If you ask me, I think those poor sisters should be left *alone*. Let them die in *peace*. Let the rest of us remember them by their kind and gentle natures, not by the grisly details of their *deaths*. And *furthermore—*"

But Pete never found out Rita's furthermore. Her call went through.

"Bill, this is Rita," she said sweetly into the phone. "When you said the loam would be delivered Tuesday I naturally assumed you meant *this* Tuesday. *This* Tuesday being now of course *last* Tuesday, I thought I should call you to find out exactly which Tuesday out of all the fifty-two Tuesdays in the year you really *meant*."

Pete kept moving, leaving Rita to run Factotum as only Rita could run it, feeling a little sorry for Bill as he went.

Rita was partly right, he thought, but then again, she was partly wrong. Pete didn't want to lose sight of Annabel's and Clara's kind and gentle natures either, but to him, fighting Paula Steigler was his way to honor those natures. Paula Steigler had no intention of honoring her aunts or of honoring Clara's wishes. Pete didn't want to let the sisters die with questions unanswered, wishes not met. Not without a fight.

Fight. Suddenly Pete was thinking of Connie again. He went into the kitchen and settled at the table in a straight-backed pine chair. He faced the screened porch with the view of the salt marsh beyond, picked up the old black rotary phone, and dialed a number he had only used a few times but had already learned by heart.

It took her a long time to answer. "Hello."

"It's Pete. I just thought I'd report in."

For a minute Pete thought she wasn't going to speak. Finally she said, "Report what?"

"I talked to Roberta Ballantine. She thinks you need a lawyer. There are certain gray areas in Clara's will that—"

"No lawyer."

"Paula Steigler's socked in at the Whiteaker Hotel for the duration. She's just ordered autopsies. She—"

"No lawyer, Pete. I appreciate what you're trying to do. Actually, no I don't. I don't appreciate it. So cut it out, all right?"

Pete mulled over this response. There wasn't much that was equivocal about it. He decided to change tack. "I could

40

use you around here next week. Andy's baby-sitting for the Coddingtons, Rita has a thesis to type, I've got two boats to—"

"Next week?"

Pete detected a faint whiff of alarm. *Why?* The Bates house? Was she afraid he was going to suggest she go back to work at the Bates house? That was easily fixed. "Yeah. To paint Ernie Ball's boat. We're way behind getting it into the water. I could use you in here Monday."

"Monday?"

"Monday. I'll see you on Monday." Before she could end-run him Pete got off the phone.

By the time Pete reached Rita's desk Monday morning, Rita reported that Connie had already come and gone.

"Where to?"

Rita raised one soft eyebrow at Pete. "Ernie Ball's. You told me you wanted her to—"

Pete spun for the door.

"Pete."

He turned around.

"I got the feeling she wanted to be alone."

"Alone?"

"And Hardy Rogers called, looking for you. The autopsy reports are in."

Pete stared at Rita. Why would Hardy call *him* with the autopsy reports? Pete retreated down the hall to his favorite kitchen phone and dialed the doctor's office.

Hardy Rogers was one of those people who never seemed to believe in the advanced technology of the phone. He hollered into it so loudly that Pete considered opening the window and listening direct.

"Half right," Hardy barked. "I was half right. Annabel died just like I told you. Coronary. she died first, too, just like I said, which is all that matters to anybody else, I suppose. I was wrong about Clara, though. She died of too much digoxin, not too little."

"Too *much?*"

"Don't get all wound up over it. Digoxin can run along at near toxic levels all the time. Accidental toxicity and death is not uncommon."

"Now wait a minute here, are you trying to tell me that Annabel dies of a heart attack and *coincidentally* Clara dies right after her of the toxic effects of her own medication?" Once again the ugly blotches on the upper side of Annabel's body reared their ugly head. What was going on here?

Hardy may or may not have been wondering the same thing. His answer came after a considerable delay. "I'm just trying to tell you *what* happened. I can't tell you *why* it happened." He paused again. "But I can make a good guess. If you want me to."

"Yes, I want you to."

Hardy apparently chose to ignore the testiness in Pete's tone. "I told you before that I thought Clara missed her medication after her sister didn't come to give it to her. So maybe she tried to give it to herself. Clara was getting confused. She was damned unsteady. She could have taken too much without knowing it, crept up over the toxic mark, and died. Furosemide and digoxin are both little white pills—maybe she mixed them up."

Pete mulled that over. It was neat. But was it *too* neat? Here Hardy on the one hand says Clara can get out of bed and roll Annabel over; on the other hand he says she can't uncork two bottles of pills and shake out one of each. It all left a pretty big question in Pete's mind, but all of a sudden he thought of an even bigger question.

"So why are you telling *me* this?"

This time the delay was so long that Pete began to doubt the excellence of all this telephone technology himself.

Finally Hardy coughed. "Because you're the one with all the questions. And because I told you at the house that Clara's lungs filled with fluid and she drowned from inside. And even though I assured your wife there were plenty worse ways to do it, she didn't seem to care much for the idea. This way out's even easier. I wanted her to know that. I also didn't want her to hear something different about how it happened and think I lied. The digoxin probably set up a heart block. Clara's heart just stopped, that's all. She went out nice and easy—you see that your wife understands that."

So Hardy was concerned about how Connie was taking this. Why?

But now Hardy set off on a path of his own. "I told Annabel," he said. "I told her it was too much for her. I told her she needed some help. I told her to let Dotty Parsons do more. I—"

Hardy stopped, as if he suddenly realized there was no longer any point in talking about the town nurse now. "You tell your wife what I said."

"I will," said Pete.

As Pete set off for the Bates house he suddenly realized he had briefly forgotten, for the first time in two years, that Connie was no longer his wife.

Ernie Ball's boat was upside down on concrete blocks, a wooden-hulled nineteen-footer badly in need of bottom paint. It didn't look like it was going to get it any time soon, either. Connie stood next to it with the sander in one hand, switched off, none of the hull yet taken down past the old paint. Something about her, the way she had failed to hear his approach, the way her hip leaned into the side of the boat, or the way her hair, bright gold in the sun, made a perfect curtain around her face, told Pete that Rita was right. She wanted to be alone.

He tiptoed back to the truck the way he had come.

The Bates sisters were still the subject of the day on Beston's porch, but now it wasn't just the sisters' deaths that were under discussion, but their lives as well. The results of the autopsies were old news. Otto Snow was now the banner headline.

43

"Courted 'em both," Ed Healey was saying. "Couldn't make up his mind between 'em. Those two sisters had been together a long time."

"Oh, hogwash," said Bert. "Couldn't make up his mind! As if anybody in their right mind would take ossified old Otto!"

"He wasn't always so ossified, Bert. You ought to know. Or weren't you even young *once?*" Ed Healey laughed at his own joke for a while, and Pete waited for Ed's flesh to settle before sitting down next to him.

"Otto Snow?"

"Sure, Pete. You know old Otto. He's been, shall we say, attentive over the years? According to Otto, poor Clara and Annabel just sat there on the porch year after year waiting for him to say I do, only he never got up the guts to say 'I don't' to the one so's he could say 'I do' to the other! Now what's this about these 'definitions,' anyhow?"

"Delphiniums," said Bert. "She was getting soft in the old belfry. She meant delphiniums, I'll bet you ten dollars."

"Definitions," repeated Evan Spender. "Did she do crosswords, Pete?"

Pete didn't know. He added that to the long list of other things he didn't know, went inside, bought the duct tape he had come for, and left the store to try to cram a good day's work into the remaining few hours.

Factotum's list of chores was varied, to say the least. On the list for the afternoon were feeding the Pfeifers' chickens, delivering the Shaughnessy's newly caulked dory, removing two bats from the Simpsons' attic, patching the newest rust hole in his own truck, and checking in to make sure all the Coddingtons were accounted for. Pete made it through the Pfiefers' chickens and that was it.

This time when he crept up on Connie the sander was going full blast and the bottom of Ernie's boat looked like it was being made into paper.

"Hi," said Pete.

Connie turned around.

"I have something to tell you," Pete hollered over the noise of the machinery.

Connie looked away, the way a person would who'd been told mostly bad things of late.

The sander bit into the wood. Pete stepped up close and flicked it off. "Paula Steigler requested autopsies. Hardy was right, and Annabel did die first, so it changes nothing as far as the will is concerned. But what Hardy told us about Clara dying wasn't exactly right." Pete explained about the digoxin, stressing, as Hardy wanted him to, that Clara had not suffered on the way out.

Connie stared at Ernie's boat, or what there was left of it. "So how does Hardy figure she got too much medicine?"

"He thinks Clara tried to take it herself, got confused, and took too much. She was taking two types of pills that looked pretty much the same. She could have mixed them up."

Connie busied herself with the sander for a while, changing the paper, straightening the cord. "This boat's going to take me only one more day tops. I don't know what you think you've got for me to do the whole rest of the week. I've got things of my own I could be doing, you know."

"You mean the garden?"

It was the wrong thing to say, and Pete knew it the minute Connie looked at him.

She switched on the sander.

Pete switched it off again. "Connie—"

She whirled around. "When are you going to get this straight, Pete? This house should not belong to me. Didn't Hardy just tell you Clara was confused, that she couldn't even count out a couple of pills? Even Annabel thought so! Why do you think Annabel changed her will so that Simon Cole was executor? She didn't trust Clara to be able to dispose of things right! And she *didn't* dispose of it right. She left it to *me*, when it should belong to Paula, the blood relative."

Connie headed for the electrical outlet on the side of Ernie's house, but Pete caught her arm and held on.

"Listen to me. Clara knew what she was doing. Sarah and

Warren witnessed her signing that will. Do you think they'd have done that if they felt Clara was losing her grip? I've talked to Sarah. I know what she thinks. Why don't you ask her yourself? Ask Warren Johnson? And do you think Annabel would have gone along with Clara's plans if she doubted the sense of it? Sarah said Annabel knew what Clara was doing. Who would know better than Annabel what mental state Clara was in? Simon Cole was probably made executor because things have become more complicated these days. Clara was older. Annabel was older. Annabel probably didn't want to burden Clara with a lot of technical details. Doesn't that make sense to you?"

"No. I didn't do anything for Clara. It makes no sense that she left this house to me."

"Oh, come on, Connie. I could find you ten people this afternoon who could tell you what you've done for Clara."

Connie snorted. "If you're going to stand there talking all day, you might as well do this job yourself. As a matter of fact—" Connie faced Pete squarely. "You don't need me. This is ridiculous. Here. I quit." She handed Pete the sander. She walked away. She jumped into her beat-up TR-6 and in a flash she had disappeared around the bend.

Pete started toward the truck, planning to go after her, but then he stopped to think. What could he do when he caught up with her? Talk to her some more? Something told him she wasn't exactly in the mood. But her attitude worried him—it was too self-effacing, too un-Connie-like. But what could he do about *that?* Maybe he could get her to see that Clara was merely giving value for value, paying for love with love. Maybe Pete could do the most for Connie if he took his own advice and talked to Warren Johnson. And maybe he could do the rest of it, too—find those ten people who could vouch for what Connie had done for Clara. Wouldn't that also lay the groundwork Roberta Ballantine had mentioned, just in case Connie changed her mind and decided to fight Paula Steigler over the will? While he was at it, there were a few other things Pete could do, like talking to Simon Cole about how he came to be executor in Annabel's will, maybe talk to Dotty Parsons, the town nurse. If she'd been involved at all, she could probably speak for just how confused Clara Bates really was.

If he couldn't keep Connie busy, at least he could keep busy himself.

Chapter

6

Pete found Warren Johnson first. He was just climbing out of the mail Jeep in front of the Beamish house on Shore Road, puzzling over a handful of mail.

Pete pulled his truck in behind Warren's Jeep.

Warren looked up and then back down. "I don't know Pete. You'd think people'd have the hang of this ZIP code system by now. Look at this. First three letters, no codes. And look at this here. 'Shore Road.' That's all. 'Shore Road.' It's a darn long road, Pete. What if some other Beamish moved onto Shore Road and I didn't know it?" He waved the offending envelope at Pete, and then, seeming to realize that he was violating every rule of confidentiality by showing one party's mail to another party, he shoved the envelope deep inside the stack.

Pete didn't think it would be possible for anyone by any name to move onto Shore Road, or onto Nashtoba, for that matter, without everyone on the island instantly knowing all about it, but Warren wasn't through worrying about it yet.

"As we speak there could be some other Beamish looking for this self-same letter, and here I stand, handing her correspondence over to the wrong Beamish altogether."

"There can't be too many *Prudence* Beamishes, Warren."

Warren Johnson looked up, momentarily encouraged. "That's true, I suppose."

Pete pushed on. "You witnessed Clara Bates's will, Warren?"

Warren frowned. "Is there a difficulty?"

"No. No. Not really. You do remember the day?"

"Sure I remember it. I was delivering their mail—an electric bill, a bank statement, a piece of personal correspondence from Washington, as I recall."

"And Clara and Annabel asked you to witness the wills."

Warren nodded. "Sarah Abrew was visiting at the time. Annabel asked if we would witness them signing their wills."

"Did Clara seem okay to you? Mentally, I mean? In sound mind and all that?" Pete had no doubts that a man who could remember three pieces of mail from a month ago would be able to remember the mental state of the person involved, but still, Warren's frown deepened.

"Soundness of mind! Are you sure there is no difficulty? Soundness of mind! I don't know that one person can state with any certainty that another—"

"I just need to know if you recall feeling at all uneasy about Clara's state of mind."

Warren's forehead cleared. "Not a bit of it. There, you see, that'd be the thing. If something seemed funny about Clara or the will I'd have felt some uneasiness. No, Pete, I don't recall any uneasiness about the situation. I'm sure I'd have been uneasy if there seemed to be anything wrong with Clara's mind." But then Warren frowned again, as if he were afraid he should have been worrying all this time and he hadn't.

"Everybody else thought she was fine, Warren—don't

sweat it. I just wondered, that's all. The will is being contested and it might—"

That did it. Warren's forehead almost turned itself inside out in knots. "Contested! Oh, Lord. Oh, Lordy Lord."

Pete did what he could to reassure Warren that his witnessing was not going to be called into question, but he was saved only by the arrival of Prudence Beamish, who had finally gotten tired of waiting at her front door for her mail. Warren immediately began to question Prudence as to whether she was indeed the one and only Prudence Beamish on Shore Road, and before Prudence decided to knock Warren down and steal her mail Pete left to track down the town nurse.

Dotty Parsons was small and round and sleek. She wore a crisp nurse's uniform when she was on duty or off, and had a thick gray rope of hair that was so constantly neat it must have been attached to her head with a staple gun. Her office was full of pigeonholes, and every single speck of paper in it was holed in nice and tight. She might have seemed efficient to the point of coldness if her eyes hadn't filled with tears the minute Pete mentioned Clara Bates.

"I'm going to miss her awfully," said Dotty. "There she was having to submit to some pretty humiliating routines and yet she always had a smile and a perky word for me. They don't often come like Clara, I can tell you that."

"She was completely bedridden by the end, wasn't she?"

Dotty nodded. "I think that's what bothered her most—that she couldn't be a help to Annabel. She had tried to get up, had fallen and cracked a rib, and made more work for Annabel in the end. She never tried it again."

So who moved Annabel? But Pete wasn't here to ask that particular question. Pete wasn't allowing himself to *think* about that particular question. Both Willy and Hardy had dismissed it. Pete would have to, too.

"Clara's mind," he said instead. "She was weak physically, but was she sharp mentally?"

Dotty Parsons chuckled, a deep chuckle that worked itself

out from the compressed white cylinder that was her chest. "Now Pete, keep in mind I'm sixty-two myself! 'Sharp' changes its meaning a bit when you reach my age! But Clara was sharp enough. She knew when she wasn't, so I guess that means she was. Most of the time." Dotty's round eyes flattened a hair. "Why do you ask?"

Pete sighed. "I'm not sure why I'm asking, Dotty. You heard about the will?"

Dotty nodded.

"Paula Steigler's fighting it. Connie seems to think Clara made some mistake by leaving the house to her. She's planning to let it go. It seems a shame. Paula's going to tear it down, put in a road, and build six houses out back. I want to show Connie that Clara was in her right mind when she made her will, and I want Connie to be able to show anybody else the same thing if she changes her mind about going to court."

Dotty pursed her lips. She even did that neatly—a perfectly symmetrical rosebud appeared. "To my way of thinking Clara leaving that place to Connie is proof right there of the soundness of her mind. I wouldn't question Clara's mind on that one minute. Not one minute. I could tell you a thing or two about that mind on Paula Steigler, though!" The rosebud straightened into a tight line and then cracked open. "Dr. Rogers sent me over to try to give some help to Annabel. Annabel wouldn't let me do much—just a bath now and then—but one day I was there when Annabel had called Paula up. She told her about me being there, and the next thing you know I get a call from that Paula myself. She wanted to know how much I was charging. Can you beat it? Not how her aunt was *doing,* mind you, but how much I was *charging.* I told her she'd be better off worrying about how much a nursing home would cost if Annabel gave out. Do you know what she said? She said, 'Nursing home! There won't be any nursing home!' Somehow I don't think Little Miss Paula meant she was planning to move in and help out, do you?"

Pete didn't. "Hardy Rogers feels Clara tried to take her own medication and took too much by mistake. He said that with digoxin there's a fine line between—"

"Very fine, very fine." Dotty Parsons turned away from Pete and extracted a notebook from one of the pigeonholes. First try, of course. Pete thought of the state of his desk back at Factotum and sighed.

"Now let me see. Here are my notes. Furosemide twenty milligrams, one tablet twice daily, and—oh, yes—the digoxin prescription, point twenty-five milligrams, one tablet daily. It ran down to nothing, and then it was filled May thirty-first. That means there should have been—" Dotty looked at the ceiling and counted. "Thirty-six pills left. Plenty for Clara to get mixed up with, I'd say."

"But she would have had to be confused to take too many?"

"I'm confused enough to take too many! I really do not understand how so many people manage to take the right pills as often as they do. Do you?"

Pete supposed he didn't, but Pete didn't take anything more than an occasional aspirin. It was pretty hard to get confused on that.

"I do think it's a shame Connie's giving up the house. I know how much it meant to Clara to have Connie taking care of her gardens—she was just tickled to death about that. Will you tell Connie for me that I think it would be a crime to let the niece mow it down? Will you tell her that?"

Pete looked at Dotty with gratitude. Another witness. "You bet I will. Do you know what Clara might have meant by a reference in the will to Connie's help with definitions?"

Dotty looked puzzled. She shook her head. Pete thanked her, and left her to get back to her work, her first task being to immediately refile the notebook in the very pigeonhole from whence it had come.

The next thing Pete wanted to do was to stop by the Bates house and look for Clara's pills. Thirty-six pills should be remaining, and Pete wanted to find out if that were indeed the case.

Pete pulled up in front of the Bates house and got out of the truck, the sisters' keys in his hand. He had been carrying the keys around for a week, but now as he approached the front door he almost wished he didn't have them. He didn't want to go in. But wasn't standing on the porch where the dead Annabel had lain just as bad? Pete turned the key in the lock, pushed open the door, and walked in.

Nothing had changed. The plush chairs with their neatly pinned antimacassars remained the same, as did the hooked rug and the lace curtains. Pete moved on to Clara's bedroom. Everything was painfully the same there—the unmade bed, the desk, the table . . . There were no pills on the bedside table.

Had there ever been? Pete couldn't remember. He went into the bathroom and opened up the medicine chest. There were two bottles with Clara's name on them: furosemide and digoxin. Pete picked up the digoxin bottle. Fifty tablets, the label said. Take one daily. If the prescription had been run down to nothing, then filled May thirty-first, there should indeed be thirty-six pills left as Dotty Parsons had said. Pete struggled with the childproof cap, spilled out the remaining pills into his hand, and counted. Fourteen. He counted again. Still fourteen. He looked around in the medicine cabinet for more pill containers. Nothing. He returned to the bedroom and looked in the bed, on the bedside table, in the rolltop desk, and all over the floor for any of the missing pills. Nothing. He made up Clara's bed neatly and felt a little better. He returned to the bathroom, put the pills back on the shelf, and shut the medicine cabinet door.

Then he looked at the medicine cabinet.

The digoxin was in the medicine cabinet.

The medicine cabinet was in the bathroom.

According to two independent accounts, Clara Bates had been unable to get out of a bed that was in a bedroom twenty-five feet away.

Clara Bates didn't take too many digoxin. Somebody who could walk from the bedroom to the bathroom and back again *gave* Clara too many digoxin. Who had given Clara Bates twenty-two digoxin pills?

The same person who had moved Annabel's body?

Pete opened the medicine cabinet, removed both bottles of pills, and placed them in his pocket.

He relocked the front door to the house and double-checked the back door before he left with the keys.

Chapter

7

Connie couldn't say she was exactly surprised when Pete's truck pulled up in front of her apartment again. She also couldn't say she was exactly displeased. Her two rooms had seemed kind of empty all of a sudden, the day kind of long. She met him at the door and led him upstairs.

"Hi," he said. "How are you?"

The question annoyed her. "All right. I'm all right." Why wouldn't she be?

Pete looked at her closely, and the look annoyed her, too. It was a look that implied maybe she wasn't all right, but if she wasn't, Pete didn't say anything about it. Instead he did what he did around her a lot—he started talking about something else.

He pulled two bottles of pills out of his pocket.

Clara's.

"I found these in Clara's medicine cabinet. Is that where she usually kept her pills?"

Connie couldn't stop staring at Clara's name on the labels. She nodded.

"You didn't ever see them on Clara's bedside table, or anywhere handy where Clara could reach them herself?"

"Annabel always put the pills away. She never wanted Clara to feel like an invalid. She didn't want it to look like a sickroom. Annabel was careful to put things like pills away."

"So." Pete stared at the pill bottles in his hands.

"What?"

Pete's head shot up. He smiled. "Nothing. I just wondered, that's all."

That *really* annoyed Connie. "What the hell do you mean? What about those pills? I know what you're saying— you're saying Clara couldn't have gotten those pills after Annabel died, aren't you? Is that why you asked me the other day if she could get up?"

"Sort of. Yeah. I guess so."

"So what does that mean? *Annabel* loused up the dose? Is that what you're saying?"

Pete seemed a little surprised, either at the idea or that Connie had thought of it. "I suppose so," he said. "There are twenty-two pills missing, though."

Connie looked out her window. "Annabel hadn't been feeling well. Clara said she hadn't. I bet Annabel was getting Clara's pills when the chest pains began. She might have dropped the pills, lost some down the sink."

"Maybe."

But Connie could see that for some reason Pete didn't think so. Connie knew him, and she knew he didn't think so. "Why not?"

Pete squirmed around in the doorway.

"Why not?"

"Because Annabel died first."

Yes, Annabel died first. There was no question that Annabel had died first. If only Annabel hadn't, if only Paula Steigler had inherited the house. But no, by loving this one lonely old lady Connie had loused things up again, had robbed Clara's only relative of her due, had set the island on its ear with scandal once again.

But Connie couldn't think about this now, not with Pete here peering into her face. She would have to think about something else, she would have to cling to being analytical. "So maybe it took a while for Clara's pills to take effect."

"Annabel was going out. Or coming in."

"Maybe she was going to get help. The Coles next door."

"Maybe. Probably."

But Connie could tell that Pete still didn't believe it. Why not?

"What is it, Pete? What aren't you telling me?"

"Nothing. I don't—"

"You don't think Clara messed up the pills. You don't think Annabel did. Why not?"

Pete shook his head, backing away. "No. Nothing."

Connie grabbed his shirt to hold him. "Tell me, dammit. Why don't you believe either of these things?"

"Because someone moved Annabel's body."

Connie let him go.

"Hardy thought Clara did it—that she got up to look for Annabel, rolled her over, strained her own heart, went back to bed, and died. Actually, that's why I asked you if Clara could get up."

"She couldn't. I told you she couldn't. She never moved Annabel's body. When did you find this out? How do you *know* this?"

Pete started babbling on about some crazy marks on Annabel's upper side.

"And when the hell were you thinking of telling *me* all this?"

"I'm not sure I should have told you now."

"Why not?"

"I didn't want to—"

"Upset me? Up*set* me? Is that what you were going to say?"

Pete shook his head, but not convincingly.

57

Of *course* that was what he was going to say. And of *course* it would upset her, but not as much as it would have if he hadn't said a word and she'd found out about it later. And she *would* have found out about it. Around here everyone found out everything sooner or later. But what, exactly, had Connie just found out?

Someone moved Annabel's body. Clara never moved her—Connie knew that—but someone had. Who? *Why?* Connie pictured it: a shadowy figure on the porch rolling Annabel over, leaving her there, dead, with Clara alone inside.

For how long?

Until she died.

Suddenly Connie felt a peculiar fatigue overcome her. She had felt something like it, briefly, once or twice before, but never quite like this. All of a sudden she wanted to go to sleep. She *had* to go to sleep. "Will you go?" she said to Pete. "I think I'm going to take a nap now."

"Connie—"

"Really. I just have to go to sleep." She turned for her bedroom before he had taken a single step toward the stairs.

Pete drove away from Connie's disturbed on two counts. First, he was worried about Connie. Sure, plenty of people did this napping thing, but Connie had never been one of them. But what could he do? Nothing, except to dwell on the second deeply disturbing thought. Connie insisted that Clara could not have gotten out of bed to move Annabel's body. Add that to the fact that twenty-two digoxin pills were missing from a bottle that Clara herself could not have reached. He should take the bottle to Willy McOwat, have him check it for prints, tell him about the missing pills. That might change his tune! Or would it? Was the chief going to have some logical explanation that any moron could have thought of? Maybe before he made a fool out of himself again in front of the chief he should check this out a little more. Pete looked at his watch. It was seven-thirty. He swung onto Main Street and down the side road to Hardy Rogers's office.

The office door was locked, but Pete could see the doctor inside, moving slowly back and forth across his office, tidying up at the end of the day. Pete banged on the window glass. Hardy jumped, startled, then moved, frowning, to open the door.

"Why the hell can't you people squeeze your problems in during daylight hours?" he snapped, but he followed it immediately with "What's the matter with you?"

"Nothing. It's Clara. *And* Annabel. We really have to talk."

"We don't have to do anything," growled Hardy, but he opened the door wider as he did so, and Pete followed him in.

They settled, as usual, on either side of Hardy's desk. "What is it now?"

"About Clara. I checked with Dotty Parsons. I went back to the Bates house. I found Clara's pills in the medicine cabinet in the bathroom." Pete put the two bottles on Hardy's desk. "The digoxin is twenty-two pills short."

Hardy's eyebrows twitched. "And?"

"And I'd like to know what happened to them."

Hardy slammed the desk with a hairy hand. "Christ on a raft, what do you think happened to them? They got dropped. They got spilled. They got short-changed at the pharmacy. What's your point?"

Pete cleared his throat. "It just seems to me that when someone dies of too much digoxin and twenty-two pills of it are unaccounted for—"

"So Clara took them all. So what the Christ is the—"

"Clara didn't take them all. Connie and Dotty Parsons both insist that adrenaline notwithstanding, Clara couldn't get out of bed. *At all.* So how was Clara going to get into the bathroom and take twenty-two pills out of the medicine cabinet?"

Hardy looked at Pete without speaking.

"And that leads us to the second question. If Clara couldn't get out of bed, who moved Annabel's body?"

Still Hardy didn't speak.

"Clara really *couldn't* get out of bed. That time she tried it and cracked a rib was the last time she tried. Annabel got burned and cried out for Clara, but Clara couldn't get to her. Nothing would get her adrenaline moving more than that."

Hardy plucked at his long white eyebrow hairs in silence for some seconds. "I admit to you, I hadn't been out to see Clara in over a month. Perhaps she had deteriorated further than I knew. Perhaps she couldn't have moved Annabel's body after all. But I ask you again, Pete, what do you think happened? What do you wish to prove? Suppose a delivery boy found Annabel, panicked, and ran. What do you accomplish by tracking *him* down? Annabel was dead already."

"But was *Clara?*"

This time Hardy slammed both hands onto the desk and stood up. "What's the goddamned difference? She's dead now, and glad of it, I expect. And if you don't leave off with all this foolishness I might just join her myself! What in the blue blazes are you thinking happened over there? Another murder? Two murders? Of a couple of old women? Who did it? And what for?"

Yes, there was that point. That same old point. Who did it and what for? Even the thought of Paula Steigler didn't put Pete quite all the way over that particular hurdle. Paula Steigler thought she inherited, but she must have known she wouldn't have to wait forever to do so. Why kill her aunts now?

Pete stood up. "I'm sorry. You're right. I guess I'm starting at the wrong end."

"Either end is the wrong end, Pete. Let it alone. Go home. Let *me* go home, for chrissake."

Pete picked up the two bottles of pills and left.

But as he got into his truck in the parking lot he noticed that Hardy didn't rush down the hall to the door. Through the dimly lit office window Pete could see the doctor still sitting at his desk, his hands folded in front of him, his knobby-knuckled thumbs rotating over each other first forward, then back, eyes staring into space.

Right, thought Pete. It's easy enough for you to say forget about it, but there you sit, thinking. About what?

About who did it?

And what for?

Pete found the police chief at home. He handed over the bottles of pills and the latest chapter in his story. The chief seemed to consider it just that—a story, but he took the bottles promising to check them for prints.

Unofficially, of course.

Chapter

8

The next morning Pete set off to talk to Simon Cole, the neighbor of the Bates sisters and the would-be executor of Annabel's estate. The Cole house sat a fair distance from the Bates property, partially screened by trees.

It was Simon's wife, Ella, who answered his knock. Ella Cole was that tired, faded-looking type who always seemed to melt into the woodwork. She was of medium height, weight, and complexion, her only memorable feature her dyed dark hair with a Paula Steigler-ish red glow around the roots. The minute she heard what Pete wanted to talk about, she turned around to fetch her husband.

Simon Cole was also of medium height and build and as colorless as his wife, but somehow he made his presence felt and, Pete suspected, remembered. He waved Pete into an extremely uncomfortable wing chair and took the other one himself. He leaned forward with his elbows on his knees, hung his head, and shook it from side to side.

"Hard to believe about the sisters."

"Yes, it is," Pete answered, but did Simon really mean it the way Pete meant it? It *was* hard to believe about the sisters. Too much of what had happened was too hard to believe. "I found the wills when I was looking for Paula Steigler's address. I assume you knew Annabel had made you executor?"

Simon Cole nodded. Beside him, Ella Cole frowned, and even the frown melted into her features as if it had always been there.

"Yes, Annabel was getting a little concerned about Clara's ability to cope. She felt Clara would need someone like me to handle the technicalities. She knew we didn't want just anyone coming in here tearing up the property, and this way I could have a say in what went on. Our part of the deal, of course, was to look out for Clara after Annabel died. That's what we promised Annabel—that we'd look after Clara."

Ella Cole made a hissing noise next to them, the sound of a teakettle just before the boil.

Simon glared at her.

"Was there any legal arrangement about Clara?" asked Pete.

Simon shook his head. "Annabel knew we'd do right by her. There was no—"

"We?" said Ella. "I like that."

"Ella," said Simon.

"You mean to say you intended to take care of Clara here at home?" asked Pete.

Simon shook his head again.

Ella snorted.

"I think Clara would inevitably have been moved into a nursing home," said Simon. "She was no longer—"

Ella snorted again.

Simon glared at her again. "My wife seems to think she knows more about these arrangements than she actually—"

"I know taking care of Clara killed Annabel. I know that!"

"That's enough, Ella."

Ella stood up. It looked like a good idea to Pete. He stood also.

"Thank you," he said to both the Coles. "I just wanted to confirm these things firsthand, since it looks like Clara's will is being contested."

Simon nodded. This wasn't new news. But then again, was anything around here?

Apparently not.

"I wish your wife well," said Simon. "I hear there's some development plan afoot, and I imagine it's no secret that we'd rather not see something like that around here."

Ella Cole burst out laughing.

Pete got into his truck and backed out of the Coles' drive, but he didn't go very far. Something made him stop as he passed the Bates house. Yesterday he had found Clara's pills. What other secrets did that abandoned house still hold? Maybe the chief wasn't ready to go poking around in there, but what was to stop Pete from giving it a quick once-over?

Pete walked across the porch, his footsteps echoing on the hollow floorboards. He selected the Bates keys from his own and put the key in the lock. It grated painfully as he turned. He swung open the door.

From the kitchen came the sound of a closing cupboard door.

Pete charged down the hall. As he ran he took in a fleeting impression of general disarray in the house, and then he saw the man running out the kitchen door.

Pete ran after him.

Pete did a lot of physical labor that kept him in good shape, but this guy he was chasing must have been some kind of track-and-field star. The man reached the stone wall at the edge of the lawn and hurdled over it. Pete scrambled after him, his wrists and ankles raked by the thorns on the rambler roses that covered the wall, but the fellow ahead just kept on going. They tore through the field of fully leafed daylilies, and Pete would have lagged further behind if the man he was pursuing hadn't kept looking back, slowing down as he did so. Soon Pete was close enough to see better, to see that this "man" was really a boy, maybe seventeen or eighteen, long-legged and slim, with flowing red hair that would have hit his shoulders if it hadn't formed a flaming contrail behind him instead.

"Hey!" Pete shouted, but he didn't have the wind to shout anything else. At the far end of the field was a bank of brambles, and the boy tore up the bank and dropped out of sight. Pete scrambled after him. When he finally got to the top of the ridge he stopped. Ahead of him was a scrub pine forest thick with woodbine and bull briars.

The boy was nowhere in sight. It could have been either the June breeze or the running boy that left the softly wafting branches behind.

Pete combed the woods for an hour but he knew it was no use. All the boy had to do was burrow down, stay still, and listen for the sound of Pete ripping his way through the brush.

Pete went back to the Bates house, more slowly this time. The first thing he did when he got there was to sit down at the kitchen table to breathe.

Then he looked around. A small square of glass in the kitchen door was broken where the boy must have reached in to undo the lock, and almost every drawer and cupboard in the kitchen was open and ransacked.

Pete went into the living room and amended his earlier impression of "general disarray." The furniture cushions were askew, the end table drawers and several decorative boxes were all open. Even the corner of the braided rug was flipped back. Pete went into Clara's room and found much the same there—the bedclothes piled on the floor, the desk open and pillaged, the bureau drawers open and their contents scrambled. Upstairs in Annabel's room it was the same.

Pete sat down on Annabel's stripped bed, stunned.

This was no burglary. On Annabel's bureau her jewelry

box was upside down but the contents were still heaped where they had fallen. The television, the radio, small gold picture frames, the few valuable antiques were all here. What had the boy wanted? Had he found it? Pete doubted it. He had still been searching when he'd heard Pete come in and had bolted empty-handed out the back.

Finally Pete went to the phone and did what he probably should have done when he'd first come in—he called the police.

The first thing Willy McOwat did on entering the house was to glare at Pete.

"Don't look at me. *I* didn't do it," said Pete, and then he told the chief everything he had seen and done on entering the house. The chief wrote it down as Ted Ball stared around the disheveled room, wide-eyed.

"Okay, Ted. Check out the neighborhood. See if anyone's seen anything of Pete's redheaded track star. Check out any strange vehicles."

"Want me to search those woods?"

"No point. *Now.*" The chief glared at Pete again.

Ted left.

The chief began going over the rooms inch by inch.

There were plenty of other places Pete could have gone next, but almost as if his truck were one large piece of iron and Connie's apartment the magnet, that was where he ended up. It was close to twelve noon. Pete had it in mind to see if she wanted to get some lunch, but when she opened the door, breakfast seemed to be the more appropriate subject.

It was her hair that disturbed him. Pete knew Connie's hair. Connie's hair was fine and straight. It was the kind of hair that looked like it hadn't been combed if it hadn't.

It hadn't.

Pete frowned at it, and Connie, seeing his look, yanked her fingers through it as she led him up the stairs. It didn't help.

"Are you just getting up?"

Connie looked at the clock. "Of course not," she said, but she looked like the clock had surprised her.

"Did you eat yet?"

"Of course I did."

"Which? Breakfast, lunch?"

Connie looked at the clock again. "Both," she said, but she said it like a question.

"Maybe you'd like to eat again. Or get a cup of coffee." Something about her made him doubt the wisdom of filling her in on what had just gone on at the Bates place. "I've been talking to the Coles—"

But even at that, something in Connie's sea green eyes shut down against him. "Why? Why did you go to the Coles?"

"I—"

"I don't think you're right about Annabel and Clara. I've been thinking a lot about it. I think we moved Annabel when we came in. I think I maybe put away the pills. The Coles didn't move her."

"I never thought they did," said Pete, and then immediately began to wonder if maybe, after all, they had. Simon had seemed anxious to shut Ella up about *something*.

"So what are you saying? They didn't just leave Annabel on the—"

"Okay," said Pete again. He held out a hand, to do exactly what, he didn't know, but Connie drew back from it.

"I have to go now," she said. *"You* have to go."

"Okay. Listen—" Pete didn't have a clue what he wanted her to listen to, but he knew he'd say anything right then to get that horrible panic to leave her eyes. "Connie. Maybe I'm wrong. What I said before about Annabel's body."

"I know. I know that. I just told you you were wrong, didn't I? Nobody *moved* her. Nobody left Clara there to—"

"No, no they didn't." Pete could see the panic receding. He tried again. "Do you want to get some coffee? I want to talk to you about Factotum. Things are getting busy."

Connie shook her head fast. Too fast. "I can't talk now. I have to go out." She looked at a nonexistent wristwatch. "I have to go out right *now.*"

"All right." Pete left. He pulled around the corner and parked where he could see her door. He sat there for forty-five minutes, but Connie never went anywhere.

Chapter

9

What was the matter with her? Pete wondered for the millionth time. It was more than just grief. Was it what he had said about Annabel's body, Clara's pills? Was she unable to accept that something was wrong with the deaths —was that it? Okay. If that was it, he wouldn't say another word about it. Was that why she didn't want him around, because she was afraid he'd try to talk her into it, try to *force* her to accept that something was wrong? Okay. It was his fault for bringing the whole thing up in the first place. He wouldn't talk about it again.

But that was only part of it. Why was Connie so upset about a little thing like inheriting a house? Okay, maybe it wasn't such a little thing, but still, it shouldn't make her this upset.

Pete was only diverted from his worries about Connie when he saw a flash of red out of the corner of his eye that turned out to be Jack Whiteaker's golden retriever, but the dog served to remind him of the redheaded boy. What had that boy expected to find in the Bates house that hadn't been there?

Pete was only diverted from his worries about the redhead when he walked into Factotum and caught the look in Rita's eye. It was a look similar to the one she had used the time her sixteen-year-old daughter, Maxine, had brought home a twenty-eight-year-old motorcyclist. With no helmet.

"You have a visitor." She nodded toward the lumpy rattan couch.

Paula Steigler's silky suit hissed as she stood up. "Hello, Pete." She smiled. She seemed to hiss when she did that, too.

"Hello."

"I wonder if I could interest you in lunch."

It's always the way with lunch, thought Pete. When you're starving, you get shot down. The minute you've lost your appetite, someone crams it down your throat. But still, he could stand to find out a thing a two from Paula Steigler.

"Okay," he said.

This time Rita's look was more in keeping with Bambi's mother's when Bambi first wandered off in the forest alone.

"Well," said Paula, picking over some unidentifiable casserole of red glop at Martelli's Italian restaurant. "I suppose Factotum's still too busy to consider another job. A very large one. For the future. Contingent, of course, on a certain outcome."

Pete's mouth was halfway around a meatball sub. He peered suspiciously over the sub at Paula.

"I hear Factotum's done some construction. This place, for example." Paula glanced around Martelli's sun-soaked dining room.

Pete chewed, swallowed, spoke. "What outcome?"

"The will, Pete. The will. Six houses. That would keep Factotum hopping for some time."

Pete sat up straight. The will.

The one thing that had been removed from the Bates

house. The one thing that someone might want to find. And burn. Someone like Paula Steigler. But Paula Steigler knew Pete had taken the wills, hadn't she? Or had she hoped to find one more, a newer one, a better one? Did she know a red-haired boy? Had *she* sent the boy to ransack the place in the hopes of finding another, newer piece of paper, one that favored *her?*

And then it dawned on Pete what Paula Steigler had just said.

Six houses. She was offering Factotum the job of building the six houses. "I wouldn't be too sure of this will business," said Pete. "You'll be contesting something that stands pretty solid."

"Does it? Or should I say, must it? I take it this Connie Bartholomew is your ex-wife. What's an ex-wife in the greater scheme of things, after all? Factotum's been involved with my aunts enough over the years so that you'd be a credible witness to my many visits to my aunts, my financial support in their times of crisis, their ongoing concern for my welfare—things like that."

Pete put down his sub, no longer hungry. He took a long swig of his Coke to clear his throat. He opened his mouth to tell Paula Steigler a few things. Instead he pulled his wallet out of his pocket, left a lot more money on the table than was called for, and walked out the door. Behind him he heard the angry clang of a fork on a plate.

It was time to get serious. If Connie wasn't ready to face up to the facts about Clara and Annabel, she certainly wasn't ready to fight Paula Steigler, but Pete was. If Paula was going to send people to break into and vandalize personal property, if she was going to beat the bushes—*bribe* the bushes—looking for false witnesses to her attachment to her aunts, Pete could certainly line up a few for Connie, just in case she changed her mind. He already had three witnesses to the soundness of Clara's mind or her attachment to Connie: Warren Johnson, Sarah Abrew, and Dotty Parsons. It was time to line up a few more. Maybe he should go back to the Coles. Who better to know who visited the sisters and who didn't? And there had certainly been something about Simon that made Pete a little curious to talk to Ella, alone. But somehow the idea of the Coles twice in one day seemed too much. Instead Pete decided to talk to Otto Snow.

Pete found Otto out working in his yard. Otto's bald, speckled head was just visible over the hedge he was trimming, and Pete walked through the picket gate and met him on the other side. Much to Pete's embarrassment, the minute he mentioned the Bates sisters, Otto's pale blue eyes filled with tears.

"To this day I can't believe it," he said, as if the sisters had died forty years ago. "Not both of them. Not my Clara. Not my Annabel. Look at me. I don't know what to do with myself these days." He looked up at Pete, apparently seeing a certain denseness there. "I'm trimming the hedge," he explained.

Pete decided to pursue the handy opening. "Connie used to do the yard work for the sisters. The garden was her special pride. She and Clara spent a lot of time talking over their plans for it."

"I know, I saw her there often. For years. Then, of course, there was the problem between the two of you and she went away."

Pete looked at Otto in surprise. Most people, Pete included, had seen Connie's leaving as the thing that had come first, and any problems between them resulting from that act. After much pain and even more soul-searching Pete now knew Otto's sequence of events to be closer to the facts. But how had *Otto* known? Pete felt his face grow hot. "Connie's back now. She'd taken on Clara's garden again. Didn't Clara mention it?"

"Of course she did. It was pretty near all she talked about. It was what kept her going these last few months."

"Do you happen to know what Clara might have meant by a reference in her will to Connie's helping her with definitions?"

"Definitions? No, I don't. She didn't do puzzles. Isn't

Connie going to make out okay? I'd hate to see that place go to the niece, somehow."

"Me too. I don't suppose you know much about this niece? You were at the sisters' house often. Did you ever run into her there?"

"Never. At Christmastime I recall Annabel wrapping a package for Paula. When she asked Clara to sign the card, Clara said they'd better include their last names so Paula would know who they were." Otto chuckled.

"Did the sisters talk about her? Did they ever fill you in on her goings on?"

"Never. I don't think they knew much about her goings on. Either that or they knew enough not to care for what they knew."

"Still, if Annabel had outlived Clara, Paula would have been her heir. She must not have disapproved too strongly."

Otto mulled that over. "I suppose to Annabel it didn't much matter what she did or didn't do since that niece was all the family she had left. Family was important to Annabel. That's why—" Otto turned his face away.

"But to Clara it was different?"

"To Clara it was different. Connie spent a lot more time with Clara than she did with Annabel, and Clara and Connie were more . . . more . . . alike, I'd say. They bucked each other up, laughed at the same jokes, you know? Had the same interests. Put 'em in a room together and they'd talk all day. I guess what I'm trying to say is that to Annabel, family, meaning Paula, was to be put before friends, meaning Connie. But to Clara, Connie *was* family—at least more family than her real family was. Excepting Annabel, of course."

Pete changed the subject. "Do you know any high-school-aged boys with long red hair? Down to here? Tall, thin?"

"Long red hair? High school? Why, no. I don't think so. Why do you ask?"

"No reason." Pete saw no need to upset Otto with tales of break-ins. The story would be all over the island soon enough.

73

Suddenly Otto peered hard at Pete, his eyes drier now. "We all felt sure once Connie came back you'd get together again. Why haven't you? We sometimes do the wrong thing even when we mean well, you know."

"I know that." *Boy,* did he know that!

Otto wrapped his short, thick fingers around Pete's arm as far as they would go. "You wait too long, you'll lose your chance, Pete."

Was Otto talking about Pete or about himself? Pete decided to find out. "I hear that you courted both Bates sisters, Otto. That you couldn't make up your mind to choose just one. Is this true?"

"I couldn't choose just one," repeated Otto, as if he'd repeated it many times. "I never asked. I never asked." A vague sort of haze came over his features. "If only . . . if only . . ." Otto snapped to. "I could have been married, Pete—happily married, all these years."

But to which one? Pete wondered.

Otto didn't say.

Pete left Otto's and returned to Beston's Store, where a full-fledged battle was raging on the bench.

"All you old fools think about is the past!" said Bert. "Preserve the past, preserve the past. Afraid of every little change. Preserve the *rot*—that's what you really mean. That old house is going to fall down around her ears faster than it would if she took a bulldozer to it. Now here's Pete. Pete, tell these old coots what it would take to fix up that house so's it'll last into posterity and preserve the sacred memory of a couple of old hens!"

"It needs a roof," said Pete. "No big deal."

"*And* new gutters. *And* a paint job. And a new furnace— you said so yourself on this very porch not—"

Pete turned his back to Bert and his face to Ed and Evan. "Have either of you seen Paula Steigler around much this past year?"

Evan shook his head.

Ed Healey pursed his chins. "Can't say as I have. Not until lately, of course. Not until after the sisters died."

"I saw her at the town hall not a month ago," said Bert.

Pete reluctantly turned around to face the other way. "Doing what?"

"How the hell do I know? Saw her traipsing up the steps as I traipsed down. I didn't see any call to grill her about her business, but then again maybe I should have, just so these old biddies'd have something to jaw about all day."

"I think I did see her," said Evan. "Now that you mention it. At Wren's. That was about a month back, too."

Wren's. Wren Realty. And the town hall.

Pete asked his last question. "Has anyone seen a teenage boy with long red hair around town?" Pete motioned to his own shoulder.

Bert snorted. "I tell you where you *don't* need to look— the barber's!" He snorted again, pleased with his own joke.

But none of them had seen any such hair or any such boy.

Myra Totabush, the clerk at the town hall, knew all about Paula Steigler, and in particular knew all about her visit to them approximately a month ago.

"She came in here on an errand for Annabel, she said. She wanted to find out how many buildable lots there were on the property. Annabel never sent her, of course. I knew that at the time, and I made sure to check up on it later, kind of cageylike. But it's public information. I told her what she wanted to know."

"How many buildable lots are there?"

All of a sudden Myra seemed to forget all about this being public information. "What do *you* want to know for?"

Pete considered several choice retorts, discarded the choicest, and settled for second best. "None of your business." He was amazed when it worked.

"Six. But only if the house comes down to make way for the road."

So it was just as Paula had told him. It was just as Paula

had discovered herself, not a month before the sisters died. *Both* sisters. At once. Coincidentally. Suspiciously coincidentally.

And that wasn't even taking into consideration the fact that someone had moved Annabel's body.

Pete asked Myra about the red-haired boy, but got a bewildered shake of the head for an answer.

James Wren Realty was the oldest and, currently, only surviving realty company on the island, the new realtor Nate Cox having left recently under something of a cloud. There wasn't much going on around the island these days, realtywise, so it wasn't surprising to Pete that the younger James Wren, who usually twiddled his thumbs behind the desk while his father roamed the island, remembered Paula Steigler's visit and almost every word of their conversation to boot.

"She inquired as to the approximate market value of her aunts' house," said James, who was distinguished from his father by use of his full name and long, convoluted sentences. "We discussed the comparative options, existing house unrenovated with land in toto, existing house renovated with land, etc., razing existing house and selling undeveloped subdivided house lots, razing existing house and developing lots for sale on speculation—the latter, of course, being by far the most profitable for the owner."

"To the tune of?"

James Wren, Jr., gave Pete the tune.

Pete gave a long, low whistle to go along with it.

Pete asked futilely again after the red-haired boy, and drove away mulling over the numbers he'd just heard. Paula Steigler had heard the same ones not a month before her aunts died. What had *her* response to it been? A month later her aunts die, both of them, of supposedly natural causes. Was that Paula Steigler's response? Was that the answer to what he'd been struggling with all along, the *who did it,* the *what for?* And if Paula *had* done it—*how?* Sure, Paula could have given Clara the extra digoxin pills, but first she would have had to kill Annabel. Could she have done that and made it look like a heart attack? True, Annabel's body had been moved, but it had been moved *after* she had died. Maybe Paula had given *Annabel* something earlier and then returned later to make sure it had worked. But whatever she had given her, it had not shown up on autopsy, and besides, *Paula* was the one who had ordered the autopsies. Why would she do that if she had killed the aunts herself? Was her method so foolproof that she could risk the medical examination without fear of discovery? Would, *could* Paula Steigler do such a thing? All he knew about Paula Steigler was that she would attempt to bribe a man into selling his wife down the river.

He was soon to find out one more thing about her.

Chapter

10

Connie looked at Pete, mildly curious as to why he seemed to be watching her so intently. She was getting more used to these daily visits—was, in truth, beginning to kind of depend on them—but still, they seemed to wear her out somehow. He'd already hinted around about her coming back to work at Factotum, but Connie just didn't have the energy for that kind of work right now. There had been another reason, once, why she didn't want to go back there, but right now she couldn't quite remember what it was. She said no to the job offer and leaned back in her chair, watching Pete as he talked. It was nice to watch Pete. There was something so solid about him. Solid and yet spare. Comfortable. But he seemed to talk so much these days. It was exhausting to listen to someone talk this much. Maybe that was why she was having so much trouble listening. She was tired. Connie yawned. "Who are you talking about again?"

Suddenly Pete looked unhappy. Upset. Connie hated to see him upset. She looked away from him.

"Otto. Otto Snow."

"Oh, Otto." Why was Pete talking to her about Otto Snow? Still, Connie put her mind to the subject of Otto, trying to keep up her end of the conversation. "Annabel told me once she was sorry she hadn't said yes to Otto long ago."

"It's hard to say yes to someone who hasn't asked."

"Who hasn't asked?"

The soft creases in Pete's forehead tensed up. *"Otto.* Otto Snow."

"Oh, Otto *asked,* all right. Otto asked plenty. Annabel told me so."

Pete leaned forward. "Are you sure? Otto told me he never asked her. He told me he never could make up his mind whether to ask Annabel or Clara so he never asked either one."

"Otto asked Annabel. But I'm not supposed to tell anyone. She doesn't want Clara to know." But now Clara was dead. So was Annabel. Suddenly Connie felt very tired indeed. She yawned again. What *were* they talking about? Otto. That's right, Otto Snow. "He asked Annabel," she said. "He asked her a lot."

Pete looked doubtful. He changed the subject. "Do you know a teenager with long red hair? Down to here? A guy?"

Connie concentrated. Sporadically. "No, I don't know anyone like that," she said finally.

"Oh." Pete seemed disappointed, but it didn't slow him down much. He kept asking these *questions.* "About Paula Steigler. Did you run into her at the Bateses' much?"

Paula Steigler. Connie tried to concentrate on Paula Steigler. No, she hadn't seen Paula Steigler. She hadn't *ever* seen Paula Steigler, and she told Pete so—not in all the years she'd been in and out of the Bateses'. All the years . . . Suddenly Connie didn't want to talk about this anymore. She stood up. "I think you'd better go."

Pete didn't much look like he wanted to. It was curious

that Pete was so wrought up about all of this, and all Connie wanted to do was to go back to bed. Finally Pete got up and walked toward the stairs, but slowly.

"Thanks for coming," said Connie. It took a lot of effort to say that, but still, the brown eyes in front of her remained unhappy. Connie turned away from them.

"I'll call you," said Pete.

Connie waved over her shoulder. She went into her room and lay down on the bed. She never heard his feet on the stairs, or the door close behind him.

She slept.

Pete *was* upset. But he was well aware as he turned the truck and drove with a vengeance toward Otto Snow's that most of the reason he was upset was because of Connie, not because of Otto Snow. He didn't like what was going on with her—he didn't like it one bit. She was too distracted. She was too . . . too what? Too detached. He supposed it was better to be detached than to be obsessive over her grief, but still, there was something real about grief, and Pete felt that Connie could deal with her grief, that *he* could deal with her grief, better than he could with this . . . this drifting. He didn't understand it. He didn't like it.

Then again, he didn't much like what he was, or wasn't, learning about this red-haired boy, and he didn't much like what he had just learned about Otto Snow.

Still, before Pete got as far as the turn for Otto's, he found himself leaving the road and heading for the Bates house, Connie still firmly entrenched in his mind. If only she would snap out of this whatever-this-was and start thinking about the Bates house, start putting her energies into saving the Bates house, he knew she'd feel better about things.

The Bates house. Pete parked the truck in front of it and looked at it with a fresh eye. It was nothing much—not if taken in the greater scheme of things: a smallish Victorian farmhouse made to look larger by the sprawling front porch and the peaks in the roof. Yes, the porch was sagging, and yes, Bert, the roof *was* leaking, and yes, the garden was parched-looking and already overrun with weeds.

So, speaking of obsessions, why was *Pete* so obsessed with this house? Why was he so obsessed with Connie taking possession of it? Why, when he looked at this house, instead of just remembering two nice old women who were dead, did he also remember Connie and himself drinking out of the hose? *Was* it garden magic? Was it because this was the very last place they had laughed, had fun, been comfortable with each other that it had become, at least for him, a symbol of, or a key to, all their future happy times? Pete sighed. Maybe happiness was no longer possible. Not for them.

Pete got out of the truck. He had planned to go inside, to pick up the mess he knew was waiting for him there, but the closer he got to the porch, the less he felt like crossing it, the less he felt like opening that door and looking inside. It was a *big* mess in there. Suddenly it seemed like an insurmountable mess. He turned around and walked out into the gardens instead.

Pete could barely tell a weed from a wisteria, but still, he could make sure that they didn't die of thirst. He uncoiled the hose from the side of the house, turned the faucet, and nothing happened. Then he remembered the leaky faucet, about Connie having to turn the water off from inside the basement after every use. Pete fished around in his pocket for the keys to the house. Yes, as he suspected, among the other keys on the ring was an old and rusted key to the bulkhead padlock. He unlocked it, climbed in, and turned on the water at the main tap. He found the sprinkler attachments, set them up, and began to give everything, weeds as well as wisteria, a good drink.

After some minutes of gazing at the ground and reliving his memories, good and bad, Pete's attention was drawn to the Coles' station wagon driving away from their house. Simon was in it. Ella was not. This was what Pete had been waiting for, a solitary talk with Ella Cole. He left the garden to do its drinking and walked down the road.

Ella Cole met Pete at the door. This time she seemed a little more cautious. She didn't ask him in.

"I just wondered," began Pete, and watched as Ella's face closed against him, similar to the way Connie's had of late. "Something you said when I was here last gave me the impression that you weren't all that keen on your husband's arrangement with Annabel Bates."

"I never said that."

Pete examined Ella Cole's bland features for any hint of that earlier show of rebellion. He decided to try to stir it up again. "Didn't you? I'd say your husband thought you did. But maybe you'd rather not say anything unless he's around."

Ella blinked. Yes, she saw her chance, one she must not have gotten too often, the chance for a little free speech, and suddenly the simmering teakettle Pete had noticed the other day boiled over.

"And why should I be keen about that arrangement? Don't you think it wasn't plain as day what my half of it was going to be? Oh, sure, Simon got to play the mighty landowner disposing of all those acres any old way he saw fit! What did I get? Drudgery! Day in and day out! Mopping up after some old lady who isn't even kin! I told you before, taking care of Clara killed Annabel, and it would have killed me, too. *We'll* do this, he says! *We'll* do that. He can just leave that *we* right out of it! It's *me* who'd do every last bit of taking care of that old woman. Don't you believe different for a minute!"

"But he mentioned a nursing home—"

"Nursing home! What would he get out of putting Clara in a nursing home? The state would take the house to pay the nursing home bill. But if we kept Clara here—if I worked my fingers to the bone feeding her and dressing her and cleaning her up—*then,* he figured, we'd make out in the end, see? *Then,* he figured, old Clara would leave us what the sale of that place brought in. And don't you think for one minute Simon didn't know just how much that was! He'd got it all figured out! Six house lots with houses on 'em? He'd sit pretty for the end of his days. *I'd* be long dead, but *he'd* be on easy street till kingdom come—when he's a hundred and eighty, no doubt!"

Pete coughed. "But I thought he said he didn't want to see a development go in next door. I thought that was why he was hoping Connie would inherit."

All of a sudden Ella Cole seemed to think she'd said too much. Either that or she had the ears of a rabbit. She stopped talking. Soon afterward Simon Cole's car wound its way around the far turn on its way home, disappearing from view temporarily at the bend.

"You go," Ella Cole hissed at Pete. "You get out of here. Forget anything I told you."

"Just one more question," said Pete. "Have you seen a young man with long red hair around?"

"The police have already been here about that."

"What did you tell them?"

"Who says I told them anything?"

"Did you see him?"

"Who says I'll tell you? I want you to get!"

Pete got.

All the way back to Factotum he mulled over what Ella Cole had said. The day before, Simon had talked about a nursing home for Clara. He had bemoaned the idea of a six-house development. One, if not both, of these Coles was lying. So, apparently, was Otto Snow.

But *why?*

Had one of these people moved Annabel's body? Had one of them given Clara too many pills? Who? Simon Cole?

But *why?*

There were only two motives for murder, after all—love and money. Simon Cole fit in very nicely with the second. But Simon Cole's only hope of getting hold of the Bates money was if Clara Bates lived. Didn't Simon know the contents of Clara's will—that Connie, not he, would inherit and control the property? What if Annabel had somehow led him to believe that he was executor of *both* wills? Maybe Simon had planned that Annabel would die but Clara would live. Maybe he had somehow killed Annabel in such a way that it had looked like natural death, but had gone back and moved her while making sure it had worked, just as Pete had earlier suspected Paula Steigler had done. If that were indeed the case, Simon Cole must have sweated off a few pounds once Clara was killed. But why was *Clara* killed if Simon so desperately wanted her to live?

But wait. Wasn't there another person handy who might *not* have wanted Clara to live? Suppose *Ella* Cole had gone next door and found Annabel dead. Suppose she had realized in a flash what Annabel's death meant. What had she called it? "Drudgery. Mopping up after some old woman who wasn't even kin." Suppose Ella Cole rolled Annabel over just to make sure she was really dead. Suppose she then went to the medicine cabinet and found Clara's pills. Suppose she explained to Clara that Annabel was dead, that she was going to take care of her from now on. Suppose she started her care right then with a dose of pills. An *over*dose of pills.

It fit. Every last little troubling, niggling question that had been festering in Pete's mind was answered with this gruesome explanation. Except for one.

Why had Ella Cole blabbed everything to him? Had she been so upset, so confused, so guilty that she'd felt the need to explain? Had she then realized she'd said too much, led him far enough down the path to be able to reach the end on his own? Was it then she had panicked and told him to leave?

So. What did this mean, practically speaking? What was Pete supposed to do now? He needed to talk this over with someone. He needed to know if he was crazy or if he was on the right track. For talking purposes, the first person he consulted used to be Connie, but Pete knew he shouldn't talk this over with her. He had already thrown her off balance with his discussion of the moved body, the unreachable pills. Connie wouldn't be able to handle this at all.

Suddenly Pete felt very much alone.

Chapter

11

Rita Peck leaned back into Pete's porch rocker, put her feet up on the porch rail, and watched the sinking sun turn the creek in the marsh to gold.

Rita's daughter was late, as usual. Rita was getting ten years older and about one day wiser with each single year of being mother-of-a-teen, and she'd learned to take advantage of moments like this. That's why she was sitting on Pete's porch, treating herself to a relaxing moment. At least that was one of the reasons she was there. The other reason had to do with being the mothery sort. If she couldn't be home starting her own dinner, she decided to make sure somebody ate a little something right here.

The hall door slammed. Pete dropped something on his kitchen table. Rita raised a hand over the back of the rocker and called, "Out here!"

Pete came out onto the porch and looked at her in surprise. "What are you doing here this late?"

"Waiting for Maxine. Catching up to myself. Get us something to drink and sit down, will you?"

Pete got a beer for himself and a glass of wine for Rita, returned to the porch, and sat down in the rocking chair beside her. He took a sip of beer and sighed. "Good idea, Rita, good idea."

"There's cold ham and potato salad in the fridge. And two nice tomatoes. I assume you haven't eaten."

"No." Pete sounded surprised again. He was always forgetting about food. It drove Rita crazy.

"By the way, I saw Paula Steigler talking to Warren Johnson today."

"So?"

"Paula Steigler. And Warren, the witness to the will?"

Obviously Pete had other things on his mind. "Know any teenage boys with long red hair, Rita? Down to here?"

Rita shook her head. "But if you want to know anything about teenage boys, Maxine's the expert."

"Maxine!" Pete seemed to perk up.

Then Rita blew it. "How's Connie?"

Pete stood up and leaned into the porch rail as if he were trying to expand his floor space by a foot. His straining shoulders pulled his shirttails out of his jeans, and Rita had to stop herself from tucking them back.

"I don't know, Rita. Something's just not *right*. She—"

"Hey!" Maxine hollered from the hall, and Rita found herself wishing for the first time in her life that her daughter had been later.

But Maxine always cheered Pete up. "Out here, Max," he called. "Grab a Coke."

Rita opened her mouth to explain that Maxine was on a health food kick and didn't drink Coke anymore, but before she could get the words out Maxine appeared on the porch, sucking down a Coke.

"What are you doing?" Maxine asked her mother.

"I'm sitting down. Is it against the law for mothers to sit?"

Maxine rolled her eyes at Pete.

"Hey," Pete tactfully interrupted them, one of the things

he did best. And often. "Do you know any guys about your age, Maxine, with long red hair, down to here? Tall? Thin? Can run like a racehorse?"

Maxine's eyes lit up. "No, who is he?"

"That's what I'm trying to find out."

"Jason Pierce has red hair, doesn't he?" Rita chimed in.

"Jason *Pierce?* With his head practically *shaved?* About two feet *ten?"*

"Sorry," said Rita.

"I don't think that's him," said Pete.

"And Gary has red hair but not that long. It couldn't be him, either. I don't know anybody like that. Not around here."

And that meant there was no such animal around. Rita was sure of it. Nashtoba's only school ran from kindergarten through grade twelve, and if there were any redheaded boys in it Maxine would know it. She had pretty well cased out most of the boys from the schools on the Hook, too. Rita was sure of *that.*

"Hey," said Maxine to her now. "Let's go, will you? I have to get going. I'm meeting Anna at eight."

"Get in the car," said Rita. "I'll be right out. *And don't touch those keys!"*

Pete was teaching Maxine to drive. For some strange reason it didn't seem to be aging *Pete* any, but Rita was getting grayer and grayer.

"So," said Rita, once Maxine had gone. "What are you going to do?"

"About what?"

"About Connie."

Pete sighed. "I don't know. I do know that Clara was in her right mind when she left Connie her house, and everyone else knows it, too—even Paula, probably. But not Connie. I think at some point she'll come around to this realization, but then it might be too late. I think I'd better look out for Connie until she decides to look out for herself."

"And you're going to eat."

Pete frowned at Rita. Then his face lifted. "Ham. And potato salad?"

"And some nice tomatoes. And May's homemade wheat bread."

Pete got up, heading for the kitchen, and Rita followed, watching as Pete set out the food. The milk bottle followed the rest of the food onto the counter, and Rita sighed in contentment. There was nothing quite like the sense of satisfaction she got when she saw all four basic food groups represented in one meal.

After Pete had eaten he went back out to the porch. It was late enough to be dark, and dark enough so that Pete had very little in the way of visuals to distract him from the darkness of his own thoughts. He rocked harder and harder. He thought harder and harder. He worried more and more. Finally he rocked so hard he launched himself onto his feet and out the door toward the beach.

A car's tires whispered on the sand-covered road and Pete, halfway across his lawn, turned in surprise. This road was a dead end. Not many cars drove down it this hour of the night unless they were coming to see him, and these days *no one* came to see him. Not at this hour of the night. Nevertheless, the strange car turned into his driveway, and a strange, starched-haired silhouette was illuminated as the driver-side door opened wide.

Paula Steigler.

For a second Pete considered hiding there in the dark, but then he thought of a few things he'd like to talk to Paula Steigler about.

"Over here," he called.

She came over there. She came pretty damned close to him over there, too. Pete backed up.

"We need to talk," she said.

"Okay. I was just heading for a walk on the beach."

Pete could just make out the downward slant to Paula's

head as she looked at her shoes. "I'm afraid I'm in heels."
She giggled. She wasn't, or shouldn't have been, a giggler.
"And panty hose."

So? Pete wanted to ask. Connie would never have let a
little thing like heels and panty hose keep her from a walk on
the beach. But then again, you didn't find Connie in panty
hose and heels too often in the first place. Pete turned
reluctantly back toward the house.

They settled awkwardly on either end of the living room
couch—not a room Pete frequented much since it had been
taken over by Factotum, but somehow his usual slouching
around the kitchen table didn't seem like Paula's speed.
After a few seconds' hesitation he offered her a drink.

"Love to. What do you have?"

"Ballantine Ale."

It had been Connie's drink. Apparently it wasn't Paula's.

"Perhaps a cold glass of water."

Pete got Paula a glass of water and himself an ale. That
was his first mistake.

"I confess to shock and dismay at your abandoning me at
yesterday's lunch," began Paula.

Since Pete had been pretty shocked and dismayed himself, he didn't answer.

"I think we've somehow gotten off on the wrong foot. I
think I might have misinterpreted something you said, and
I'm *sure* you've misinterpreted me."

Pete just shrugged and drank his beer, but Paula seemed
to find that an acceptable response.

"I'm sure I don't know why, but you seem to feel your
ex-wife—" She looked at Pete over the rim of her as yet
untouched glass. "It is your *ex*-wife?"

Pete nodded.

Paula giggled again. She wasn't getting any better at it. "I
confess I was beginning to wonder! But apparently you seem
to feel she is somehow entitled to my family's property."

"Clara seemed to think so."

"I'm sure I don't know why. Do you?"

"Clara and Connie loved that garden. They worked in it

together for years. This spring Connie came back to work there, and she and Clara planned it and worried over it for hours. Connie did the work, but it was still Clara's—"

"The garden. You're telling me this really is all about the *garden?*"

"No, it isn't all about the garden. They were friends. More than friends." Pete, thinking of Otto's remarks, fell just short of adding that Connie was more like Clara's family than her real family was.

"Friends. And I'm her niece. And you seem to see nothing wrong with a *friend* walking off with everything that should, by law, belong to me?"

Pete was, on occasion, a nervous drinker. He downed his beer and stood up. "I seem to recall reading someplace, in a will or something, that according to *law* that place belongs to Connie."

Paula Steigler stood up, too. All she'd had was a glass of water, but still, she teetered sideways toward Pete. Pete's already limited street smarts were further dulled by one rapidly consumed ale, and he grabbed her to steady her. That was his second mistake.

All of a sudden Paula was all over him.

"Ex-wives are so *distant,* don't you think, Pete? Don't you think it's about time you looked around for someone a little closer at *hand?*"

It was such a corny gambit, it was so trite, that Pete was instantly angry at Paula for pulling it and at himself for falling for it. He pushed her away. "So what are you trying to say, that those panty hose *do* come off, but only if there are six house lots in the offing?"

Paula Steigler's face suddenly looked like something Pete had first come across at the age of six on Cruella DeVille.

She turned and stormed toward the door.

"Hey," said Pete. "One more question." But he waited until she stopped and turned to ask it. He wanted to see her face. "Your redheaded friend? The one who can run? The one who trashes houses?"

The face of Cruella DeVille disappeared, but nothing replaced it. Paula's face was blank.

Pete had to admit that her puzzlement seemed real—at least, as real as anything else about her.

Despite being made to feel the fool the last time he tried it, Pete decided the next morning to talk again to the chief of police. After all, the man was supposed to be his friend. If you can't look foolish in front of your friends, where can you?

It helped a fair amount that when Pete walked into the tiny cedar-shingled police station, Willy was looking pretty foolish himself. He was up on a chair behind the dispatching desk with a rolled-up newspaper in his hand, and the dispatcher, Jean Martell, was holding on to his belt as Ted Ball hollered directions.

"Over there! Wow! It just took off like a *shot!* There! By the lamp! Oh, you missed it."

"Missed what?" asked Pete.

The chief looked over his shoulder. He seemed relieved it was only Pete.

"The biggest spider I've ever seen in my life!" said Ted Ball, his face very red from all that watching. "This big *black* thing." He shuddered.

Jean Martell, who had never taken her eyes off the ceiling, finally turned away in disgust. "It's back inside that crack up there. You'll never get him now."

The chief climbed down from the chair, and Jean sat down in it, apparently not too concerned about the evil that lurked above her head. Ted Ball continued to stand on the far side of the desk, staring at the ceiling.

"What's up?" Willy asked Pete.

Pete didn't say anything. The chief and Pete had developed a fairly sophisticated silent communication by now, born out of necessity by the finely tuned eyes and ears of Jean Martell. Willy led Pete out of range of Jean's radar and into his office.

Pete decided to solidify his position as the currently less

foolish-looking of the two. *"Black* spider, huh? I hate those."

Willy just looked at him.

Pete decided this was as solid as his position was going to get. He cleared his throat and went on. "I'm here about the Bateses again."

The chief didn't look as skeptical as Pete thought he would, and Pete thought he might know why. "Anything turn up on that redhead?"

Willy shook his head. "By the time we got in on it he'd had plenty of time to get off the island, if that's where he came from. Nobody seems to have seen him. Except you."

Pete squirmed.

"And there was no real damage to the house. Whatever he was trying to do, he wasn't trying to wreck the place. He was looking for something. Granted, he didn't much care how he left the place when he was through, but nothing was broken or destroyed."

"I figured he was looking for something. And he didn't find it, did he?"

Willy doffed an invisible hat to Pete. "So what else do you want to know?"

Pete cleared his throat. "Anything on the pill bottles?"

"Other than your fingerprints, you mean? On file as elimination prints from a previous murder investigation? Don't you get tired of this?"

"Yes. Don't you?"

The chief didn't answer.

"Did you find anything in the house?"

"Some unidentifiable prints, presumably this redhead's. Nothing else exciting."

"So what are you going to do?"

"About what? The redhead? We'll keep a—"

"I told you where I found those pills. Twenty-five feet away from a bedridden woman. Clara never got up and took any twenty-two pills. She never moved Annabel's body. I've talked to Hardy. Even he agreed."

Willy looked out the window at the beach plums in the

dunes as if he were seeing them for the last time. Pete figured he probably did that often. The locals had reacted to this off-islander the way they reacted to all off-islanders, only worse; it was a far cry from your Southern-hospitality type of welcome, and his first few murder cases hadn't exactly helped things. Yet. "Has Hardy changed his opinion about the natural causes of the deaths?"

Pete shook his head.

"I'll have a talk with him. But you see that unless *he* does, I'd be kind of crazy if *I* did?" He looked hard at Pete again, wanting Pete to see, and Pete had to admit he did. Contradicting the highly respected local physician's decision wasn't going to help Willy with the locals any, but still . . .

"But still," said Pete.

Willy rubbed his huge hands over his thinning hair. There'd been a lot more hair when he'd first come here.

"I'll talk to Hardy." Willy stood up. He looked so miserable that Pete felt he needed to explain.

"It's just that there are all these questions. And this kid wrecking the house."

"The kid wrecking the house could be unrelated. And it's one thing to raise the questions. It's another to find the answers. It's also another thing altogether when you start asking yourself what those answers are going to solve."

Pete looked at the chief in surprise. He didn't sound much like the Boston homicide cop he had once been. As a matter of fact, he sounded a lot like Hardy Rogers. Maybe the guy was going to fit in around here after all—maybe he was going to finally become, instead of the efficient, by-the-book law enforcement machine the selectmen had hired him for, the bastion of common sense that the island needed him to be. But what was it going to cost?

Two dead old women.

"I'll talk to Hardy," the chief said again. "But unofficially."

"You officially looked for the redhead, didn't you?"

"That's different, Pete. Surely you see the difference? The house was vandalized. I can go after the redhead in the open. What will people think if I start going house to house asking questions about the deaths of those two sisters?"

And Pete knew, without having to wait around to ask, that the chief wasn't going to do anything more about the Bateses. Yes, he'd ask around every now and then about the redhead. He'd pay an unofficial call on Hardy Rogers. Hardy would explain Pete away somehow—he'd stick to his "natural causes" guns. The chief could then breathe a sigh of relief and go home.

The question was, why couldn't Pete? Was it just his natural curiosity, or was it his affection for the Bates sisters? Or did he really think something evil needed to be avenged? How much did it matter to *him* that they found out whatever it was the red-hair had tried, and failed, to find? How much did it matter to him how and why the two old women died? That they had died, yes, that mattered. Did it matter how? Was it worth the price of a whole lot of pain and suspicion? Pete thought of Connie. What would it do to her if she found out that someone had killed Clara or Annabel? Connie had never before been a person who needed to be shielded from pain. In their life together they had faced outside adversity shoulder to shoulder. Their *inner* adversity had been another matter. Pete had simply refused to admit it might exist. But the Connie of recent days was not the Connie Pete had known for so long. Connie wasn't handling the deaths of the Bates sisters well. If it turned out to be murder, he doubted she'd be able to handle that at all. Maybe it was time for Pete to become a bastion of common sense himself.

Chapter

12

Connie got up off the bed where she had been lying for too long and walked into the kitchen, then stared at the sink trying to remember why she'd come. Hungry? Was she hungry? Not enough to get worked up over. Dishes? There were only two, a cup and a spoon. Breakfast. Yesterday's. They could be left till after lunch. She opened the refrigerator and stood in front of that for a while, forgetting the minute she saw it what was in it. She shut the door and walked back to the bedroom.

There was a knock on the door.

Pete. It would be Pete. He'd come in, he'd sit down, he'd talk to her for a while, he'd connect for her all these crazy scattered dots. She was beginning to hinge her day, her mind, her focus on the sight of Pete's face at her door.

She went down the stairs and opened the door—not that she had to, since it was never locked.

"My name is Paula Steigler."

Connie looked at the probing face in front of her. She didn't much like it, but she couldn't at the moment think of anything she could do about it. She held open the door.

Paula Steigler strode up the stairs, into Connie's living corner, and sat down in the one chair. She looked around. "So this is why you're after my aunts' place."

Connie didn't know what that sentence meant. She didn't answer it.

Paula Steigler slanted a look up at Connie. "Your ex-husband and I were talking about you last night."

Connie could make more sense out of that. Paula Steigler had been talking to Pete. Last night.

"We were trying to figure out what you were doing still hanging on around here. He seemed to think it was the garden. He says you like the garden?"

A direct question. Easy. "Yes," said Connie. "I like the garden."

"And just because of this . . . this *garden* you think you have a right to take the house, the entire property, away from me? Is that what you think?"

Connie should have told her then that she didn't want to take the property away at all but it seemed like a lot of work. Again she said nothing.

Paula Steigler walked over to the window and the loose panes of glass rattled. "I can't believe this. I can't believe that because of some lousy garden—"

She whirled around. "You know what I think? I think you're nuts. And so was Clara! And I'm going to prove it, too. I can't believe this. I just can't believe this. Here I was, cruising along, laying out my plans, and there you were, already down the road ahead of me, blowing up my bridges! This unbelievable, this unfathomable, this *ridiculous* mess is all because of you. It's all *your* fault." Paula stomped to the stairs and turned, waiting to hear what Connie might have to say for herself.

Connie shrugged. Paula wasn't going to get any argument from *her*. After all, this was just what she herself had been saying all along.

It *was* all her fault.
Maybe a lot of *other* things had been all her fault, too.

Rita Peck stepped out of her little Dodge Omni and
reached back in to remove the stack of amended menus she
was delivering to the Whiteaker Hotel. Factotum was short-
handed, and Rita, who usually stayed cemented to the desk,
was doing an errand or two at lunch to catch them up on a
few jobs. It didn't help any that Pete kept roaming around
the Bates place and Connie's place and Otto's place and the
Cole place, but she was used to Pete by now. Of course, Rita
knew that Pete was used to *her,* too. It was one of the most
comfortable things about their very comfortable
arrangement—that they were used to each other, that they
made allowances for each other, that they helped each other
out when the chips were down. That was why, when Rita
saw Paula Steigler and Warren Johnson walking out of the
dining room at the Whiteaker side by side, she nearly
dropped the stack of menus in her rush to get back to
Factotum to tell Pete.

"What?" said Pete when Rita told him.
"Paula *Steigler*. And Warren *Johnson.* The *witness.* I told
you I saw them together before and you hardly listened.
Now look what's happened! *Lunch!"*
Pete frowned.
"I ask you what Paula Steigler could be doing with Warren
Johnson, what in your wildest *dreams* could she be doing
with little Warren *Johnson,* that wouldn't amount to no
good?"
"Oh, I don't know, Rita. What could she get out of
Warren? He already witnessed the will. He can't take it
back."
"Can't he?"
"What are you driving at, Rita?"
"I'm driving at this. Paula Steigler is getting Warren
to . . . to . . . to do *something."*

"Well, you let me know when you figure out what, all right?"

Rita rolled her eyes at the ceiling. Maybe she was nuts, but she was going to keep a nice sharp weather eye on Paula and Warren from now on.

Pete had been right. Hardy Rogers had not retracted his verdict of deaths by natural causes, and Willy McOwat was officially letting it go at that. Pete and the chief shared a late-night beer in a quiet booth at Lupo's, and Pete listened to the chief tick off one by one the reasons why Hardy was probably right.

"Proof," said Willy. "Even if someone did do something to one or both of the sisters, I'm not going to get anywhere without proof. So I start openly investigating this thing and I come up with no proof. What have we gained? This island is crazed enough already without me stirring up more suspicion and fear."

Pete could see that point.

"And if I wanted to sneak around quietly on this, assuming first of all that I *could* sneak around quietly on this—"

"You couldn't," said Pete. "Not around here."

"See what I mean?"

Pete saw that point, too.

But then Willy leaned across the booth and started grilling Pete about the Bateses. At least it started with the Bateses. Then it moved on to Paula Steigler and Otto Snow, and it finished up with the Coles.

When Pete finished talking, Willy leaned back against the booth and stared at the ceiling for a bit, then he leaned in toward Pete again. "Of course, I can see why you might want to clarify a particular legal point. Considering your own personal interest in your ex-wife's personal interest in that will."

Pete stared at the chief. "What legal point?"

Willy mentioned a particular legal point that he thought might be troubling Pete.

* * *

"So do I have this right?" Pete asked Roberta Ballantine the next morning. "If Annabel, half owner of the house, were alive, she could have held on to the property, even if Clara had gone into a nursing home. But if Annabel were dead and Clara owned the entire house, the house and property would have been taken by the state to pay the nursing home bill."

"Assuming, of course, there were no funds elsewhere to pay for the nursing home care. Clara would then have had to apply for the state and federal assistance program, and the house would indeed have been forfeited."

Pete mulled that over. "But what if Clara got better and wanted to come home? She wouldn't *have* a home."

Roberta Ballantine just looked at Pete.

"So the state assumes if you go in, you don't come out?"

"The state assumes you owe them for your care. Your assets are dissolved to pay that debt, whatever those assets may be. These laws are always changing, even as we speak, but there are ways around this existing one. With a little forethought, a little planning, properties can be transferred into a relative's name, into a trust, but it has to be done thirty months in advance of any nursing home admission. If three years ago the Bateses had foreseen that one or both of them might need nursing home care, they could have transferred title to their home to the niece."

A niece who would have sold it out from under them on the spot?

Pete thanked Roberta Ballantine and left. Ella Cole had been telling the truth about this particular point, at least.

It was questionable whether Pete would have pursued things much further if he hadn't driven down Otto Snow's street and seen him hard at work on his hedge.

After about five minutes of delicate attempts to get some answers out of Otto, Pete began to feel like he was grappling with an eel. Finally he decided to get tough.

"I heard, Otto, that you really did ask Annabel to marry you but she said no." Pete couldn't have put it much plainer than that.

Otto blinked. "I don't know where you got that idea, Pete. Unless Annabel misled you, for some reason."

Pete gave up. He was no good at badgering old men.

He went to see Connie instead.

Connie's little TR-6 was parked in the street, but there was no answer at the Coolidge apartment. Pete banged on the door louder, thought he heard something, and shoved the door open, calling as he went. He walked far enough up the stairs until he could just see her through the archway into the bedroom, curled up on her side on the bed, eyes open wide.

"Oh, it's you." She propped her head on her hand. "I thought it was Paula again."

"Steigler? What's she—" Pete stopped, alarmed at the sight of Connie.

She didn't even bother to get up. She dropped her head into the crook of her elbow. She looked thin. Tired. Haunted. "She wanted to know if it was because of the garden."

"If *what* was?"

"If I was trying to steal her property because of the garden. I told you, Pete. I told you she'd say that, that it was her property and that I—"

"Come on, Con. What's the matter with you? Of *course* she's going to say that. But she's wrong. Everyone on this island thinks so. *I* think so. Clara thought so. And it's not just because of the garden."

Connie didn't move.

Pete sat down on the bed. Connie rolled over on her back, folded her arms over her, and looked at Pete with a face so expressionless he wouldn't have believed it was hers. It scared Pete to death. He reached out and gave her a shake.

"What are you doing lying around in here all day? This isn't healthy. I mean it. Will you get up and get back to work?"

Connie didn't answer.

Pete wracked his brain for Factotum jobs that might pique

101

her interest, things that were far from the Bates house, things that didn't involve gardens. He had made enough mistakes already in bringing up his concerns about the Bateses. He wasn't going to fall into that trap again. "Lee-Ann Mason needs swimming lessons. You're still certified, aren't you?"

Somewhat understandably, Connie didn't get too excited about giving Lee-Ann swimming lessons.

"And Felix Fleming needs someone to dig up information on the glaciers that formed Cape Hook."

Connie didn't seem much interested in glaciers, either.

Come on, Pete yelled at himself. *Is this the best you can do?* Something outdoors, in the sun, something active . . . "James Wren has some lawn furniture that needs to be rewebbed." So now he was into rehab for the mentally ill. So great. Pete gave up on the subject of work. "When did you eat last, anyway?"

Connie looked with some confusion at the kitchen, and that did it for Pete. He gave up on asking. He went into the kitchen and pawed around, but most of what he found was unfit for human consumption.

He returned to the bedroom. "I'm going to the store," he said.

Connie didn't move.

Pete left for the store, but when he got as far as the phone booth at the gas station he got out of the truck and called Hardy Rogers.

"She's not eating," said Pete.

"Not eating?" Hardy boomed into the phone after him.

"And she's sleeping all the time."

"Sleeping, too?"

"And she won't *do* anything. She just lies around all the time! She doesn't even get dressed!"

"Not getting dressed."

"And this stuff about Annabel and Clara. I don't know, she—"

"I suppose she's her own worst critic, too?"

"Yes," said Pete. "Yes, that's the other thing! She acts like everyone else walks on water and she doesn't count for *squat*. And it would take a hydraulic lift to get the corners of her mouth to turn up! I don't know, I'm worried about her."

"Been coming on for a while?" It was one of those questions Hardy sometimes asked that wasn't a question at all.

He's right, thought Pete. This *has* been coming on for a while.

"It might be a grief reaction," said Hardy. "But it could be real depression, too."

Depression. Just the word made Pete feel depressed.

"Sometimes a death can trigger it. That doesn't mean there's nothing more *to* it. If things don't pick up soon some therapy could help her sort it out."

"So what should I do?"

"Get her moving."

"That's *it?*"

"That's most of it. That's the place to start. Call me back if she won't budge."

"All right."

Pete went to the market, mulling over what Hardy had said as he shopped. If he were going to get Connie moving he was going to have to come up with something better than swimming lessons or glaciers, he could see that.

Pete returned to Connie's apartment with a selection of foods that would have made even Rita proud. He went into the bedroom. Connie hadn't budged.

"Why don't you get in the shower and get washed up and dressed?"

Connie just looked at him.

Get her moving, huh? It seemed a little . . . well . . . simplistic, but Pete did what he was told. He grabbed her upper arms and pulled her up, a move that in the old days would have set off a wrestling match for sure, but this time he was met with a limpness of flesh that was appalling. Still, it got her to her feet, and Pete pushed her into the bathroom.

Now what? Pete was unsure enough of this new ground to doubt the wisdom of hopping in the shower with her. He pointed to the rusty metal shower stall. "In there." He closed the door after her.

Pete went into the kitchen and began to make a grilled cheese and tomato sandwich. When Connie appeared he was pleased to see she'd done part of what he'd ordered—she sat down at the kitchen table fresh from the shower, wrapped in a robe, with her hair in a towel. Still, Pete suspected that the minute he left she'd flop back into bed without ever dressing at all. He decided to press on. "Oh, no you don't. I'm not sitting down to lunch with somebody who's not even dressed."

Connie got up and went into the bedroom. When she came out, in a T-shirt and shorts, Pete had a glass of milk waiting at her place.

"Drink it."

She looked at him. She took a sip.

"*All* of it."

She took another.

He brought her the grilled cheese and tomato sandwich and sat down across from her until she ate a quarter of that, then managed to talk her into eating the whole half. He peeled a banana and handed her that. She ate two bites. Pete decided to let it go at that.

"I think I'll take a short nap," she said.

"Sure," said Pete. "After you do the dishes, right?"

Connie gave him a puzzled look, but at least it was a look with some sort of expression in it.

She did the dishes.

Then she took a nap.

Pete left a note on the kitchen table. *Back at six with steak.* Then he went to tell Willy about his conversation with Roberta Ballantine.

The minute Pete opened his mouth around the name "Cole," the chief stood up and walked around his desk until he stood beside Pete. "I could use a beer, couldn't you?" A heavy hand landed on Pete's shoulder and maneuvered him toward the door.

"It's a little—"

"I'm through working for the day," said Willy. By this time they were in the hall. "I'm through *working*," he said again, in front of Jean Martell, and finally Pete got it. Willy wasn't working. Not when he was talking to Pete about the Coles.

Over a late afternoon beer at Lupo's, Pete filled the chief in on his visit to Roberta Ballantine.

"So Ella Cole told the truth about *that,* anyway," said Willy. "It makes me wonder what else she might say if, in front of her husband, you got a few of those same sparks to fly."

Pete looked at the chief. The chief looked straight back.

Pete pushed back his chair and set off for the Coles' place.

Pete tried, but something, or someone, had miraculously turned Ella Cole into a dutiful wife. She even stood two feet behind her husband and echoed his every thought like the mere shadow she had become.

"I believe my wife might have misled you the other day," began Simon Cole. "There was never any intention on our part, there was never an expectation on Annabel's, that we would care for Clara here. Clara would have gone into a nursing home. Our responsibility, as far as any arrangement I had with Annabel was concerned, was to see that she went into a proper home, to see that I could get the most out of the property next door so that Clara would have the best care available."

"Yes," said Ella Cole, without a single snort. "The best care available."

"I see," said Pete. "And I suppose developing the property next door would get Clara the best care."

"Not necessarily," said Simon.

"No, not necessarily," said Ella.

Simon turned around and smiled at her. It seemed to embolden Ella to branch out on her own.

"Simon would have looked into all the possibilities, of course," said Ella. "Whatever was best to do for Clara, that's what Simon would have done."

"Even if it was to keep her here?"

"I don't think that would have been necessary," said Simon.

"Not necessary at all," said Ella. Pete listened for a little hiss of that old teakettle, but all he heard was his own labored breathing. He tried his hardest to interject a few seed pearls of dissention between them.

"I suppose even if you did have to keep Clara here, even if you did have to take care of her yourself"—here he looked pointedly at Ella Cole—"she wouldn't have lived too long."

"Oh, I don't know," said Simon. "As long as she got the proper care—"

"Yes, as long as she got proper care," said Ella, but not as if she were being sarcastic about it. "And besides, Dr. Rogers said that although she certainly wasn't going to get any better, she wasn't necessarily going to get much worse."

"Yes, but when Clara died, Hardy Rogers hadn't seen her in over a month. She'd gone downhill pretty fast in that space of time, I believe."

The Coles exchanged a puzzled look. "A month?" asked Simon. "Hardy hadn't seen in her in a month? Who told you that?"

Pete began to feel a cold draft on the back of his neck. "Well—"

"Hardy was out here just a few days before they died. He was out here checking over Clara—when was it, Simon?"

"Let's see."

Simon Cole thought.

Pete shivered.

"Wednesday!" said Ella. "The Wednesday before they died. They died on Saturday—or at least they were *found* on Saturday. Hardy was here Wednesday. I remember because I shop on Wednesday mornings. I came home with all my shopping, and he very nicely strolled over the lawn and helped me carry in the bags. That's when he said that about Clara not necessarily going to get a whole lot worse."

"That's right," said Simon. "You told me about that, and about him carrying your bags. Wednesday, then."

Wednesday. Hardy Rogers had checked Clara over on Wednesday, three days before she died.

And Hardy Rogers had told Pete to his face he hadn't seen Clara in over a month.

Chapter

13

As Pete left the market he almost dropped his grocery bag full of boneless sirloin, asparagus, and French bread when Rita grabbed his arm and pulled him halfway into the street.

"Look!" she hissed. "Do you believe me now?"

Warren Johnson was standing on the sidewalk with his hands full of mail and Paula Steigler was hanging on to his elbow.

"Oh, Rita, I don't know. What could Paula Steigler get Warren Johnson to do that—"

Rita stopped Pete with one of those looks he'd seen her give her daughter Maxine when she came home late talking about flat tires.

"Pete. For heaven's sake. Open your eyes."

And Pete *did* open them. A flash of long red hair had just caught his eye far down the street. Pete shoved his grocery bag into Rita's arms and tore off after the hair.

"Pete!"

Pete couldn't answer her. He needed to save his wind. He started right out with the rhythmic breathing exercises he'd taught himself in gym class twenty years ago, an in-and-out count to the word *Oklahoma*. He sprinted past the market, past Wren Realty, past the town hall. He was pacing himself well this time. In. *Okla*. Out. *Homa*. He was going to catch this punk this time! He rounded the corner of the library, where the hair had just disappeared, lunged over the remaining few feet, grabbed the hair, and yanked him around.

Or her.

"Ow! Hey! What the hell!" Tricia Cleary's snapping blue eyes were contorted in pain.

Pete couldn't answer her. He didn't have any wind. He stood still and breathed for a second or two. *Okla. Homa.*

"Pete? Pete!" Tricia Cleary flung back her shoulder-length red hair with one hand and eyed him. Somewhere along the line the pain in her eyes had been replaced by something other. "What is this, your new caveman technique?"

Pete backed up. "Are you all right?"

Tricia Cleary advanced. "I'm all *right*. My hair seems to have stretched, my scalp seems to be tingling, I'm a little *confused*, but I'm basically all right." She looked narrowly at Pete, still breathing hard. "But how are you?"

"Okay," said Pete. He tried to remember if that stupid Oklahoma trick had worked better in high school. "I'm sorry," he said. "I thought you were this kid I was chasing."

"So who's the lucky kid?"

Pete backed up more. "Nobody. I'm sorry."

Tricia advanced more.

Finally there was nothing to do but turn around and run the other way.

Pete *Okla-homa*-ed himself back down Main Street to Rita.

"I suppose you're not really crazy," she said. "I suppose you'll explain this to me someday?"

"Yes," said Pete. "I will." He collected his bag of groceries and drove to Connie's.

The trip was a short ride made long by the many mental

miles Pete managed to cram into it. Tricia Cleary. It hadn't been Tricia at the Bateses' that day. It hadn't been a girl. It hadn't been anyone Pete had ever seen before, he was sure of that. What had the boy been looking for? *Was* it the will? Pete didn't know, and he decided to stop thinking about it. What else could he do, search the house for it? Whatever *it* was? The police had searched the house. The boy had searched the house. If it had been in the house, one of them would have found it. Besides, Pete had plenty of other worries, and he spent the rest of the ride trying to figure out which of them—other than Connie, of course—was bothering him the most.

Was it the fact that Otto Snow, for absolutely no reason, refused to come clean about his proposal to Annabel? Maybe Otto's pride had been hurt by Annabel's repeated rejections. Or maybe Otto had some other very good reason to lie. Just because Pete couldn't figure out what the reason was didn't mean it didn't exist, wasn't perfectly satisfactory. But what if he had a reason that *wasn't* so satisfactory? What if he was trying to throw Pete off the track? *What* track? The track that would prove that Otto killed Clara? Pete started to laugh, but he didn't feel like laughing so much. Why *not* Otto—just because he was teary-eyed and old? Suppose Otto kept asking Annabel, and Annabel kept refusing? What if Annabel kept refusing because of her invalid sister? What if she couldn't bring herself to leave Clara? Wasn't *love* the most famous motive for murder? Couldn't Otto have eased Clara out of life to free Annabel for himself? Had Otto somehow not known that Annabel was already dead, that Annabel had died first?

But these terrible suspicions of Otto didn't bother Pete as much as they should have. Other suspicions were bothering Pete more.

The Coles, for example. So now Ella was backing up her husband's story. So what? So maybe Simon Cole had talked to her, had told her that now the sisters were dead there was no point in working herself up over the might-have-beens. Maybe he convinced her that now was the time to put her shoulder to the wheel and keep the husband out of jail. Or the *wife* out of jail. Maybe Simon had finally made Ella see how her own mouth was going to hang her.

Yes, the Coles, alone or together, were enough to worry about, but still there was something more.

Paula Steigler, for example. Pete had believed her puzzled look when he had mentioned the redhead, had believed that Paula Steigler knew nothing about him at all. But Pete kept learning other things about her. She would bribe Pete with jobs and with sex. She would harass Connie. Would she tamper with Warren Johnson, the witness to the will? How? And would she *murder?* Yes, Pete was plenty bothered by Paula Steigler.

But still, there were bigger bothers out there, and finally Pete forced himself to face up to the newest one. Either the Coles had lied in unison about Hardy's last visit to the Bates house or Hardy Rogers had lied. Pete preferred to think the Coles had lied, but no matter how hard he searched for a *reason* for them to lie, the search was fruitless. Besides, the Coles had sounded genuinely surprised when Pete suggested the doctor hadn't been there in a month. They had readily supplied details of the Wednesday visit—details of conversation, details of Hardy carrying the grocery bags. How could they have anticipated Pete would mention Hardy Rogers? How could they have known Hardy would have mentioned a visit to Clara? Simon had questioned it first— Pete remembered that—but Ella had been first in with the details. If they were lying, it was a slick job. Too slick for the Coles.

It left only one other option.

Hardy Rogers had lied.

The more Pete thought about it, the more it seemed to be the truth. Hardy had said he hadn't seen Clara in over a month, but as Pete thought back over the conversation, Hardy hadn't sounded all that convincing. He had sounded defensive. Why? Because he wanted Pete to leave off with the questions? Because he didn't want anyone upset? *Was* that all there was to it? Hardy had seemed concerned about

111

Connie's reaction to the sisters' deaths. Had he seen where she was headed? Was that why he had downplayed all Pete's questions? Had he known Pete would run straight to Connie with his concerns? Had he known Connie wasn't going to be able to handle this? Had he foreseen this depression of hers long ago?

Suddenly all these other bothers faded under the weight of the biggest one of all, and Pete was right back where he always seemed to start.

Connie.

Yes, Hardy had been right to worry about Connie. He had seen the signs long before Pete had. He had warned Pete. Pete had tried, but he hadn't been able to keep Connie from sinking into this black pit of depression.

Connie.

Pete turned the truck down Pease Street, advancing slowly on Coolidge's garage. The first thing he saw was Paula Steigler's car parked right smack in front of Connie's door. He bolted out of the truck and up the stairs.

Nobody seemed too surprised to see him. Paula sat in the rocking chair, and Connie stood in front of her bedroom door.

"Get out of here," Pete said, but it was Connie who turned around and went into her room. Paula didn't move from her chair.

"Why? We're just visiting. I was just explaining to Connie a few of my lawyer's thoughts on the validity of my aunt's will."

Pete walked past Paula into Connie's room. "Are you all right?" It was strange to be talking to Connie this way, stranger still to have her stare so meekly back.

"I was also explaining to her that I saw no point in her continuing her interest in Clara's gardens since they'll all be bulldozed up when the road goes through."

Connie's eyes flickered.

"I also told her that Clara was certifiably off her nut by the end. She probably didn't know who Connie *was*, let alone what she may or may not have done to get her mitts on her land."

Connie winced.

Suddenly Pete was furious. He whirled around and strode back out to the other room.

"I said get out of here." He had moved fast. He hadn't slowed the closer he got to Paula's chair. Pete would have stopped before he slammed into Paula, he wouldn't have laid a finger on her, but apparently Paula wasn't too sure of that fact. She jumped up out of the chair.

"Go. And if you come here again, the police will see you out."

Paula Steigler went.

Pete turned back to the bedroom. Connie was still standing just inside the door. *Get her moving,* Hardy had said. But how? By doing what?

Then Pete remembered something Sarah Abrew had said to him once—that nothing ever went away by the avoiding of it.

"Come on," he said to Connie. He waited patiently for a count of one. She didn't move. He took her by the arm and pulled her out the door.

"Where are we going?"

"To Clara's."

He wasn't going to lie to her. He wasn't *ever* going to lie to her. He wasn't going to humor her or shelter her or avoid things around her anymore. Connie was able to take life. She was able to take death. Whatever this other thing was that she *wasn't* able to take, Pete didn't know, but he was suddenly sure he knew one way to help them work it out.

At Clara's Pete opened the truck door and led Connie right into the middle of the half-rotting, half-overrun, abandoned garden.

"This is what's become of Clara's garden. It doesn't much matter what Paula Steigler does to it if it's going to look like this, does it?"

Connie stared at the ground.

113

"I said *does* it? Is this better than a road? Is this what Clara expected you to do? Do you think she thought this is what it would look like once she left it to you?"

Connie started to cry. *Really* cry. She didn't put her hands over her face when she cried, she just screwed up her face and made noises that would scare a moose. Because she didn't cry much it wasn't something she or any observer ever got used to. Looking at her, listening to her, Pete had a moment's doubt about the correctness of his strategy. But before he could do anything really stupid, like get down on his hands and knees and beg her to stop, Connie was down onto hers, ripping things out of the garden.

Weeds, Pete hoped.

Chapter
14

The next day was Sunday. Pete wasn't exactly what you'd call a workaholic, but he'd been known to put in extra hours and extra days as the need required, especially when he'd spent most of the regular hours on something as unproductive as murder.

But Pete never hustled out on Sunday. On Sunday Pete read the paper from front to back, with the exception of the economy, real estate, automotive, and opinion pages. Pete knew what the economy was doing by how busy he was Monday through Saturday. He owned all the real estate he ever wanted to own. He hoped—fruitlessly, he knew—that he'd be able to die in his old Jeep truck, and if there was one thing he got plenty of on Nashtoba, it was opinions.

Rita knew about Pete and Sunday. Andy knew about it. Therefore, Pete was much puzzled, not to mentioned slightly annoyed, when eight-thirty that Sunday morning he heard clanging around in one of Factotum's cluttered rooms.

Pete jumped up and was just about *at* the kitchen door when he heard a softish knock from behind it. He opened the door.

"Sorry," said Connie. "I thought you'd be up."

Pete was so happy to see her he didn't even bother to remind her it was Sunday. "Hi! Come in!"

Connie shook her head, a head freshly combed, still damp from the shower. "Can't. I want to get to work. I just needed to get some of my stuff." She looked at the floor. *"Your* stuff. To work in the garden."

Pete held up his fingers. "Two minutes. Give me two minutes and I'll go with you. Coffee?"

Connie shook her head again, still interested in the floor. She looked better, but not right. Not yet. Pete yanked the coffeepot off the stove and snapped off the burner. "Two minutes," he said again. He charged back into his room, tucking in his shirt, and scrambled for his sneakers.

Connie set Pete to dividing the Siberian iris.

"Dig these up," she ordered, pointing to a long vista of green clumps. "See how there's nothing in the center? You have to get rid of that. Chop them apart like this." Connie jabbed the shovel into one of the clumps. Nothing happened. "Your shovel's dull." She looked over at the bulkhead and the rusted padlock she had snapped shut all those days before. "I wish I hadn't locked it. Clara's got a good, sharp spade."

Pete pulled out his keys and separated the Bates keys from them. He gave them to Connie, bulkhead key out. She went off to the cellar, returned with the spade, and handed the keys back to Pete.

Pete raised both hands. "Hey. Your house. Your keys."

"No." Connie jabbed the keys at Pete's stomach so hard he made a mental note to check himself later for an extra belly button. He took the keys.

Connie attacked the roots of the Siberian iris with Clara's spade, successfully this time. "Then we replant them along here. See?"

"Got it," said Pete, and he set in happily with the spade, glad the sun was shining, glad Connie seemed able at last to form a cohesive thought, glad for this chance for the two of them to get in touch with the earth.

In an hour he was sweating and filthy, the ragged rings of iris seemed practically untouched, and Connie, hard at work ten yards away, hadn't spoken a word. After two hours Pete stopped to realign his spinal column. He walked over to Connie. She was staking up some tall purple flowers that had collapsed over the ground.

Pete strolled up behind her. "What are those?"

"Delphiniums."

He should have known.

Connie looked first at the plants, then at Pete. "So what happened, Pete?"

"I don't know. They fell over, I guess."

Connie shook her head impatiently. "Clara. Annabel. What happened to them? Clara couldn't get up. Who moved Annabel? What happened to the pills?"

"I don't know. But I told the chief about it, and I told Hardy about it, but the chief doesn't want to do anything official unless Hardy changes his tune. I guess I'm going to—"

"Let it go?"

Pete wasn't too crazy about the way Connie said that.

"I don't know," he said. "I wouldn't mind letting a few iris go. Maybe a few delphiniums. Want to knock off for today?"

Connie shook her head. She picked up a long green garden stake and a bristly ball of twine.

Pete picked up the spade.

On Monday they weeded.

Pete, not as up on his weeds as he could be, carefully skirted masses of fragile-looking, jagged leafed plants with white blossoms and red berries only to look over and see Connie pulling them up.

"Damned wild strawberries—they take over the place."

Pete pulled the plant nearest him, and not only the plant in his hand, but two others that had been attached by runners, came with it, kind of like two-for-one night at Lupo's. He looked over at Connie to report this minor coup, but Connie was staring at the Coles' house.

"You said you talked to the Coles. Why?"

"I don't know. I just wanted to know if they'd seen anything, noticed anyone around."

"Anyone who moved Annabel, you mean. And gave the pills to Clara."

Pete looked at Connie cautiously. This was the stuff that had set her off before.

"Simon Cole was executor in Annabel's will," she said. "Annabel must have trusted him."

"I guess so."

"Do you?"

No lies. No humoring. "No," said Pete.

"Why not? What did Simon say?"

Pete told her.

"Do you think Ella Cole killed Clara so she wouldn't have to take care of her?"

"I don't know."

"Do you think Simon found Annabel dead? Do you think he moved her? Then he killed Clara so he could get her property?"

"Simon didn't get Clara's property, you did." The minute Pete said it, he tensed. Would she fly off the handle again at the mention of the unwanted inheritance?

"Right," said Connie. "I forgot." She went back to tearing things out of the ground.

Pete wanted to tell her about the redhead. He wanted to take her inside and show her what the kid had done to the house, but he was afraid there might be such a thing as too much truth too fast. He didn't want to send her spinning back into her dark hiding place again.

He decided, for now, to say nothing more.

* * *

On Tuesday they warm-weather mulched. It was the very first day of July. The weather was holding. The garden was starting to look better.

So was Connie.

"What's in this mulch stuff?" asked Pete.

"Shredded pine bark."

"What's it for?"

"Keeps the moisture in. Keeps the weeds out."

"Good." Pete was starting to see weeds in his sleep.

"About Otto," said Connie.

Pete looked at her in surprise.

"Did you talk to him again after I told you he proposed to Annabel?"

"Yes. I told him right out I'd heard he asked Annabel and been refused, but he never would admit it."

"He asked her. She said no. I think it was because of Clara."

"You're sure?"

"Otto asked her. More than once. Why would Annabel lie about that?"

"Why would Otto?"

"I don't know," said Connie. "Do you trust Otto?"

"I don't know," said Pete.

"Do you think he might have killed Clara so that Annabel would marry him?"

"Not unless he somehow missed seeing Annabel, dead on the porch. Annabel died first."

"Oh, right," said Connie. "I forgot."

On Wednesday, she remembered. They were feeding the roses.

"What's in this stuff?" asked Pete.

"Five-ten-five fertilizer. Sprinkle it six inches from the crown."

Pete began to shake fertilizer into the air about six inches above the plant.

Connie grabbed the bag out of his hands. "Crown! *Crown!"* She pointed to the base of the plant.

Pete redirected the fertilizer. "Whose dumb definition is that?" he grumbled. "The definition of a *crown* should be something at the *top.* The definition of a *foot,* or a *shoe,* or a *base,* on the other hand, would be—"

Pete stopped talking, because Connie had stopped listening.

"The definitions." she said.

Pete straightened up.

"I told Clara. When she couldn't garden anymore, I told Clara that she could still be just as happy if she changed her definition."

"What definition?"

"Her definition of *happiness.* To Clara, *happiness* meant working in her garden. When she began to have trouble doing the work, I told her she shouldn't make herself miserable over it, she should adjust her definition, that's all. I told her to redefine *happiness* as a *walk* in her garden. We talked about it again, later on. She wondered what definition she could use when she couldn't even walk. I think she knew what was ahead of her. I told her there were lots of other definitions of happiness—watching out the window as her plants came into bloom or spending a rainy day in bed with a book."

Or hiring your wife instead of living with her?

"So it worked," said Pete. "You helped. She remembered."

But Connie shook her head. "It may have helped her then. I don't think the whole of *Webster's* would have helped her once Annabel was gone."

But something, some altered definition of her own, seemed to help Connie now. She was never one for explaining how she felt, but now a backlog of words and emotions spewed into the air as she struggled to sort things out. "I have to remember that. I honestly don't think Clara would have *wanted* to live without Annabel. What would have been ahead for her then? Ella Cole? A nursing home? I don't know why this is hitting me so hard. Clara is dead, and maybe I don't want her to be, but maybe this is how *she'd* want it, you know? But this stuff about the will. Everybody thinks I was friends with Clara so I could snag the place."

"*Nobody* thinks that."

"Paula Steigler does. And I bet you Bert Barker had a—"

"And there's a pair of opinions to lose sleep over."

Connie shook her head stubbornly. "It ruined it. I can't explain it. I thought this was the only thing I'd done that I didn't screw up. I thought this was my one untainted act of love. And then she ruined it."

Her one untainted act of love? What did *that* mean? Pete was afraid he knew. *"Connie,"* he began, but he stopped, unsure which way to turn.

"It ruined it," repeated Connie.

Pete struggled with a good-sized wave of impatience. "Paula Steigler can't ruin something that—"

"Not Paula Steigler. Paula's not to blame for any of this—she's just trying to keep what she thinks is hers. *Clara* was the one who ruined it when she left me this place. But it's not Clara's fault either—not really. If I hadn't let you hire me—"

"What the *hell*—"

"No. Wait. I kept thinking I shouldn't have let you hire me, I should have left Clara alone." She looked up at him. "I should have left *you* alone. But then you brought me over here and I saw this place, and I knew what Paula Steigler wanted to do with it, and suddenly it seemed clear what Clara wanted me to do with it. It seemed okay again."

Connie looked out over the garden, and Pete followed her gaze. After five days of backbreaking toil, it was just now beginning to look like it should.

"I think it's going to do all right," said Connie.

"I think it's going to do great."

"If I get to keep it."

Yes, thought Pete. That would be the way of it. Connie finally decides to fight for it, but loses it in the end. But he said out loud, "You'll keep it. I've talked to Roberta

Ballantine. We've resolved a lot of the foreseeable problems already, and now you remember about the definitions. It proves that Clara was making sense."

"But it's only my word about the definitions."

"And Clara's. Hers is the word that counts."

Connie nodded. Then her face clouded. "When you told me about someone moving Annabel, I couldn't stand it. I can't now. I keep picturing it, someone coming along, finding Annabel, leaving Clara there alone to wonder where her sister was all that time. Someone leaving Annabel *dead*, on the steps, leaving Clara to . . . to—"

"She didn't suffer. Hardy made sure we knew that she—"

"I know that. I *know* that." Connie walked a few feet away from Pete and turned around, as if she needed to be at a safe distance to say what she was struggling to say next. "But all this business about someone moving Annabel. About the missing pills. I can't . . . maybe if I hadn't been mentioned in the will none of this would have happened. If I'd just stayed away from here, if I'd never come back to the island at all—"

"Wait a minute. *Wait one minute.* Clara wanted *you* to have this place. She—"

"I know that! I know that! But if I wasn't here, if I hadn't been *hanging around—"*

"Connie." Pete stopped. He didn't know what to say next. He didn't know where to begin. Pete had been pretty good at blaming Connie for leaving him, but not as good as she suddenly seemed to be at blaming herself for coming *back*. "Your getting left the place can't have anything to do with who moved Annabel or what happened to the pills. Whatever happened to Annabel and Clara probably happened because somebody *else* thought they'd been left the place. Can't you understand that?"

Connie bent down to the ground and said something into a plant.

"What? I can't hear you."

She looked up. "I need to know what happened to Annabel and Clara. Can't you understand *that?"*

Yes, Pete could. And it answered his old question. Now it mattered a whole lot how and why two old women died.

Connie turned away, and she remained still and silent so long that it made Pete nervous.

"Are you all right?" he asked finally.

"No," she said. Then she shot him a shaky smile. "Unless of course you'd care to adjust your definition of 'all right.'"

"Temporarily?"

"Temporarily."

"Okay, then."

Connie seemed to give herself a mental shake. "So what's next?"

Pete looked around. "More mulch?"

"No," said Connie. "Otto Snow."

Chapter

15

On the way to Otto Snow's, Pete and Connie discussed the best way to approach Otto on the subject of his proposal to Annabel.

"I know he proposed," said Connie. "Annabel told me. If I just tell him what Annabel told me, he'll have to come clean, right?"

"I don't know," said Pete. "Maybe our approach should be a little more oblique."

But Connie had never been too good at oblique.

This time she wasn't too good at *alive*.

"How nice to see you again," said Otto when he answered the door, but it didn't look like he meant it. His eyes flitted back and forth between Pete and Connie so fast that it looked like a nervous twitch. "Would you care to sit down?"

Pete and Connie sat on each end of Otto's couch. Pete noticed that Connie seemed to sink into the corner of the couch as if she weren't there, but he didn't worry about it. You always knew when Connie was there.

"Well, Otto," Pete began, "I guess you wonder why we're here."

Otto didn't look like he'd wondered much.

Pete began again. Obliquely. "We're trying to figure out just what the situation was with Annabel and Clara before they died. To help with the legalities." Pete left a pause there for Connie to jump in.

She didn't.

Pete rambled on, getting less and less oblique. "For example, we understand Clara was completely bedridden at the time of her death. If you had married Annabel, would Annabel have moved in with you?"

Otto just blinked.

"Would Clara have gone into a nursing home? Did you and Annabel ever talk about that?"

The freckles on Otto's head suddenly seemed to get darker. Or did his skin get whiter? "I never talked about any such thing—Clara, nursing homes, marrying Annabel. I never did."

Good, thought Pete. Now he's said it. This is where Connie chimes in.

He waited.

No chimes.

Pete decided to move sideways to another subject to give Connie time to collect her thoughts. "Maybe you could help us with one other thing. The police may have talked to you already—"

Yes, the skin definitely went whiter.

"Do you remember when you saw the sisters last? We found them on Saturday, the fourteenth of June. Do you remember when you saw them before that?"

"I saw them all the time. I saw them the week before, I'm sure of it. Yes, the week before." Otto began to pink up again. He didn't seem to mind talking about *this*.

"Do you remember which day?"

"Let's see. On Thursday I usually go to the market. I stop off on my way to see if I can pick up anything for them. So I suppose it would have been Thursday. I don't like to travel on the weekend, you see." He made the half-mile trip from his house to the market sound like a two-day ordeal.

"Since Clara was confined to her bed, you probably spent a lot of time alone with Annabel?"

"Oh, I went in to see Clara. She couldn't come out to the parlor, no, but I saw Clara plenty. I always saw Clara, too."

Pete looked at Connie again, but still she said nothing.

"So the last time you saw them would have been Thursday, June twelfth."

"I believe so. Thursday. Yes."

Pete sighed. What was he doing here? What was he supposed to be asking next? The hell with it.

"Otto," he began, "the other day we discussed your proposal to Annabel. Earlier you said—"

Connie stirred on the couch. *Thank God.* Pete paused so she could cut in.

She didn't.

In Connie's mental absence, Pete opted for use of the royal "we."

"We were told that you did indeed ask Annabel to marry you, many times, but that she refused. Isn't this so?"

"Why I don't know who would ever tell you that," said Otto. He eyes flitted to Connie. So did Pete's. Connie didn't seem to notice.

"But you did propose to Annabel," said Pete, and to his horror Otto's eyes began to water.

"I never proposed. I never proposed."

It was too much. Pete stood up. "All right, Otto." He walked to the door.

Connie got up and followed, like a good child who had been seen and not heard.

"I'm sorry," Connie said once she was safe in the truck. "I don't know, my mouth wouldn't work. Something's wrong with me. I can't—"

"No big deal," said Pete.

"He's lying, though. Otto's lying. Why?"

"I'm beginning to suspect we'll never know."

"We *have* to know. We have to find out who moved Annabel's body, who did what with Clara's pills. And what else do we have to find out?"

"Why Hardy lied."

"What?"

Pete groaned silently. He'd forgotten Connie didn't know about that yet. "Hardy told me he hadn't seen Clara in over a month before she died. Ella Cole said he was out there just a few days before."

"Why?"

Pete shook his head. "I don't know. I think maybe Hardy's trying to keep something from us. It might be something he thinks we'd rather not know."

"I *have* to know."

Pete did, too.

He drove back to the Bateses.

Paula Steigler's car was parked in front.

"What the hell is she doing here?" Pete threw open the truck door and got out. He was halfway over the lawn toward Paula before he'd realized Connie had taken another route, *away* from Paula.

Paula Steigler was walking around the garden, her high heels sinking drunkenly into the grass as she went.

Pete strode over.

"So," she said. "Is this your handiwork, or has the wilting violet finally waked from her trance?"

Connie, a wilting violet? Pete would have laughed if Connie wasn't right then slinking out of sight around the far side of the house.

"Connie did all this, yes," he said. "She'll continue to look after her property."

Paula looked in the direction of Connie's disappearance. "She doesn't look quite up to the job, if you ask me."

That got Pete mad. He swept his arm over the neat roses and the weed-free, warm-weather mulched flower beds all around. "What do you call this? She did this in one week. She's going to put this garden back the way it was."

Paula raised an amused eyebrow. "Good luck."

She wobbled back toward her car.

Pete went around the back of the house to look for Connie. She was standing on the back step staring at the board Pete had nailed over the broken pane of glass in the door.

"Who did this?"

Pete decided it was time to tell her about his phantom redhead. After a second's hesitation he also told her a little bit about the condition of the house.

"I want to go in."

Pete fished out the keys and opened the door.

Connie's first sight of the ransacked house worked almost as well on her as her first sight of the neglected garden.

She turned into a tall gold flash. She righted living room cushions, replaced drawers, straightened rugs.

Pete started with the kitchen.

He looked up when Connie appeared in the doorway.

"You're sure he didn't find it? You're sure he didn't leave with whatever he was looking for?"

"Pretty sure. Willy's pretty sure, too. When I caught the kid he was still looking. In the kitchen."

"So it's still in this house. Maybe in this kitchen."

"Whatever *it* is."

"But Willy looked, too. If he didn't find it, I doubt if we can."

"Don't be so sure," said Pete. He walked to the nearest drawer and pulled it open. "Of course, it would help if we knew what we were looking for. It has to be something small. He's not looking for a piece of furniture, for example. Or a lockbox. Look at this. He's pulled out all the dish towels from this two-inch-deep drawer. What would fit in there, what would he be looking for that might be stuffed between a couple of dish towels?"

Connie joined Pete at the drawer. "A safe-deposit box key, maybe?"

"Good idea. Did they have any jewelry, any old coins, any bonds?"

Connie shook her head. "I don't know. They didn't wear jewelry around the house. Maybe Sarah would know. But what else could it be? Why else would someone break into a house where two dead old—" She stopped on a wobble.

Pete hurried over it. "Or a will. I was thinking maybe someone was looking for another will."

Connie shot up out of the drawer. "A will! Another will! That's it! It has to be it!"

"Don't sound so disappointed."

"I'd *pay* you to find another will. I'd pay you to *write* one."

"Or maybe someone was looking for an incriminating letter."

"Incriminating? About Clara? About Annabel? I don't think so."

"It wouldn't necessarily have to incriminate *them*. It would have to incriminate whoever was looking for it."

"The redhead."

"Or someone who hired the redhead. Paula Steigler, maybe."

They stopped talking and bent to their work, searching through the unrifled parts of the kitchen, finding nothing. Then they began to put everything back. Connie was sorting the silverware in the last drawer, Pete was inside the last cupboard replacing plastic wrap, tin foil, sponges, and garbage bags, when Connie straightened up and stood still, hands on hips, thinking.

"Wait a minute. Aren't we starting at the wrong end here? We're assuming whatever it is is still in this house because the redhead didn't find it. But maybe he didn't find it because it wasn't in the house in the first place. Did you ever think about that?"

Pete hadn't. "You mean maybe the redhead just *thought* it was here, but it wasn't. It never was."

"Or maybe it was once, but somebody took it out long ago. Or maybe somebody took it out just recently, just before the redhead arrived. Maybe somebody else came and got it, somebody who didn't get caught. Or maybe it got thrown out with the trash. Hell, anybody could have—"

Pete scrambled out of the cupboard so fast most of the plastic wrap and tin foil came with him. "Trash! I forgot about the trash! I took it to the dump that first day!"

"The dump? You took it to the dump?"

"Remember Annabel told you the barrel was full? That's why I came with you that day."

"She was spring cleaning," said Connie.

They looked at each other in silence.

"You used to *like* the dump," said Pete.

Slowly, without use of hydraulic lift, the corners of Connie's mouth turned up.

They stopped at Factotum to pick up a couple of clam rakes and two pairs of rubber waders. Connie got out of the truck at the dump, clambered into the waders, and looked around with high spirits. Yeah, she *did* like the dump. You found a lot of neat stuff in the dump. The smell wasn't *that* bad—not if you didn't hang around too long.

"Over there," said Pete, pointing to the northwest corner of the landfill. "I dumped the Bates stuff over there. We'll know it right away because it's the neatest garbage around. Brown paper bags, tied both ways with about a hundred yards of string, you remember?"

"I remember," said Connie, looking out over the sea of garbage. "But isn't it going to be pretty far down by now?"

"Oh, I don't know, everybody recycles most everything these days."

Pete waded in.

Connie followed.

They found a lot of neat stuff. An antique apothecary jar that was perfect except for a crack, a wooden footstool that still had three good legs, a striped awning with hardly any tears, and three teakettles with only partly burned out bottoms.

They also found out everybody *didn't* recycle.

"Look at this!" Pete hollered, as he tossed an aluminum can onto high ground. "And this!" A glass jar followed. "And *this!*" A plastic milk container went sailing through the air.

Connie learned how to duck and rake at the same time. She also learned that "too long" at the dump came a lot sooner than she thought. She started to breathe through her mouth. Her throat was so raw by the time she found Annabel's telltale garbage that it took her three tries to attract Pete's attention.

He waded over.

"Yuck." The collection of brown paper parcels in their wads of string were soaked through from within and without, and nicely rancid. Pete retrieved a barrel from the truck. They tossed in the garbage and headed home. Pete and Connie were pretty rancid, too. They kept the windows open on the way.

They rinsed off the rakes and waders in the hose and collected heavy rubber gloves. They dumped the trash barrel onto Factotum's lawn, straddled the mess, and began.

Some of Annabel's garbage *was* garbage. Pete, always the chivalrous sort, collared the most sopping parcels for himself, and Connie tackled the others.

They didn't find any wills.

What they did find were coffee grounds, orange peels, pork chop bones, chicken bones, cardboard containers, what appeared to be the contents of a vacuum cleaner bag, unopened letters asking for contributions, old catalogs, pencil shavings, four half-finished letters in Annabel's hand, and Annabel Bates's marriage license.

Connie found the letters and the license, since she was sorting the dry bags, but Pete knew right away that she'd found something of interest—she grabbed him by the shirt and nearly pulled him into her lap. She shoved the paper at him, reading it over again with him.

"This certifies that on the thirteenth day of September, in

the year 1932, Alfred Edison Standish and Annabel Ethel Bates were by me united in marriage at Monroeville courthouse, according to the laws of the state of Maine."

Annabel? Married? In *Maine?*

Then Connie read the half-finished letters. Each one was dated June first of that year. Each one began "Dear Alfred," in varying shades of Annabel's sensible hand. Each one ended not far from where it had begun.

"Dear Alfred," ran the first. *"I have waited every day since my letter to you in the hopes of receiving your reply or my letter returned undelivered. Neither has happened, and as I consider why, I feel that perhaps you expect more from me than those few short words that reached you. Perhaps I should have explained more fully why—"*

The first letter ended there.

"Dear Alfred," began the next. *"Having received no reply to my previous letter, I feel called upon to attempt to communicate with you again. Forgive me, please, for being so bold. I would not have written at all, not wishing to cause you to remember any part of our painful past, if the matter mentioned in my last letter had not come up."*

That was the end of the second letter.

"Dear Alfred," began the third. *"I have wondered why you have not answered my letter, and I think perhaps I know. You have not forgiven me. I beg you to consider what the years that have past have been."*

That was it for the third.

The writing in the fourth letter was more bold, more certain, more Annabel. *"Dear Alfred,"* it began. *"It does not matter that you do not forgive me. I have forgiven myself."*

Annabel had actually signed this letter, but still, she had never mailed it.

She had thrown it out, along with the marriage license.

Rita Peck walked beside Evan Spender along the harbor in the soft summer night. They had just finished dinner at Martelli's. Rita had had a little red wine. When she pulled

Evan behind the bait and tackle shop he assumed she'd had a little too *much* red wine.

"*Well,* now."

Rita shushed him. She peered around the bait shop. Paula Steigler and Warren Johnson were just slipping onto the beach and into the dark.

"Come on!" Rita, hopping on first one foot and then the other to pull off her shoes, dragged Evan onto the beach.

Rita peered into the dark. Yes! Paula Steigler was leaning on Warren Johnson. *Hanging* on Warren Johnson.

"What the—" Evan began, but Rita shushed him again. Clinging to the dark fringe of the dune, she pulled them onward after the two figures ahead.

It didn't take Paula long. Soon two dark, heavily breathing shapes were pumping away in the sand.

Before Evan could possibly have known what hit him, Rita was pulling him backward the way they had come.

Pete was pooped. After he and Connie had found Annabel's marriage license and letters they had gone back to the Bates house, pouring over every piece of paper in the two desks, checking every shoebox, every nook and cranny that might hold the next clue to the tale—a divorce paper, a death notice, more letters, perhaps. They'd come up empty.

They had gone home to their respective showers and respective thoughts, and Pete was finally drifting off to sleep in the privacy of his lonely bed when Rita Peck and Evan Spender came pounding on his kitchen door.

Pete got up and ushered them into the kitchen. He couldn't catch what Rita was babbling on about. First he tried to slow down her speech, but when that didn't work he tried to speed up his hearing.

"Paula Steigler was what?"

"With *Warren Johnson,*" said Rita. "I *told* you. I *told* you. You didn't believe me, did you? Well, now I have proof. Don't you *get* it? Don't you see what she's trying to do?"

"I'd say she did it, Rita," said Evan.

Rita rolled her eyes at him. "Warren *Johnson*. One of the two witnesses to Clara Bates's will. Don't you see what she's doing? If she can get Warren to say that Clara *wasn't* in her right mind, the score is even. Sarah for, Warren against."

All of a sudden Pete's hearing, and his brain, woke up.

"You might want to have a talk with that man," said Evan.

"I might want to have a talk with that *woman,"* said Rita in such a way that Pete was suddenly glad he was a man.

Still, Pete felt Rita and Evan were jumping too fast and too far to conclusions. "Just because Warren Johnson and Paula Steigler are together doesn't necessarily mean Warren's going to change his opinion about the state of Clara's mind."

"Doesn't it?" asked Rita. "Paula Steigler and little Warren Johnson? You think she just picked him up out of the *blue?* Little *Warren?"*

"He wasn't her first choice," said Pete modestly.

"I don't care if he was her *last* choice. All I care about is that he's her *present* choice! Honestly, Pete. Wake up, will you? Aren't you going to at least *talk* to him?"

Pete looked at the clock. "Do you mind if I don't do it right now?"

"Oh, for heaven's sake!" Rita turned to leave.

"Hey!" said Pete. "Wait. Either of you ever hear of an Alfred Edison Standish?"

"No," said Rita.

"Who is he?" asked Evan.

"Annabel Bates's husband." Pete picked up Annabel's marriage certificate from the kitchen table and passed it around.

"Annabel's *husband!"* Rita sat down in the kitchen chair. Pete sat down across from her.

Evan took one look at Rita's astonished face and went to the refrigerator for a beer.

* * *

"I don't know," said Connie the next morning on their ride to the garden. "I don't know anybody who *does* know. Sarah, maybe?"

Pete shook his head. "Sarah didn't know. She said they never married. And Bert kept calling them spinsters."

"Oh, *Bert.*" Connie snorted. Pete was relieved that Bert's opinions had sunk in her estimation back to where they belonged. "Maybe Sarah knows, but is keeping it secret for Annabel's sake. Clara never said a word about Annabel being married. Maybe Annabel was divorced. In those days nobody got divorced. Maybe she got married in Maine, got divorced in Maine, came home, and pretended nothing had happened."

"If she were divorced, you'd think that paper would be saved, not just the marriage license. And why, after all this time, did she decide to throw the license out? And write to Alfred?"

Connie sighed. "I wish I'd found a goddamned will." Then her eyes lit up. "But if she were married, maybe there are some other relatives who—"

"Give it up, will you? It's yours. You're stuck with it. Unless—" Pete told Connie about Paula Steigler and Warren. She kind of liked that. Pete could tell. But in no time at all they were back to Annabel and this Alfred Edison Standish, whoever he was.

When they pulled up to the Bates house, though, the sight that met them put Alfred right out of their minds.

The garden was destroyed.

There were tire marks everywhere. Someone had gotten in a car and driven it over the garden about a million times. The delphiniums were flattened. The sawed-off green leaves of the Siberian iris, the iris that had caused Pete to take two aspirin after he'd divided them, were crushed into the dirt. The rosebushes were snapped off and crumpled, and those annuals that had survived their earlier neglect might as well not have bothered.

"I knew it," said Connie. She seemed frozen to the spot.

"Come on," said Pete. He picked up what was now half of

a garden stake, straightened up what was left of a delphini-um, and bolstered the plant with the stick as best he could.

"It's no use," said Connie. "She'll just do it again. Or she'll do something worse."

"No she won't. Not if she sees she can't scare you off." Pete moved on to the next fractured stick, the next trampled plant.

"Maybe she *can.*"

"Can what?"

"Scare me off." The words were spoken in a voice Pete didn't know.

It scared *him,* but he kept on going. After he'd propped up five plants he felt movement beside him.

Connie knelt down and began to pack the dirt tightly around the roots.

Chapter

16

Connie could feel it the minute Pete began to fidget. She followed him doggedly for three more plants and then straightened up. "What?"

Pete straightened up also, leaning into the crick in his back. "I'm thinking we might not be doing the right thing just now. I'm thinking we should maybe leave this the way it is." He waved a hand at the destruction around them. "This is evidence. Evidence of a crime. We should get Willy."

"No." The word was out before Connie even figured out why she said it, but she knew she meant it, and Pete was getting that obstinate look, so she said it again. "No." It wasn't that she didn't want the police chief here, although she didn't. It was what would happen after that that bothered her the most. Connie knew who had done this. She could *feel* who had done this. Pete knew, too. If the chief found enough evidence to bring against Paula Steigler Connie would have to file a charge, and there they'd be,

Paula Steigler and Connie Bartholomew, out in the open and head to head at last. "Why did you attempt to destroy the Bates garden," the lawyer would ask. "Because this golddigger was trying to steal it from me," Paula would answer. "And what do you have to say to that, Ms. Bartholomew." the lawyer would ask. "Not a hell of a lot." Christ, she hadn't been able to say boo to Otto Snow—how was she going to stand up to someone like Paula Steigler?

"Come on," said Pete, as if Connie hadn't said no once, let alone twice.

Connie shook her head. She could pretend it was out of strength of will that she declined to agree with Pete. She could pretend it was because she was smarter. She could pretend whatever the hell she wanted to pretend! She didn't want anybody asking her all these questions about Clara's garden. She didn't want Paula Steigler stirred up any more than she already was.

"Come on, Connie," said Pete. He was starting to sound a little impatient. "Let's get Willy."

"No." After all, either it was Connie's garden or it wasn't. If it *was* Connie's, then she could do whatever she wanted about Willy. If it *wasn't* Connie's garden it was Paula Steigler's garden, not Pete's, and Paula could drive around in it all she wanted. *"No,"* she said again. She bent down to her work. She could feel Pete watching her. She ignored him, but it didn't seem to phase him any.

"I'm leaving now," he said. "If you want a ride—"

"I can still walk."

"Okay, then, walk."

When he was halfway to the truck Connie called after him.

"Instead of talking to Willy you should talk to Sarah about Annabel! Or you should talk to Hardy Rogers! Ask him why he lied!"

Pete just looked at her.

"And Warren Johnson! You should talk to Warren Johnson!"

Of course, the most sensible answer Pete could have given

her was "Why don't *you* talk to Sarah and Hardy and Warren Johnson?" but Pete didn't give it. Maybe he was remembering how well she had done with Otto. He said nothing. He resumed his walk to the truck.

"Are you going to see Willy?"

"Maybe."

Maybe, my ass, said Connie, but not out loud. The thought itself, coupled with the withholding of its verbal execution, were the perfect symbols of her recently improved but still extremely shaky state of mind.

Pete wasn't stupid. He also wasn't blind or deaf. He was beginning to get better at figuring out, around the things Connie did say, what she wanted to say and didn't know how. Today, for example. Connie was afraid of Paula Steigler. She was afraid to go head to head with Paula Steigler with an actual legal charge, but at the same time she wanted him to talk to Hardy Rogers and Sarah Abrew and Warren Johnson. She wasn't out of the woods yet, but she wasn't giving up yet, either.

And neither was Pete; his route out of the woods was just a little straighter, that's all. He put aside, but just for the moment, Sarah and Warren and Hardy in favor of the chief of police.

"Now let me get this straight," said Willy, after Pete, learning something about the ropes by now, had hauled Willy out of his office and into Lupo's. The bartender, Dave Snow, was starting to look at them funny when they showed up in the middle of normal working hours this way. When Willy ordered a mineral water instead of beer and Pete ordered a cup of coffee, even the waitress Tina Hansey seemed to know something was up.

"You have evidence of another vandalism, one that I could in clear conscience look into openly. *Should* look into openly. But this time you want me to run out to the Bates place *un*officially. You want me to hurry out there, as a matter of fact, to catch some of this evidence your wife is busily destroying as we speak. Is that it?"

"She's not my *wife*," said Pete testily.

Willy just looked at him.

"All *right*. I'm asking you, as a friend, to saunter out to the Bates place as inconspicuously as you can, because Connie doesn't want to do anything official about it. That's all."

"All right, all right. Jeese. Creeping around in a garden. I used to be a big, important homicide cop, and here I am—"

"You might still be a big, important homicide cop."

Willy looked at Pete again. "Paula Steigler, huh?"

"Paula Steigler."

They tossed off their mineral water and coffee and left Lupo's, almost on the run.

You didn't see much in the way of official police procedure on Nashtoba, and even though Willy repeatedly told Pete this was about as unofficial as it could get, Pete was impressed. They stopped at the station on the way, and Willy unofficially borrowed a camera and a large cardboard box. The box clanked as they walked. They parked around the bend from the garden and crept around the house.

Connie was gone.

The first thing the chief did once he reached the garden was to stand still.

"What are you doing?"

"Looking."

"Oh." Pete looked with him. Connie had done little if anything after Pete had left, which told him she had thought things over a bit and reached a sensible conclusion. Good.

"We straightened up those plants," said Pete, waving at the few sad-looking stakes. "Everything was really flattened. Her car did it."

"*A* car did it," corrected Willy. First he pulled out the camera and took some shots. Then he got out a notepad and pencil and began to draw. Then he moved in close to one particular patch of bare dirt, picked off a couple of leaves, pulled out a ruler, and began to measure, write, *and* draw.

Pete crept up behind him. "What are you doing now?"

"Description of the tire tread. Width of impression. Distance between impressions."

"Oh," said Pete.

Willy returned to the car and retrieved the cardboard box. He pulled out a can of silicone spray and a flat piece of cardboard, crouched over the particular tire track in question, and gently deflected the spray off the cardboard over the dirt. Next he pulled a metal frame out of the box and centered the best part of the tire's print inside it. Out came a rubber bowl, a bag of plaster, a jug of water. He mixed the plaster right on the spot, and breaking the fall of the mixture with the spoon, poured it over the patch of dirt until it was a half inch deep. He fiddled in the carton again and pulled out small squares of wire mesh.

"Now what are you doing?"

"Strengthening the cast." Willy lay the mesh on top of the poured plaster, remixed the remaining plaster, and poured again until it reached the top of the metal frame. He stood up. "Now for the next thirty minutes while that dries, let's collect a little dirt," and much to Pete's surprise, the huge bulk of the police chief lowered itself onto all fours and began to spoon dirt from the various garden locations into individual Ziploc plastic bags.

"This is *un*official?" asked Pete, following the chief closely, but careful to stay behind.

"Unofficial. But if anyone decides to turn it official, we're prepared. We have a tire impression to match to a tire and dirt samples to match to any dirt found on the tire." The chief sat back on his heels and looked around again. "Of course, some hairs or threads or fingerprints would be nice. Somebody could have stolen the car."

Stolen the car! And, of course, Paula Steigler would be the first one to think of that. Pete's spirits sank.

But the plaster was now dry. The chief lifted out the most perfect impression of a tire tread, albeit the *only* one, that Pete had ever seen, and Pete was so sure it would prove to match the tires on Paula Steigler's car that his spirits picked up. Even if Paula Steigler weren't arrested for this it wouldn't help her any in her fight over the will, and wasn't that the point?

But just then Pete happened to remember something, or someone, that *might* help her in that fight over the will. Warren Johnson.

The chief packed up and took off.

Pete went to find the mailman.

Pete came upon Warren Johnson, not trodding along his mail route, but standing on the steps of Beston's Store.

Standing next to him was Paula Steigler.

"Fax," Paula was saying to the three stone faces on the bench in front of her. *"F-A-X. Fax."*

"Don't believe I'm familiar with that term," said Ed Healey. "How about you, Ev?"

Evan Spender shrugged.

"Bert? You heard of this *faxing?*"

Paula Steigler looked incredulously from one blank face to the next. The bench sitters could look pretty doltish when they tried. "It's used to send documents via the telephone lines," said Paula. "Instantaneously. I need to send a document to a business office in Boston. *Today.* I am sure on this entire island there must be one establishment in possession of a fax."

"Today, huh?" said Ed. "Too bad you didn't think of it yesterday—you could have sent it regular mail."

"Hah!" said Bert. "You think it'd get there today if she mailed it yesterday regular mail?"

"Wouldn't it, Warren?" asked Ed.

Warren Johnson cleared his throat. "It all depends, Ed. It *might* have gotten there today, but it all depends on just where you mail it *from* as well as *to.* Now if you was to mail it from the post office right over there, Paula, depending of course on what *time* you—"

Paula. It sounded cozy. Too cozy. But the object of all that coziness didn't seem to be in the mood. She whirled on Warren.

142

"I don't care where, when, how, or what you do with your mail! I need a *fax*. A simple *fax*. If you weren't such a—" Suddenly she stopped midstride. Pete could almost see her pulling on her own reins. She started off again, more evenly paced this time. "Warren. *Dear* Warren. Perhaps we could ask somewhere else. I'm sure if you wracked your little brain you'd know just where to try next."

Warren looked up and down the street, his forehead a washboard of wrinkles. "I don't know, Paula. I've got all this mail to deliver. You've already set me a good deal behind with this faxing as it is. I just don't know, Paula."

There she was again. Cruella DeVille. Warren blinked a few times in the face of it, but by the time he was all squared up and ready to take it straight on, Paula Steigler was gone, her heels rattling the loose floorboards as she went.

"I'll go part of the route with you, Warren," said Pete, and he gave Warren a good firm nudge in the right direction, the one away from Paula. After some lingering backward looks, Warren set off down the street.

"Faxing," said Pete after they had gone a good ways away from the porch. "What do you suppose Paula's in such a rush to fax off?"

"I don't know," said Warren. He looked extremely confused. Pete made a mental note to collect his own mail from Warren before he left.

"I don't know what she wants to fax, unless it's my testimony, but I don't see what's the big rush on that."

Pete stopped walking. "Testimony?"

"Testimony about Clara." Warren flashed Pete a look that was a pathetic mix of pride and confusion. "I've been seeing a bit of Paula. We've talked a good deal about her aunts. It's only natural, her wanting to talk about the aunts. She misses them something awful."

"Warren, you don't mean you've—" Pete stopped, unable to formulate just the right phrase. "Warren," he said again. "Just what testimony are you planning to give about her aunts?"

143

"Oh, only that I witnessed Clara's signature on that spur-of-the-moment will I described to you earlier on."

"What spur-of-the-moment will? What makes you think there was anything spur-of-the-moment about that will? For all you know Clara had that written out months before you signed!"

Warren drew himself up to a stop and looked at Pete with surprise. "So you didn't realize it either, huh? I didn't realize how it must have been myself, till Paula and me got to talking and I got to see it more clear. This is how it was. Old Sarah Abrew decides to drop in on the Bateses spur-of-the-moment. I come by, spur-of-the-moment, with the mail. Clara all of a sudden, spur-of-the-moment, whips out the will. Doesn't that sound pretty spur-of-the-moment to you?"

"Not necessarily, Warren. You arrive there every afternoon like the *tide,* Warren. Clara could have invited Sarah over anticipating that you would be there, or she could have noticed that she had her two witnesses she'd been waiting for over a period of—"

"That's the other thing me and Paula kind of worked out. Clara sure wasn't the best historian, was she, Pete?" Warren said the word *historian* as if he'd just learned it that morning and was trying to show off.

Pete started to lose his cool. "Best historian! When was she not the best historian?"

"Y'know at first I thought she was darned clear-headed, but now I know I didn't consider the facts thoroughly at the time. Now that I've thought it over some, I see the inconsistencies—"

That sounded like a new word, too. *"What* inconsistencies?"

"Inconsistencies," Warren repeated, starting to sound a little testy, but then again, so was Pete. Warren diverted off the sidewalk to a mailbox and then rejoined Pete. "For one example, these inconsistencies about her mail. You can't cotton the mess that woman made of ZIP codes! She had considerable correspondence, let me tell you, and either she left the ZIP codes off altogether or she jumbled up the numbers in one of those lottery drums or something. I forgot all about the ZIP codes until—"

"For God's sake, Warren! ZIP codes? You're going to testify she was of unsound mind because she loused up a couple of ZIP codes? *I* louse up ZIP codes. I leave them off all the *time*. Come on, Warren!"

Warren Johnson stopped walked and frowned at Pete. "I don't recall seeing your mail without the proper codes."

"Oh, Rita always fixes it. She obsesses over things like that. Now why—"

Warren huffed himself up like a bird. "There's no call to say she's *obsessing* just because she likes to use the proper codes."

"All right, all right. Not obsessing. She's not obsessing." Pete looked away from Warren and took a deep breath. Warren was dead right. This was serious stuff, this ZIP code business. It was going to hang Connie if Pete didn't think up some way to convince Warren that Clara was not the one who was nuts.

He tried again. "Warren. Say Clara Bates asked you to witness the will because Sarah was there at the time, and she finally had two people present who were not involved in the will themselves. There's nothing spur-of-the-moment—"

"In my opinion a will's a legal document. You want to make a will, go talk to a lawyer."

"Your *opinion* is not proof in a court of law. Clara held a different opinion, all right? Now what else, if anything, made you feel, *all of a sudden,* after you talked to the niece Clara wrote *out* of the will, that Clara was out of her mind when she wrote it?"

Warren didn't speak to Pete for two more houses' worth of mail. He returned from the second house looking grim. "Don't think I don't understand the gist of that little remark. You think Paula's trying to use me, don't you?"

Pete thought about that for a few seconds before answering, not because he was in doubt of the right answer, but because he was unsure if he really wanted to break it to

Warren exactly what Paula Steigler was like. Pete had never seen Warren Johnson date anybody before. If Pete convinced him Paula Steigler was using him he'd probably never date anyone again. But still, what was Warren going to get from Paula Steigler in the long run? More hurt and pain than the truth told to him right now would ever cause him. "Yes, I do, Warren. I do think she's trying to use you."

"And I suppose *your* opinion is proof in a court of law?"

"Yes, Warren, in a way. I mean, in a way, I do have proof. We both know what Paula Steigler's getting out of you—testimony that might reverse Clara's will and get Paula the property. I *think* I know what you're getting out of Paula, because she offered me the same thing for *my* testimony, assuming I'd doctor it up the way you did yours."

"Doctor it up!" That buckled Warren's head all right. "Nobody got me to *doctor* anything! And I'll have you know there was no talking about her aunts at *all* until long after . . . until certain commitments were made!"

So Warren had gone for it hook, line, and sinker. How brutal was Pete going have to be to shake him loose? Hell, he'd already gone this far, he might as well finish him off. "Paula offered me those same 'commitments' a week ago, Warren, only I couldn't see trading Clara's last wishes for a second-rate roll in the hay."

Warren pulled himself up to his full five feet four and a half inches and for a second Pete thought he was going to get a sock in the mouth. "I'll thank you to take that back."

Pete didn't take it back. He braced himself and went on. "That was Paula's second offer. Her first offer was money. She offered me the construction contract on the six houses she's going to put up once she tears the Bates place down."

"Hah!" said Warren. *"Hah! You* just made up one last thing too many. The only reason Paula's fighting that will at all is because she can't bear to see her aunts' house pass out of the family. She wants to live in that house all her life. She wants to raise her family there. She—"

Warren blushed. Clearly he was counting on it being *his*

146

family she was planning to raise. Pete knew it was best not to let him count on that too long.

"Check it out, Warren. She's going to tear down that house you think she loves so much. She's going to subdivide, build, and sell out fast. She's already looked into the subdivision at the town hall. She's talked to Wren Realty about the market value of six houses there. Check it out."

Warren Johnson blinked. He looked kind of like someone who'd been socked in the mouth himself. "I'll thank you to excuse me from continuing this conversation," he said. He carefully looked to the right and the left and then crossed the street to the other side.

Pete had to admire a man with that much class.

It would remain to be seen if he had anywhere near as much smarts.

Chapter

17

Connie didn't stay more than two minutes in the garden after Pete had left. Her heart wasn't in it, and besides, she wanted to talk to Sarah Abrew about Annabel.

It was hard for Connie to talk to Sarah these days. Whereas Clara and Annabel had reminded Connie of things that had gone right in her life, Sarah Abrew, *Pete's* Sarah Abrew, seemed to remind her of all those things that had gone wrong.

Pete, for example.

And Sarah had never had any qualms about telling Connie just *where* she had gone wrong. On days when Connie was thinking straight she knew that Sarah was telling Pete all the places he'd screwed up, too, but Connie hadn't been thinking straight in a while now.

But today there was something in Sarah's hug, something in the way she held Connie's face in her warm, knotted fingers a little too long.

Yes, this was hard for Sarah, too.

Connie jumped right in and asked about Annabel. It must have had something to do with living a long time. Sarah hardly seemed surprised.

"Annabel? Married? No, I didn't know Annabel had married. Did he die?"

"I don't know," said Connie. "They were married in Maine. His name was Alfred Edison Standish. Ever heard of him?"

"Standish." Sarah shook her head. "You say they were married in Maine? I do believe Annabel and Clara used to visit friends in Maine."

But that was all Sarah knew. She didn't seem to think there was cause to dwell on it. She began to talk about Pete. As usual.

Pete's ears must have been burning.

When Connie pulled up in front of her apartment, Pete was just getting out of his truck outside.

Connie pushed open her door.

"About Warren Johnson," began Pete, but that was as far as he got.

A streak of human flesh topped by a red comet blasted through the crack in the door and knocked them to the ground. Actually, only Connie, in direct line with the door, was knocked to the ground—Pete just fell there when he tripped over Connie's foot.

"Ow!" hollered Connie. Afterward she was sorry she'd hollered. It distracted Pete from running after the redhead, kept him hovering over her foot instead. "Go!" she hollered. *"Get* him!"

"Are you all right?"

"Go, for chrissake. I'm—"

"Call Willy. Fast." Pete took off.

Connie limped up the stairs to call the chief of police, but she didn't do that as fast as she should have, either. The minute she hit the top of the stairs she was distracted by the sight that met her. She sat down, grabbed her ankle, and looked around.

The apartment was a mess.

Connie's living space was compact, and the belongings that had survived her first flight away and her second flight back were sparse, but somehow there seemed to be more of them now that they had been ripped out of their drawers and tossed on the floor.

"Oh my God," she said out loud, looking around. She only remembered about calling Willy when her eyes had gone full circle around her two rooms and come to rest by the phone.

Pete was getting pretty sick of this guy. He'd caught a flash of him turning left outside Connie's door, and Pete turned left, too, but there was an awful lot of left on Pease Street. He started to run, but soon stopped to listen instead.

He was getting smarter. About three houses down a gate banged shut. Pete cut across the lawn between two houses in the direction of the stockade fence and vaulted over it just in time to see the redhead hit the woods. But these woods were different from the woods behind the Bates house. These woods weren't deep enough or thick enough to hide anyone and they went back only as far as the next road.

Pete turned around, revaulted the fence, and collected his truck at Connie's. He circled the woods and came out on the other side as the redhead burst onto the road. The redhead saw Pete and doubled back, into the woods, where the truck couldn't follow. Pete left the truck and charged into the woods right where the redhead had entered, then stopped, looked around, and listened.

The first thing he heard was the friendly rustle of the summer breeze in the tops of the trees.

The second thing he heard was the not-so-friendly sound of his truck coughing to life and peeling off down the road.

Pete walked back to Connie's.

He stood in the middle of Connie's compact living space

and looked at the scattered contents of her few drawers, the topsy-turvy bedding, the scattered kitchen things.

"Wow."

"You lost him?"

"And my truck."

Connie's eyes opened wide.

"But that's okay. It'll be easier for Willy to find my truck than to find some kid on foot."

And Pete was right.

Willy found the truck, no problem. It was parked by the side of Shore Road, overlooking the Sound, the keys still in it.

The redhead was nowhere in sight.

Connie tossed the very last T-shirt into her bureau drawer, returned to the kitchen, sat down at the table, and sighed. Pete was still sorting silverware into its proper compartments. Connie didn't have the heart to tell him it wasn't the redhead who had dumped it every whichway in the drawer.

"So why *my* place?" Connie asked.

"I don't know," said Pete. "This guy must have heard that you inherited the house. He must have thought you took out whatever it was he was after and brought it back here."

"Whatever it was. Which we still haven't found. I still think it's a will."

Pete snorted. He'd been a little out of sorts since Willy and Ted had returned Pete's truck but no redhead. Connie decided to change the subject.

"I've been thinking about Warren Johnson," she said.

"I just talked to him. Paula's got him all twisted around about Clara's state of mind. I tried to clue him in to—"

Connie gave an impatient jerk of her hand. "I don't mean about that. I want to know why Warren Johnson didn't find Annabel and Clara. At least Annabel. He delivered the mail Friday afternoon. We found her on Saturday morning, and Hardy Rogers said Annabel had been dead for at least twenty-four hours. What about Warren's mail stop on Friday afternoon? Annabel was lying there dead. Why didn't Warren say something about that?"

"I don't think it was because he found Annabel dead, and then went in and force-fed Clara twenty-two digoxin pills."

Yes, he was out of sorts.

"I'm sorry," said Pete. "But this is getting pretty crazy, isn't it? I can't see Warren doing anything to Clara. What would he get out of it? Unless of course we're falsely assuming he met Paula only after the aunts died. Maybe Paula went to work on Warren longer ago than we think. Maybe she got Warren to do her dirty work for her."

"Are you going to ask him?"

Pete shut the silverware drawer and sat down opposite Connie. He looked tired. He also didn't look too anxious to talk to Warren. "There must be plenty of good reasons why Warren hasn't said anything about finding Annabel dead, and the best one is that he *didn't* find her. The mailbox is out on the street. He probably just dropped off the mail and kept walking. Who says he went up on the porch and saw Annabel at all? And who says the Bateses even had any mail on that Friday? Maybe there wasn't any mail, and Warren skipped right on by to the Coles'. Or maybe Warren didn't work that Friday."

"Or maybe he did." But Connie didn't press Pete again, not wanting to demand of him something she was unwilling to do herself. She asked instead about Hardy Rogers. "Did you see Hardy?"

"No." Pete was still stalling on that, and Connie knew why. To someone raised on Marcus Welby the idea of catching Hardy in a lie was not a nice thought.

"But you talked to the chief about the damage in the garden."

"Yes."

"Did he—is she—"

"I don't know. He *un*officially looked around, took a tire impression, and left. I don't think he can do much unless you file a complaint. You've got this, today, too." Pete waved his hand around him at the now neat apartment. "Why don't you make it two for one?"

Connie didn't answer. The redhead was one thing. Paula Steigler was something else.

"Or maybe tomorrow we should just stop by the hotel and have a word with old Paula ourselves. Let her know we've got the police in on this."

But as Pete spoke Connie could feel herself curling up into the age-old defensive position, arms across chest, knees pulled in. She wasn't going near any hotel that might have Paula Steigler inside.

Pete watched her. He changed tack. "Actually, you probably want to get back to work on the garden instead."

Connie wasn't too thrilled by that idea, either.

"I'll go with you," said Pete.

And was that, after all, what this was all about? Was all this panic just some ploy her subconscious was pulling to keep Pete close? Connie unfolded herself from the chair and stood up. "No. You're not my keeper. Go talk to Warren or Hardy or—" She looked at Pete more intently. Yes, he did look tired. "Isn't tomorrow the Fourth of July? Why don't you take a day off, a real day off. Go lie on the beach. Don't you ever have any *fun* anymore? I'll go work in the garden. I'll—" She sat back down again fast. Were her hands shaking? Her knees were. What was making her feel so creeped out?

"So forget the garden. We'll both go to the beach."

Connie shot back up again. *"No.* I don't need you to . . . I don't want to go to the beach. I think you should get out of here."

Connie walked purposefully to the stairs. She could hear Pete, after a second's stall, behind her. She walked him out the door, up to his truck, and opened the door for him. Pete got inside. She closed the door, but stayed there with her hand on the window ledge, not really wanting him to leave her, almost changing her mind.

153

Pete didn't move. He was *waiting* for her to change her mind, she could tell.

No. "Good-bye. Thank you." She walked away.

Pete didn't want to go. He got this strong feeling that Connie needed him right now. It was a feeling he hadn't had in a long time. If ever.

As Pete drove reluctantly away, he tried hard to occupy his mind with something other than Connie. He wasn't too surprised to find that the first "other" that came to mind was Hardy Rogers. He'd put it off long enough. He'd have to talk to Hardy about whether he saw Clara three days before she died or not.

Hardy Rogers had probably wound up his official office hours long ago, but Pete could see him through the window, in one of the examining rooms, rummaging in a drawer. Pete went to the door and knocked.

"Now what do you want?" asked Hardy the minute he saw Pete, as if Pete had just left there five minutes ago.

"I want to know when you last saw Clara Bates alive."

Hardy turned around and walked away. Pete hustled after him. When Hardy went back into the examining room, Pete went with him.

"You said you hadn't seen her in over a month, but Ella Cole says you were out there just a few days before the sisters died. Did you forget about that visit?"

Pete braced himself for a blast, but none came.

"Apparently."

"So you knew Clara never could have gotten up and moved her sister or taken those pills."

Hardy looked out from under his eyebrows and then returned his attention to an open drawer full of various-sized jars that he'd been pawing through. "I envy you, Pete. These days I seldom get that sense of certainty that rings so clear in you. How's your wife?"

"She's doing better. I did what you said. I got her moving. She's been working in the garden a lot. And she'd be even better if some of these questions could be cleared up. That's one reason I'm asking you this. It's important for her to know."

"Important as compared to what?"

"Listen, just tell me if you're going to tell me. If you're not going to tell me, just tell me you're not."

"Tell you what?"

"Why you lied about when you saw Clara."

"I thought you decided I forgot."

Pete started to get mad. For one thing, he was getting nervous that the sensible explanation he had secretly expected to hear from Hardy was not forthcoming. For another, Hardy wouldn't get his nose out of the damned drawer, and Pete couldn't tell if he was even taking this seriously or not. Besides, the constant clanking around of the glass jars was starting to get on his nerves. What were those jars *for* anyway? Recently removed tonsils? Pints of blood? Other bodily fluids that Pete wasn't so sure he'd want saved?

"So you forgot. Either way you lied. You purposely lied about when you were there, or you purposely lied about Clara's abilities to function. I think it's fair of me to want to know why, don't you?"

"No." At that Hardy looked up at Pete, and his eyes, piercing as blue blades, never waivered.

But Pete's didn't waiver, either. "Why not?"

"What the Christ does it matter? Give it up, Pete." The eyes got kinder. The hand came down on his shoulder. That was when Pete lost his cool.

"Your word is not the last word on this. You're not God, you know."

"And you are, I take it?" Hardy slammed the drawer shut and it sounded like a crack of lightening. The jars inside rolled around like thunder. The storm clouds of Hardy's eyebrows massed overhead, and Pete felt a little like Moses, just before he got sent to the desert for forty years.

He knows something, thought Pete, driving away again. He knows something, but what? Is Hardy implying that

155

what he knows would upset Connie more than not knowing would? Pete had to think Hardy was wrong about that. Connie needed, above all, to know what was what. So did Pete. And one of the things they needed to know was where Warren Johnson was the day Annabel was lying on her porch, dead.

Pete found Warren Johnson just leaving the post office at the end of his day, walking down Main Street in the direction of Beston's Store. Pete parked the truck and fell into step beside him. At the sight of Pete, Warren's forehead folded up on itself, and he looked at the ground. Despite what Hardy Rogers had said about his sense of certainty, Pete was suddenly riddled with his usual doubts.

"I'm sorry, Warren," he said right away. "I don't know what makes me think I'm the world's best judge of human nature. I think I said things before that I shouldn't have. Everyone has more than one side to him and some people are better at seeing a person's good side than others. I guess I'm not."

It was a noble speech. Warren Johnson ignored it.

Pete cleared his throat and tried again. "Could I ask you a question?"

"Free country."

Pete felt like he was six years old, out on the playground. "The day before we found Annabel and Clara. June thirteenth it would have been. Friday. Did you deliver their mail?"

Warren looked up from the ground in surprise. "Sure I delivered it."

"What did you see?"

Warren looked up at the sky. Pete looked with him. It was still a deep blue. The sky over Nashtoba was blue for about a month and a half every year, so Pete kept looking at it for a while just so he wouldn't forget what it was like. Finally Warren answered him.

"I think 'round about June thirteenth was the Cherry and

Baker catalog. And if it was Friday, the Islander newspaper comes in the mail."

"No, Warren. Not their mail. What did you see at the house? Annabel was dead. She was lying inside the screen porch with her—"

Warren stopped walking. "I didn't see Annabel! You think I'd see Annabel and walk on by? You think I'm *that* foolish?"

"No, Warren. I just want you to think back. Did you see anything strange? Anyone around the place, any strange cars, anything that didn't seem just right?"

"Why are you asking me this?"

It was a good question. Maybe because Pete kind of felt like he owed Warren one, he answered it. "Someone moved Annabel's body after she died."

Every last worry line left Warren's face for one second of surprise and then returned, doubled. Not long after that, the man who had remembered every piece of mail he had delivered three weeks ago lost his memory of everything else besides that. "I don't remember that day at the Bateses'. I don't remember seeing anything that day. It was weeks ago."

"Think, Warren. You remembered the catalog and the newspaper."

"I didn't so much *remember* the catalog and the newspaper. I just happen to know when they'd have come around due. I left the Bateses' mail in the box and went on my way. I didn't see Annabel." Warren, in a sudden burst of speed, moved away from Pete.

Pete caught up. "You didn't see anyone else around?"

"No, I told you!" Warren hurried on.

"Somebody moved Annabel!" Pete hollered at him. "After she was dead!"

"Now *that's* a pretty piece of news!" said a voice behind Pete, and Pete whipped around. Bert Barker stood behind him.

"Someone moved Annabel's body! I almost didn't think I heard you right!"

Pete knew he was doomed but he tried anyway. "That's not public information, Bert. Keep it quiet, all right?"

"Why, you afraid the chief will find out? He wouldn't find out unless you painted it across his forehead! *Hah!*" Bert seemed to like his own joke. He hastened up the steps of Beston's Store to try it out on the others.

So the cat was out of the bag. There was only one thing Pete could do now, and that was to warn Willy.

The chief wasn't at the station and Jean Martell wouldn't tell Pete where he was, which meant Jean didn't *know* where he was. Pete left a message to have the chief call him the minute he got in, resisted Jean's efforts to get him to open the bag and let out another cat, and returned to Factotum to hover around his phone.

The first phone call was from Mrs. Potts, who wanted Pete to come over right that minute to stomp up the clamshells she had collected whole and thrown in her drive. Pete stalled her.

The second call was from Maxine, who was looking for her mother. She wanted permission to go in a friend's boat to Boston and camp overnight on the esplanade to secure a good spot for the fireworks the next day. Pete told Maxine that her mother had already left.

"Oh," said Maxine. "Then maybe you could just tell her? I'll leave right now. I'll leave her a note that you figured it was okay?"

"No dice, Maxine."

"That just *figures,*" said Maxine, and hung up the phone.

The third call was from a very unhappy chief of police. At least, he became very unhappy once Pete told him his news.

"So now the whole island knows that someone moved Annabel's body," Pete summed up.

"I thought you said you only told Warren Johnson."

"And Bert Barker overheard."

"Oh. Right."

The chief was beginning to catch on to this place.

"What are you going to do?"

Willy remained silent for a second or two. "You really shook the tree, Pete, didn't you?"

"Guess so," said Pete glumly.

"Well, I guess the only thing to do is to sit tight and see if any apples fall."

True, Pete was the one who shook the tree, but the last thing he expected was that all the apples were going to fall on *him*.

Chapter

18

It was the Fourth of July. Pete wasn't really expecting Connie to collect him to go work in the Bateses' garden on the Fourth of July, but still, he was disappointed when eight-thirty came and went and Connie hadn't showed. He was so disappointed that by nine-oh-five he was parked outside her door.

Connie's car was gone. He knocked anyway, but no one answered. He pushed the door open and yelled. No one was home.

Almost on a whim Pete drove past the Bates place on his way home, and there she was, hard at work in the garden. She had even bought new plants, and was banging them out of their peat pots and settling them into the ground.

She looked up when Pete's truck came into view, scrambled to her feet, and came halfway to meet him. "Hi!" She seemed in good spirits. She seemed glad to see him. She was wearing baggy khaki shorts and the same T-shirt she wore every Fourth of July, the one with the picture of the red, white, and blue Pabst Blue Ribbon beer can.

"You didn't come to get me," said Pete. Even to himself he sounded hurt.

"I thought you were going to go to the beach."

"Why don't we *both* go to the beach?"

"I think I'd rather just keep working," said Connie. "Go home. I'm all right."

"Is that an unadjusted definition of *all right?*"

Connie looked away. "I told you the other day all of *Webster's* wouldn't have helped Clara once Annabel was gone. But I figure somewhere in everybody's life they have to look in the dictionary for *something,* right? It's okay to need *some* help, right? I mean you can't lug the dictionary around with you everywhere, but if you can count on it being there when you need it, if it's going to help you to see things differently or make sense out of things or bail you out in a jam—"

Pete didn't know what the hell she was getting at, and it must have shown, because Connie broke off with a half-strangled laugh.

"Hey, Webster. I'm just trying to say thanks, all right? Now get lost, will you?"

Webster? Thanks? Was that what she was saying, that Pete was *her* dictionary?

Pete didn't want to go. But neither did he know what to say to her. "How about lunch? Twelve-thirty?"

Connie looked off into the distance, as if she were searching for a plane, or a boat, or a train. It made Pete nervous.

"Make it six-thirty. Dinner. I'll meet you back at Factotum."

Pete agreed, reluctantly. Not that he didn't like the idea in theory, it just gave him an awful lot of time without a whole lot to do.

He'd forgotten about the recently shaken tree and all those loose apples.

* * * *

The first one to come tumbling down was Ella Cole. Pete had previously catagorized Ella as faded—now she was out-and-out white. She walked into Factotum and caught Pete just coming out of what had once been his office but was now a general repository of everything that didn't fit anywhere else. Pete never got a chance to walk Ella to the more scenic porch—she just dropped onto the lumpy rattan couch and looked at him with, yes, fear.

"My husband, Simon, didn't go moving any bodies," she said.

"What?"

Ella leaned forward. "My husband, Simon, didn't go moving any bodies. I heard. Oh, I heard! Someone moved Annabel. That's why you've been asking all those questions. After I opened my yap about Simon expecting me to take care of Clara, you think he moved Annabel. You think he did in that poor old woman next door."

"Actually—"

Ella scooted even further forward on the couch. "Let me tell you something. Maybe I was a little out of sorts with my husband that day. Maybe I said a thing or two in a speculating sort of way. That's a far cry from wanting to see that man swing at the end of rope."

"Still and all, Mrs. Cole—"

"Don't you 'still and all' me! I'm telling you, you heard nothing from me about any taking care of Clara. You heard nothing from me about any six houses and Clara leaving it all to us. Is that clear?"

Ella Cole was yelling now, and Pete didn't much like being yelled at, especially when he hadn't done anything to warrant it. He sat forward himself and lowered his own voice a half a register.

"How about you, Mrs. Cole? Did you move Annabel's body?"

Pete hadn't thought Ella Cole could get whiter, but she did.

"Me? Me?" She said it faintly and not very convincingly.

"Weren't you the one who was most upset about being left

162

with Clara on your hands? Annabel died first. Did you find her? Did you figure out what it meant for you in the long run? All that drudgery, as you put it?"

Ella Cole leaned back into the cushions of the couch as if Pete had hit her.

"*Someone* moved Annabel, Mrs. Cole," Pete went on. "You and your husband were handiest. You'd think if it wasn't one of you, one of you would have seen whoever it was who did."

Ella Cole's eyes assumed a crafty look. "Maybe we *did* see someone over there. Maybe we did."

Pete waited.

"But why am I wasting my time talking to you, Mr. Person-employed-to-do-all-kinds-of-work-whether-they-want-you-to-or-not! Making me feel something's wrong with me because I don't want to waste what's left of my health on Clara! Making me throw my husband to the wolves! Who do you think you are, anyway?" With this last thrust Ella stood up and swept toward the door. "And it's not *my* skin I'm the least bit worried about—you remember that, will you? I came here to explain about Simon. I don't want to see that man swinging at the end of a rope!"

That phrase again. Her eyes even gleamed a little as she said it, and Pete figured she was kind of getting to like the idea by now. He didn't have the heart to tell her they didn't hang people anymore.

After Ella Cole left, Pete put on his swim trunks and headed for the beach. He hated scenes. He needed to clear his head. He walked across the prickly lawn and onto the marsh, talking silently to himself as he went.

Who did Ella Cole think she *was*, anyway? Calling him Mr. Person-employed-to . . . But was he? *Was* it his business, after all, to go charging into their house, demanding to know what they knew? What business of it was his? Still, there was no call for Ella to get so uppity about it all. True, she was on a mission, a mission to save her husband from the rope. Pete grinned to himself and then stopped grinning.

Or *was* that Ella's mission? In a way, all she had done was to remind Pete of just what her husband *had* said and done that could be called into question. Maybe Ella really *was* looking to see him swing! Maybe she was that furious with him! Or . . . Pete stopped walking. Maybe Ella wasn't so much furious as smart. Maybe she had moved Annabel and killed Clara, and knew her best hope of escaping detection was to pin it all on her husband. Two birds with one stone? Her freedom, his death? And who had she seen next door? The redhead? Hardy Rogers? Paula Steigler? *Otto Snow?*

Pete reached the beach, dropped his towel, and hit the water running.

He dove and stayed under for one long, clean glide, then surfaced. He flipped onto his back, floated in the soft chop, and looked at the perfect sky. Ah. Yes. He had to remember to do this more often. What did he care who moved Annabel's body? What did twenty-two little digoxin pills matter in the greater scheme of things, after all?

Then he remembered Connie.

Pete stretched out in a long crawl parallel to the beach for a hundred yards and back, then dove under and came up close to shore. He walked up to the beach to his towel and dried off as he walked. Once back at his house he threw on a T-shirt, and grabbed his wallet and the keys to the Bates house that he carried with him everywhere on the off chance he could unload them on Connie. He jumped into the truck and was at the Bates house in record time.

"No," said Connie. "Come on, Pete. Six-*thirty*. I don't want to swim. I'm on a pretty good roll here."

"Lunch, maybe?"

"Dinner. We said *dinner."* But Connie grinned at him. It was a nice sight, and too long absent. Maybe she *was* all right. As he thought it the grin left her face in a flash. She was looking over Pete's shoulder, and the hand that held the trowel wasn't as steady as it had been the minute before. Pete turned around. Paula Steigler was cruising to a stop in the street, right behind Pete's truck.

She primped her way across the lawn and looked Connie up and down. "How nice to see you," she said.

Connie didn't answer her. Neither did Pete.

Paula looked around at the newly planted things in the garden. "How nice," she said. "But then again, I never could see the point to these meaningless, therapeutic exercises, like gardening. That *is* the point here, isn't it? Therapy?"

Connie said nothing.

"What do you want?" Pete snapped at her.

Paula's eyes widened. "Want? I don't want anything. I just came to take one more look at the place where the road will go. I think I can maneuver things to get a seventh lot if the road takes a good sharp turn right here." She stamped her heel into the dirt Connie had just finished loosening. Connie said nothing. Did nothing.

No, she wasn't all right.

"Ta-ta," said Paula. She waved, and she didn't seem to care that neither of them waved back.

Connie turned abruptly on her heel and headed for the back of the house.

Or the woods.

"Connie—"

"I'm all *right*. Dinner. Six-thirty. I'll meet you for dinner. *Go.*"

Pete didn't. At least, not until it seemed that Connie was determined to stand at the very edge of the Bates property staring at the pine trees until he did.

All well and good, but Pete would have preferred her to show some of that stubbornness when Paula Steigler was around.

But as Pete returned to the front of the house he found Paula Steigler was only just climbing into her car. She got back out as Pete approached.

"Your ex-wife insists on remaining here, I see."

"She can do what she wants. It's her house."

"And yet she doesn't *want* the house, does she? It's this garden she wants. It's the garden that's spurred her interest in the place."

165

"House, garden, it doesn't matter, since it's all hers."

"Maybe," said Paula Steigler. "But then again, maybe not."

Paula Steigler returned to her car and drove off.

Pete waited until she was out of sight and then followed suit. He pulled up to his own home just as the next apple, Otto Snow, was walking away from his door.

Otto was all dressed up to go calling in a seersucker sport jacket and a blue bow tie, but he didn't so much as wait for Pete to ask him inside before he started talking, right there in the drive.

"I did ask Annabel to marry me. Annabel told you so, didn't she?"

"She told Connie. Would you like to come in?"

"I think it's best that I do. Yes, I do think it's best."

Otto followed Pete inside, still muttering about what was best. Pete led Otto out to the porch, his favorite spot for entertaining his seersuckered and bow-tied guests. He settled Otto into one of the rockers and offered him something cold. Otto, shivering in the balmy breeze, opted for a cup of tea.

Tea. Pete scrambled around in the recesses of his kitchen cupboard and finally found a dried-up old tea bag. Salada. Connie had once been addicted to the proverbs on the tags, hooting over them at every breakfast until the one that said something about he who laughs now, cries later. After that she gave up tea.

Pete read this tag warily. "You have to grow up, you don't have to grow old." Pete felt like he was doing the reverse. He peeked out the door at his guest. He wondered which Otto had done, grown up or grown old. Pete put the kettle on the stove and returned to the porch.

Otto sat perched on the outer edge of the rocker and peered at Pete, anxious to get straight to the point.

"I knew you knew I proposed to Annabel when you and Connie came calling. I don't know what possessed me to lie."

"I don't either, Otto," said Pete, but actually he thought

he did. He felt for Otto. And just maybe he could help him out. "I think I know why you lied, Otto. Wasn't it a matter of pride? But I don't think Annabel's refusal reflected on you at all."

Otto blinked. "Annabel's—"

"She was already married, Otto. We found the license. His name was Alfred Standish. We didn't find anything to indicate they'd ever been divorced or that he'd died. I think maybe that's why she kept refusing you. I'm sure she cared for you a good deal." A good deal? Pete always talked like an old man whenever he was around one. He drove himself nuts.

Otto didn't seem to notice. "Annabel . . . married. And you think this is why she . . . refused."

"Heck, who knows?" said Pete, now doing Beaver Cleaver. "Maybe she didn't want to discuss that part of her past, even with you. She must have left him, or he must have left her. But nobody seems to have known about the marriage."

The kettle whistled. Pete went to the kitchen and poured the boiling water over the crisp bag. Apparently stale tea still worked—the water turned brown just like it was supposed to. Pete picked up the cup and returned to the porch.

The empty porch.

Otto Snow was gone.

Chapter

19

Pete sat on the porch staring at his sneakers, thinking about Otto Snow. Why had he left that way? He had been upset about the news about Annabel. True, what Pete had told Otto might have healed his wounded pride, but what must he have felt about Annabel concealing her marriage from him? And why hadn't Annabel simply told Otto she was married, instead of continually refusing him? Or had she refused him with some alternate explanation, maybe the one Connie suspected, that she couldn't leave her sister?

Otto Snow had wanted to marry Annabel in the worst way. Enough to ask her over and over again. What if Annabel had blamed her refusals on her sister? What if Otto knew that Clara, and only Clara, stood in the way of his happy home? Suddenly Pete got an uneasy feeling in the base of his brain, admittedly not his most effective organ. Suppose Otto had come to the Bates house while Annabel was out? Suppose he had come upon Clara near enough to the time when she'd be due for a dose of pills? Suppose he got them for her? Too many of them? No. Hardy said Clara had died *after* Annabel. Then again, Hardy had said a lot of things, and left out a lot more. Why? But wait. Hardy's opinion had been confirmed by autopsy, at least as to the order and time of death. *Or at least that was what Hardy had told Pete.* But even so, what if Otto gave Clara the pills, and the pills didn't work right away? What if Annabel had come home and died on the porch *before* Clara's pills took hold? Before Pete could muddle through his thoughts further, another apple rolled across his lawn and knocked on his door. Pete went inside, opened the door, and found Warren Johnson.

Warren looked even smaller than usual somehow. "Hello, Pete," he said, but he didn't sound like he expected Pete to answer.

"Hello, Warren. Come on in. Grab a chair."

Warren stayed standing.

Pete looked at the envelope Warren held in his hand. "It's the Fourth of July. You're not working, are you?"

"No, I'm not working. Social call, I guess you'd call it. Well, no, I don't expect you would call it that. Not social. Not at all." He looked at the envelope in his hand. "This here's a copy of my testimony. I made her give it to me. Not that it does much good. It's already *faxed.*" He gave the *F* word the same emphasis given to all *F* words. "She was going to tear down the house and sell the property. You were right."

"Oh," said Pete.

Warren stood up a little straighter. "Not about everything, mind you."

"No."

"And don't think I just plain took your word over Paula's just like that. I checked around. The minute you told me about Annabel I checked around."

"About—"

"Someone moving Annabel that way. It's one thing to . . . Well, let me say it's another to . . ." Warren cleared

169

his throat. "I mean, after all, *somebody* came along and moved a dead woman and walked away. I don't like that. I don't like that at all."

"Me either, Warren."

"Well, I just wanted you to know. I told her I wasn't necessarily going to stick to that testimony she faxed. I told her I was going to have to think this thing through a bit more. She seemed to think it didn't much matter if I thought about it anymore or not. She seemed to think she could throw enough question into the thing as it is. I'm sorry, Pete. Tell Connie I'm sorry, will you?"

"It's okay, Warren. You only did what you thought was right."

Warren looked at Pete for a second in silence. "I'll grant you, I *wanted* to think what I was doing was right. But I wanted to think a lot of things, I guess."

"Are you saying you think Paula Steigler might have moved Annabel?" asked Pete.

Warren looked too shocked to frown. "Of course I don't!"

"You said it was after you heard about Annabel that you—"

Warren backed up. "I never said that. I never for one minute implied what you're saying I'm implying. I just thought some about what you said. I added to what you said the fact that something . . . something *unusual* was going on about those dead sisters. Surely something is going to be done, questions are going to be asked. I felt I should make my statement as clear as possible, that's all. After all, Pete, what could I prove about Clara's mind? Not anything. Not anything at all. That's all I'm saying, Pete."

But still, to Pete's way of looking at things these days, Warren was saying a whole lot.

After Warren left Pete looked at his sneakers some more, thinking about Warren this time.

"Christ on a raft, do you need your ears blown out? I've been banging on that door for five minutes!"

Pete jumped.

Hardy Rogers's head loomed up from the lawn and through the screen.

"Come in! Grab a chair."

Hardy Rogers stomped up the stone steps, yanked open the screen door, and folded his long body into the porch rocker. He looked like Lincoln, hands on bony knees, deep-set eyes gazing out through the screen and over the nation.

Or marsh.

"So!" said Pete, in a kind of false heartiness prompted by his many questions regarding Hardy of late. "Would you like—"

"Oh, stop yapping and sit down." The blue eyes left the fields of Gettysburg, or wherever they'd been, and zeroed in on Pete. "So what in the blue blazes made you go blabbing all that business about Annabel?"

Pete looked at his sneakers. Again. "I told Warren Johnson. I didn't notice Bert Barker standing right behind me at the time."

Hardy groaned.

"I didn't just *tell* Warren, either. It occurred to Connie that Warren must have delivered the mail to the Bateses that day, and maybe Warren saw Annabel. I just asked—"

"You just *told*. And now all hell breaks loose. I suppose you know you've put your friend the police chief in a fine pickle. Why in hell don't you leave it alone and—"

"Wait a minute." Pete started to get a little ticked off. Why should he sit here and explain himself to Hardy Rogers when Hardy Rogers refused to explain anything to him? Who did he think he was? "Why'd you come over here, anyway?"

Hardy looked out over the marsh again. He set the porch chair rocking by pushing his hands against his knees. He rocked for some time, and when he looked back at Pete some of the fire had gone out of his eyes.

"It's nice here, Pete. You have it nice here. You'd think it would be enough."

"Is that why you came? To sit on my porch and rock?"

171

Hardy snorted and stood up. He did it slowly, in jerks, and suddenly he seemed old. "Christ knows why I came here. I keep expecting to find a brain inside that head. Something to reason with. Wasted trip, I see." Hardy opened the screen door.

"Reason? Go ahead. Reason me this. How did Clara die of too many pills, lying trapped in her bed with the pills in the bathroom? Who moved Annabel's body after she died? Or don't you care?"

Hardy stood on Pete's grass with his hands in his pants pockets, his rumpled coat jacket hanging from protruding wings. He kept looking at the marsh, the sea, the sky as if he had never seen them before. When he did look at Pete the blue eyes seemed dead. Cold. "You know, Pete, I care a hell of a lot less right this minute than I did just a few weeks back."

He turned away.

"Hey!" Pete hollered. "Did you know Annabel was married?"

"Married? Annabel? No." But Hardy didn't seem to care about that, either.

He kept walking.

Pete could no longer sit on the porch. His brain was making his body nervous. He was still in his swim trunks, T-shirt, and sneakers. He shed the sneakers on the porch and the T-shirt on the beach, and dove into the water again. This time he swam underwater with his eyes open, the water crystal clear but so loaded with salt that it blurred his vision. Or did it? He kept seeing Hardy Rogers standing on the lawn, caring even less now than he did three weeks before. Why? Pete burst through the surface of the ocean and set out to sea with an even crawl. There were a lot of *why*'s revolving around Hardy. Why had he lied about his last visit to Clara, about Clara's physical condition? Why wouldn't he talk? Why had he come here today? Obviously, he wanted to shut Pete up. Obviously, he had not wanted the whole island to know about Annabel's moved body. Obviously, something was up.

But *what?*

Forget it, Pete lectured himself. If Hardy didn't want Pete to know, Pete wouldn't know, it was as simple as that. Pete shook the water out of his eyes and turned for shore, this time thinking about Connie.

Webster's, huh? *Webster's.* Help with the definitions. Everyone needed to look in a dictionary for something. So Pete was Connie's *Webster's. I don't think the whole of* Webster's *would have helped her once Annabel was gone,* Connie'd said.

So maybe nobody could *help* Clara, but who would want to *hurt* her? Of course, it hadn't actually *hurt* her, not if what Hardy had said was true. She had gone out peacefully, and if what Connie had said about the whole of *Webster's* was true, she probably went out gratefully as well. Painlessly, peacefully, gratefully, like falling asleep at the end of a long, hard . . .

It came slowly. Pete was almost to shore, face in the water, about to tip his face out to breathe. Instead he stood up, his toes gripping sand.

You don't have to be feel sorry for Clara, Hardy had said. Why not?

Because Hardy Rogers knew what kind of life was left for Clara.

Leave it alone, he'd said to Pete.

Why?

Because Hardy Rogers knew. Because he'd come to the house, found Annabel, maybe broke the news to Clara and listened to her cry. Pete knew Hardy would never have crammed a bunch of pills down Clara's throat, but maybe Clara had talked to him, begged him. All Hardy had to do was bring the digoxin pills from the bathroom and leave them within Clara's reach.

But who moved Annabel? Hardy, of course. A doctor wasn't going to leave a human being lying on a porch until he'd made good and sure he couldn't do anything to save her. True, he had neglected to turn her back over, but doctors could get just as rattled as anyone else.

Pete was practically running over the marsh by now, in a hurry to get back home, but as he thought further he found himself slowing down. He couldn't quite picture it. He couldn't picture Hardy Rogers leaving the pills with Clara and walking out. What if something had gone wrong? What if she'd taken too many but not enough? What if she'd lingered, suffered? Was that possible with digoxin?

But Clara hadn't been dead all that long when Pete and Connie found her. Hardy must have been sitting by the phone, waiting for that call, and if it hadn't come soon, what would he have done—gone back and "found" the sisters himself? Or had he waited there, to be sure it went the way he expected? Someone had put the pills back in the medicine cabinet, after all.

Yes. It made sense. It especially made sense for someone like a doctor who was expected to alter the natural course of life and death every day. Wouldn't he get kind of used to it? Wouldn't the line get a little fuzzed? Wouldn't it be easy for him to figure he could work it either way? What had he said to Pete when he'd first arrived? Pete had seen him and been filled with relief. *Thank God you're here,* Pete had said. What had Hardy answered? *What's God got to do with it?* No, Hardy Rogers wasn't the type to give credit for his own hard work to God. Conversely, it seemed unlikely he'd go looking to God to take care of life's problems. And if God didn't do it, who would?

Hardy Rogers.

By the time Pete reached his little cottage he was convinced of it.

Hardy Rogers had killed Clara Bates.

Chapter

20

After most of a day of selective snipping, pulling, staking, and replanting, Connie had to admit that the compost heap looked a hell of a lot better than the garden.

The annual bed had definitely had it, the cutting bed didn't have a prayer of delivering a decent bouquet till fall, and the perennial bed certainly wasn't going to be one of next year's stops on the island tour. But Nashtoba's own contributions to the scene, the wild, haphazard thicket of honeysuckle and rugosa roses that Paula Steigler hadn't dared take on, still laughed and waved and shed their perfumes into the breeze. The hydrangea bushes, snuggling into the ell of the house, had also escaped Paula's tires and seemed to have burst into bright blue bloom just to spite the great-niece. And there were pink rambler roses crawling over the old stone wall that ran along the west edge of the property, and tight buds on the field of daylilies that Paula must have mistaken for unmown grass, and just enough cherry red verbena, white baby's breath, and blue marguerites to remind Connie that it was the Fourth of July. All in all, it looked . . . all right. Connie dropped her tools and headed for the beach to wash off in Nashtoba Sound.

Connie figured it had to be well after five o'clock and still the beach was dazzling. White sand, glittering water, blue-gold sky. Connie blinked. This particular stretch of beach wasn't all that accessible by car and the occupants of those few houses that sat within easy reach had gone home by now. Connie wanted a swim in the worst way. There was nobody in sight. She scrambled out of her clothes and dove.

She felt as if she hadn't swum in years. She beat back and forth along the shore for a quarter of an hour or so, then clambered out and yanked on her clothes over dripping wet skin. She stretched out in the sand and sighed.

It felt good. *She* felt good. It was as if some huge, gaping knife wound was finally beginning to close. Connie lay on the beach thinking about nothing, feeling everything.

It took Pete a while to face up to the fact that he'd have to talk to Hardy. There were a lot of reasons not to, and the few reasons to do so were pretty easily argued around, except for one. What if Pete were wrong? What if Hardy *hadn't* given Clara the pills? Then someone else had, and for motives much less noble.

But before Pete could leave for Hardy's he was interrupted by his second visit from Otto Snow.

Otto didn't look so hot. Pete hurried him into a chair on the porch and debated offering him that cold cup of tea. Otto didn't give him the chance.

"I'm curious as to why my little lie about whether or not I proposed to Annabel interests you so much," said Otto.

Pete mulled that over. "I guess it was *why* you were lying that interested me. If it was for some other reason than just pride—"

"Pride. Pride. You keep saying that, Pete. Why do you keep saying that?"

"Isn't that what it was, Otto? You didn't want anyone to know Annabel turned you down. Isn't that pride?"

Otto gave Pete a sad look and shook his round, bald head. "I see your trouble, Pete. I see how you look at it. I think I see why, too. It hurt you, didn't it? Hurt your pride that Connie ran away with someone else. But that didn't even occur to me. Pride? I gave up on that a long time ago for the waste of effort it was. Do you want to know why I lied? Or do I even need to tell you?" Otto peered at Pete. "Or is this what you've been doing all along? You know everything, don't you?"

It was like the wind that came before a hurricane, smelling of freshly snapped wood.

"Know what, Otto?"

"That *I* killed Annabel."

Pete almost fell off the porch. "Otto—"

"I know you're thinking I found her. I heard today that someone found her and moved her, that you knew that someone moved poor, dead Annabel. I wasn't the one who found her. I wasn't the one who moved her. I was the one who *killed* her."

So what was Pete supposed to do now, he wondered? Excuse himself and call Willy? Begin a makeshift reading of Otto's rights?

"I did it the same as if I'd shot her in the head. She never wanted to marry me, but I persisted. I *persisted*. She never would agree. Of course, I knew about her marriage to Alfred. They never were divorced. Annabel didn't want to contact him. She was afraid of what she might find, I think. She hadn't treated him fairly, she said. She'd acted like a silly child, she said. She was ashamed of what she'd done to Alfred, and no talking of mine could change it. She didn't want to write him. I begged her to. For a long time I begged her to write him, and finally she did, but he never answered. Oh, everyone kept fussing about me being over there all the time, over at the sisters'. Nobody knew Annabel was married, see, and it started to look pretty . . . odd. Finally Bert Barker said to me, 'What's the matter, Otto, can't you make up your mind?' It was easier at the time to laugh along. 'Sure, Bert,' I said. 'That's just it, Bert,' I said. 'I just can't make up my mind.' I thought that would take the pressure off Annabel, leave her secret where she wanted it to be. But I didn't like it. I didn't like it one bit. I kept after Annabel, see? I told her to have him subpoenaed. I told her to declare him legally dead. She didn't take kindly to my ideas, I might tell you. She felt it was only right that she make contact with him herself. It went on and on. I *pressured* her. I wore her down. She agreed. She was about to write to Alfred again. The strain of it was too much. I killed her, see?"

"No," said Pete firmly, but he knew it wasn't enough. He knew Otto wasn't even listening. What to do with him? Pete did his best, but in the end he did what he always did with tricky problems of this sort.

He called Rita.

Rita did much better with Otto. At least, Pete thought she did. She did something to the tea and came back with a steaming cup. She talked to Otto about how everything he had done had been done from love. Otto nodded twice. He even smiled once. It seemed okay. He got up to leave and turned to Pete.

"Don't tell her niece I killed her, please," he said.

Rita rolled her eyes at Pete. "Otto," she said. "I'm taking you home."

And she did.

Pete was left alone. He sat and stewed over Otto for a while, but finally he realized that thinking about Otto would get him nowhere. Otto had not killed anyone.

The question was, had Hardy?

It was now five o'clock on the Fourth of July. Even a doctor as busy as Hardy wouldn't have office hours on a day like today. Pete passed up Hardy's office entrance in favor of his kitchen door and found his guess correct. Hardy opened the door with a cup of tea in one hand and half a peanut butter sandwich in the other.

"You? Again?"

"I've been thinking," said Pete.

Hardy peered at him for a second. Then he raised first the cup of tea and then the sandwich in offering.

"No, thanks."

Hardy waved at the kitchen chairs, and after Pete sat down, Hardy did the same. The last of the peanut butter sandwich disappeared and was swilled down with the tea.

"Well? I get nervous when you think these days, Pete."

"Yeah, me too."

"Now that I think about it, I've always gotten a little nervous when you think. You *dwell*, Pete. You dwell. Not only over everything *you* ever did, but over everything everyone else does, too. Or did. You seem unable to excuse a person's peccadilloes. You—"

"I don't consider giving someone twenty-two digoxin pills a peccadillo. Apparently you do."

Hardy continued to study Pete.

Pete squirmed in his chair, but held his ground. "I'm not necessarily saying we've got the crime of the century here. I'm just saying this whole thing bears a closer look, that's all. If it was done with a certain . . . benevolence in mind, that's one thing. If it was done with some sort of self-interest, that's another. I think we need to know which."

"Or if?"

Pete looked at him, puzzled.

"These twenty-two pills are such a certainty in your mind? You have some proof? Before you make accusations in this country I believe you're supposed to have some proof."

"The nurse has proof. She has notes of the number of pills that should have been on hand. And I found the bottle that proves they weren't."

There was the quickest flash of something in Hardy's steel blue eyes.

Had he forgotten about the nurse's notes?

Still, he did not give way. "I asked you once to leave this alone, Pete. Now I'm asking you again."

Asked? When had he ever asked? *Told* was more like it. "I can't leave it alone unless I know what I'm leaving alone. I just want to know if you found Annabel dead and left Clara with the extra pills."

Hardy stood up. He loomed over Pete, but his eyes held nothing that Pete could consider the least bit threatening. He seemed nothing more than . . . sad. Pete stood up, too. Hardy went to the door and opened it.

Pete walked through it.

"I've been practicing medicine for a lot of years," said Hardy from behind him, almost as if he were talking to himself, but Pete turned around.

"The practice of medicine used to be built on trust. Trust that as professionals we would do our best, do what we could. What happened? When did we violate that trust? How? What do we build on now? What *is* it built on now? Now it's built on . . . Christ knows what it's built on! Of course, our legal system, our democratic system, is built on the *lack* of trust. Checks and balances. We retain the right to get rid of you. That's all right. That's all right. But everyone's always so *sure.*"

Hardy backed away from the door. Before he closed it Pete heard him still muttering. He sounded . . . old.

Connie pulled herself off the cooling sand and with one last therapeutic look at the beach she headed for the path that led to the Bates house. She had to get home, clean up, and meet Pete at six-thirty. She was looking forward to it. She was still afraid of how *much* she was looking forward to it, but even so, she could feel her bare feet pushing off faster from the sand.

Even the path through the scrub seemed different today, the scent of the honeysuckle heavier, the bayberry leaves glossier, the poison ivy less lethal. All of her senses seemed more neatly tuned. Maybe that's why she smelled the smoke while she was still deep in the path.

It reminded her of corn husks smoking on the grill. She burst out of the woods on the run to see the compost heap scattered and smoldering, the piles of dead leaves beginning to catch.

She froze. For a minute she froze, the knife wound wide open and burning. *So it's over,* she thought. *The garden's gone, the house will catch.* She wasn't surprised. It seemed, for that one frozen minute, to be no more nor less than what she deserved. She had done nothing to earn this house, this garden. Therefore it made sense that it would be taken away.

But in flames?

Then her feet were moving. She looked down, half surprised, to see her own bare feet, brown calves, long thighs pounding over the grass toward the house and the hose. She snatched the hose off the coil. She twisted the faucet. No water. She'd forgotten it was turned off from inside. She dashed for the bulkhead and stopped in her tracks at the sight of the lock. *Damn.* Pete had the key. Why the hell hadn't she taken it from him when he'd practically shoved it down her throat? She dropped down onto the wooden bulkhead and yanked and twisted the rusty old padlock, but it didn't budge. She stood up and looked behind her. The smoldering compost had burst into an impotent blaze here and there, but Connie didn't trust it to stay impotent long. The hell with it. She raced to the pile of tools on the edge of the lawn and picked up a shovel. She charged to the basement window, stepped back, and swung. The glass shattered, half into the basement and half out. She chiseled off as many rough edges of glass as she could, then grabbed the old piece of tarp she'd been using to haul the garden rot to the compost. She doubled it and draped it over the bottom edge of the window frame, got down on her hands and knees, and wiggled feet first through the tightly fitting window frame.

The basement was a hell of a lot more crowded than she'd thought.

First her bare feet landed on a couple of porcupines.

Then somebody in a cement mixer plowed into the back of her head.

* * *

Pete would have been better off swimming. On land, he paced. Onto the porch. Off the porch. Into the kitchen. Out of the kitchen.

What did Hardy want from him, anyway? Blind trust in his judgment without revealing just what that judgment had been? And he called *Pete* stubborn! And talk about trust! Didn't all this mean that it was *Hardy* who didn't trust *Pete*? Even if Hardy had killed Clara, it would have been safer for him to tell Pete then to let Pete roam around like a loose cannon, attacking every discrepancy in Hardy's story. Pete paced into the bedroom and looked at his bedside clock. It was almost five o'clock. At six-thirty Connie would come. He'd talk to her about it. Or would he? *Should* he? Pete went back to the porch.

Maybe, after all, Hardy *had* told Pete the truth. All he'd needed to say was "No I did not leave Clara the extra pills." He hadn't said that. That must have meant he did it. And what did *that* mean? And what, if anything, was Pete supposed to do about it?

At six o'clock Pete showered and ironed a white cotton shirt. He changed into his best jeans and his least mangled sneakers. He combed his hair and brushed his teeth.

So what if Pete did nothing? What happened then? Nothing. What was wrong with that? Nothing. Unless, of course, Paula Steigler, or Ella Cole, or Simon or Otto . . . He'd talk to Connie. No sense thinking any more about it until he and Connie had talked. Pete looked at his watch. Six-thirty-five. He started pacing again, but for a different reason.

At six-forty-five Pete got mad at her. Where was she? His hair wasn't even wet anymore and she still wasn't here. Connie was not a person who was late, unless she was doing something she didn't really want to do. Maybe that was it. She didn't want to come.

Five minutes later Pete got mad at himself. He was supposed to be over all this fury and this paranoia. He *was* over it. If Connie was late it was because she'd lost track of the time. She wasn't her usual self. She was probably obsessively at work in the garden without a thought to the time.

At seven Pete left. He was so convinced that he'd pull up to the Bates house and find her still hard at work, oblivious of the time, that when he first saw the smoke he thought it was a roadrunnerlike cloud of dust moving down the garden in her wake. He wasn't sure which he saw next, the flames beneath the smoke, the uncoiled but unused hose, or the broken cellar window.

Pete fumbled in his pocket for the Bates keys. They weren't there. They weren't there! He picked up the shovel lying on the ground and smashed through the wooden bulkhead planks.

There was enough smoke in the basement so that it took him a minute to see what was what, but not enough to disguise the long red hair of his track star.

The boy was leaning over a body. Pete could just see the body's feet. Bleeding feet. *Connie's* feet. The boy started like a rabbit when Pete crunched over the broken glass around them, but he didn't run. Connie's head was cradled in his hands. The gold hair on the back of her head was black, wet, oozing.

"I saw it," said the boy. "I saw a woman light that fire. A woman with dark hair, in a purple Saab. She drove by in the car and walked back. She must have left the car someplace else. She lit the fire and went around the house. I was going to go someplace and call the police. Then *she* came." He nodded at Connie. "She broke the window and climbed in, but she never came back out. I dropped through the window and almost landed on her. She must have cut her feet on the glass when she hit the floor. I think she's knocked out."

Pete brushed the rest of Connie's hair out of her face.

She opened her eyes, saw Pete, and blinked. "I think we're out of Wheaties," she said.

"I'll call for an ambulance." The redhead sprinted up the cellar stairs.

By the time they all got there, the ambulance with two volunteer firemen in it and the squad car with Ted Ball in it and the Scout with the chief in it and the fire truck with the rest of the volunteer firemen in it, the redhead was gone.

Chapter

21

Connie lay on Hardy's examining table with a man at either end. While Hardy stitched up her head Pete cleaned off her feet. When Hardy moved down to the feet, Pete moved up and rested a hand on her shoulder, as if he had to touch her. Connie wasn't sure if it was to prove she was alive or to anchor her down.

"I can't remember," said Connie. "This is bugging the hell out of me. I can't remember. I remember all those stupid sirens."

"They weren't all for you," said Pete. "Some were for the fire."

Now there were more noises in the air, a string of firecracks popping off on a beach somewhere.

"What day is it?" Connie asked.

"Still the Fourth."

"I can't remember. I swear to God, the last thing I—"

"Stop thinking about it," said Hardy. "It'll all come back in time."

"In time. Right." Connie didn't feel like she *had* time. All of a sudden she had a lot of things she wanted to get squared away. She twisted her head a little and saw a wall of white cotton smudged with blood and dirt. She reached out and touched it. It was Pete's shirt. She could feel the knot of his stomach underneath. "Are you going to Florida?"

His hand tensed on her shoulder. "Florida?"

"Florida? Who said anything about Florida? I asked if you were going to—" But then she realized she *had* said something about Florida. She was losing her mind. Again. But differently.

Pete must have shot Hardy some sort of a look because the doctor answered him quietly, as if Connie weren't in the room. She *hated* that.

"It's all right. She'll get sorted. Just feed her light till tomorrow, wake her up every hour or so tonight to make sure she comes to. Make her take it easy. No driving for a bit."

"Got it," said Pete.

"And keep her off those feet for any long spells. At least for a day or two. That dressing will have to be changed on Monday. The stitches will come out next week. And get this filled—she'll need it for tonight." Hardy handed Pete a prescription.

"Right."

Connie sat up. "I don't—" But she stopped. She was afraid she'd start talking about Tennessee or something.

"Where are her shoes?" asked Hardy.

"She doesn't have any," said Pete.

"I don't?" asked Connie. It seemed serious, not having shoes. She was sure she had shoes. Somewhere. She frowned.

"I've got it covered," said Pete.

Connie was very tall, and, lately anyway, very solid, but all that shoveling in the garden must have stood Pete in good stead. He picked her up and carried her out of the room, grunting only once.

She woke to the sound of distant voices.

"The minute we got here she fell asleep. She doesn't remember, but Hardy said she should, later on." That was Pete.

"She hit her head when she fell?" That was Willy.

"Hardy didn't think so. He thinks she was hit. With something round and flat." Pete again. "The redhead's gone? Again?"

"We were busy with other things." The chief sounded edgy. "I'm going back there now. I'll want you with me—you know where she fell."

"I can't leave. I have to wake her up in—" There was a watch-checking pause. "Forty minutes."

Connie sat up. *Boy,* did she have a headache. She lay back down and looked around.

She was home.

Factotum.

The voices drifted in and out.

"I'll stay with her." *That* was Rita Peck.

"No. I'm taking care of her." That was Pete.

"Oh, Pete, let me stay. Why do you think I hightailed it over here, anyway? The minute Evan told me." Rita again. Bossy old Rita.

"No." Stubborn old Pete.

"I need you with me." The chief again. "You say the redhead saw someone?"

"Paula Steigler. Dark hair. Purple Saab. She parked down the road, lit the fire, went around the house. Then Connie came."

Connie closed her eyes. The voices continued back and forth. The door opened. Sneakered feet crept close, but Connie couldn't seem to open her eyes. The door closed.

Pete's voice carried through it, cross now. "In *forty minutes,* Rita. And if for some reason I'm not back, wake her again an hour after that. And don't give her anything but ginger ale, maybe some crackers. Have you got that?"

There were a few more murmurs, then a more distant door opening and closing.

Quiet.

Connie drifted.

I'm taking care of her.

It was nice to be taken care of. She stretched her throbbing feet further down into the cool sheets and eased her head more comfortably on the pillow.

Pete's sheets.

Pete's pillow.

She slept.

Pete looked around him. The volunteer firemen had drenched the garden, and just for good measure, it seemed, had doused the house. The gray shingles were black with wet, and Pete and Willy slogged through a pool of water at the bottom of the bulkhead to the spot on the basement floor where Connie had fallen. There was nothing in the vicinity of the basement window that would have so neatly and yet accidentally cracked Connie in the back of the skull as she fell. Willy asked Pete about a million questions, and Pete answered what he could, but it was clear that they needed Connie's failed memory to figure out what had really gone on.

Either that or the redhead.

"You say Ted's looking for the redhead?" Pete asked again.

Willy nodded.

"He's a key witness. He saw Paula Steigler."

"He saw a dark-haired woman. Or so he says."

"With a purple Saab."

Willy cocked an eyebrow at Pete. "So he *says.* When you caught him leaning over your battered wife."

"So how'd he know she had dark hair and a purple Saab if he didn't see her?"

"Nobody says he didn't see her. Somewhere."

"How many dark-haired, destructive types like that could there be around here?"

"How many kids getting caught at the scene of the crime think up something pretty quick?"

Pete mulled that over. "You mean if this redhead set the fire, if he hit Connie, and then I showed up, he would have pretended he was just trying to help. He would have made up a dark-haired—"

"Maybe." But Willy didn't sound convinced of that, either. "Or maybe he's known Paula Steigler, the dark-haired woman in the purple Saab, for some time."

Pete wasn't convinced of *that*, however. He had asked Paula about the redhead once, and he had trusted the instinct that had believed her reply. Pete didn't think Paula knew the kid. He abandoned further speculation and put his efforts into helping Willy poke around.

There was a pile of firewood against the far wall. Willy began to go through it.

"What are you looking for, bloodstains?"

"Bloodstains. Hair."

Connie's hair. Pete shivered. He began to look also—not at the firewood, but at the few tools on the workbench, the base of the broken lamp, the croquet mallets.

No blood, no hair.

Pete started to look elsewhere, then stopped. He turned around and looked at the croquet mallets. The set was an old-fashioned one, with a wheeled wooden stand with holes for each mallet, racks for the balls, hooks for the wickets. One mallet hole was empty.

"Hey, Willy?"

They searched the basement's hiding places for the missing croquet mallet, but found none.

"Of course, it could have been missing for years," said Pete.

"Could have." But Willy took one of the remaining mallets, went upstairs, and called Hardy Rogers.

While Willy talked to the doctor, Pete thought. All the time Hardy Rogers had been stitching up Connie's head,

Pete had been too worried to think about his previous chats with the doctor that day. Now, as he listened to Willy's half of the conversation, he wondered what Hardy must have thought when he'd first heard the police chief's voice on the phone. That Pete had turned him in?

Willy described the dimensions of the head of the croquet mallet and apparently they meshed with Hardy's recollections of Connie's wound. The chief hung up the phone and called the station. He set the wheels in motion for all the fingerprinting and collecting of evidence in and around the house. He then set the two of them searching in earnest for the missing mallet.

Pete found it, still in one piece, in the middle of the field of daylilies. As he and the chief poked around in the growing dark for any other possible blunt instruments, he noticed for the first time that the Coles didn't seem to be at home.

If Paula Steigler *didn't* do this, if the *redhead* didn't . . . What if the Coles *did?* Ella Cole was dark-haired. Maybe the redhead saw Paula Steigler drive by in the purple Saab, but maybe it was the dark-haired Ella Cole who set the fire. If Ella Cole set the fire and clobbered Connie, the Coles would absent themselves from the scene, all right. But why would the Coles set the fire *or* clobber Connie? Although Connie could well have died in the basement as the smoke circled in, Pete doubted this was an out-and-out murder attempt. There was no need to set fire to the garden first if the object was only to bash Connie's head in. There was no need to bash Connie's head in if the object was just to destroy the garden and house. But the redhead had said the woman who set the fire then went around the back of the house. And went inside? What if whoever set the fire was still in the house when Connie arrived? What if he or she heard the smash of the glass and ran down into the basement to see Connie dropping out of the sky? What if whoever set the fire was about to be caught at the scene? He or she would *have* to clobber Connie or else run the risk of being identified as the arsonist. Before Connie could land, regain her footing, and turn, someone had made sure she would see nothing, no one.

So why set the fire in the first place? It made sense if it was Paula Steigler. She destroyed the garden by fire for the same reason she tried and failed to destroy it with her car. Paula Steigler knew that Connie's newly revamped interest in the place centered around the garden. If there *were* no garden, would that interest fade? Would Connie step back and let Paula contest? And win?

The Coles no longer had anything to gain by keeping Connie out. Neither did Otto Snow. Neither did it make sense for this phantom redhead to burn whatever it was he was trying to find. Unless he was trying to find it to destroy it. But then why burn the garden and leave the house intact? And despite whatever Pete might have thought about Hardy's methods regarding Clara, he certainly couldn't be expected to have an interest in whether or not Connie got the house. Besides, Pete couldn't for one minute see Hardy doing anything as illegal, as unsubtle, as setting fires, striking blows. But what if he had to set fires, strike blows to protect his own neck? Could Pete picture that? Not without some very intense, very personal pain. But how about the redhead? Pete didn't know this redhead from a hole in the wall. He didn't know what he was capable of. He knew only that he was fast, young, nice-looking, and that he seemed to have stayed around a risky situation long enough to make sure Connie got help.

The dark-haired woman hadn't.

And besides, Pete didn't *like* Paula Steigler.

Rita was a little miffed at Pete. True, he'd been under a lot of strain of late, but you'd think after all these years he'd know he could trust her to take care of Connie for an hour or two without lousing it up. *Forty minutes, Rita. Ginger ale, Rita. Maybe some crackers.* Really! Rita looked at her watch. Then she walked across the kitchen to the bedroom door, opened it, and peeked in.

Clearly, Pete hadn't been expecting company. The room showed evidence of a hastily attempted cleanup: a half-open bureau drawer spilled hurriedly inserted clothes, album jackets had been shoved into a pile on the top of the turntable, newspapers and assorted books and magazines had been corraled in one rocking chair, some muddy clothes had been draped over another. Through the bathroom door Rita could see a pile of sheets that had most likely been stripped off the bed not moments ago.

In the middle of the crisp and clean replacement sheets lay Connie, in one of Pete's T-shirts, sound asleep. Or was she? Maybe she was unconscious. Maybe she was *dead*. Rita crept closer. She could see Connie breathing. She could see her fingers clutching the balled-up sheet. She wasn't dead, but how did Rita know she wasn't out for the count? Rita leaned over the bed.

"Connie," she whispered, and jumped back into Pete's dresser when Connie sat bolt upright in bed.

"Ohhh." Connie grabbed the back of her head and then let go, fast. She blinked. "Where am I?"

"Pete's."

Connie touched the bandage on her head. "What happened?"

"Someone set fire to the Bateses' and hit you on the back of the head. That redhead found you. He saw a dark woman in a purple Saab. Don't you remember?"

"No. Sort of. I don't know."

"When Pete got there you were lying in the basement with your head conked in. The redhead was leaning over you. Pete thinks you broke in to turn on the water and someone knocked you out. You cut your feet on all the glass when you landed. The redhead called the ambulance and they took you to Hardy's. Hardy stitched you up. The police chief and Pete are at the Bateses' now, trying to figure out who did it, and I'm here to keep an eye on you till he gets back. We're not supposed to let you sleep too long or give you much to eat. Do you want some ginger ale?"

As Rita talked Connie's eyes had gotten rounder. Then

they got darker. Greener. *Furious.* She seemed about to vault out of the bed, but changed her mind and staggered more sedately onto her feet. Once she was standing she didn't seem to like it. She looked down at her bandaged feet, saw the clothes on the chair, and hobbled over to them. She pulled on the muddy shorts.

"Hey," said Rita. "Where do you think you're going?"

Connie didn't answer. She was rummaging around in Pete's drawers as if she'd rummaged there many times before. She surfaced with a pair of white gym socks and pulled them on over her bandaged feet. She snagged a pair of high-top basketball sneakers out of the bottom of Pete's closet and pulled them on. Connie's feet were big, but not that big. She sat on the bed and laced them up, tying them tight around the ankles. She stood up, feet splayed. She looked like a fuller-figured Olive Oyl.

"Where do you think you're going?" asked Rita in her best mother-talking-to-recalcitrant-teen voice.

"Purple *Saab.* Dark *hair. Paula Steigler.*"

Connie took off out the door.

Rita didn't hurry after her too fast since she knew Connie didn't have a car.

She sauntered to the door, hands on hips, speech all ready just as Connie pulled out of sight in Pete's truck.

Chapter

22

The chief held the croquet mallet between two fingers and turned it around. The next thing Pete knew he was moving. Fast.

"Where are we going?"

"The Whiteaker Hotel."

"Paula Steigler?"

"Paula Steigler."

The chief climbed into the Scout on one side. Pete climbed into it on the other. They took off for the hotel.

The Whiteaker Hotel was the only really classy place of accommodation on Nashtoba, and even so, it had been built in the early 1900s and had been through a lot. Still, it's owner, Jack Whiteaker, seemed to pump enough of his own apparently ready cash into the place so that every July Fourth the long wooden veranda floor glistened with fresh enamel paint, the white-clothed tables inside and out glowed under lantern light, and the three tiers of Victorian gables withstood the tremors caused by a full house worth's of feet. The Whiteaker sat right on Far Harbor, overlooking the mainland of Cape Hook. Every Fourth of July its porch was jammed with tourists and islanders alike, there to eat, drink, and watch the Cape Hook fireworks over the harbor.

The hotel parking lot was packed. Still, it didn't take Pete two minutes to recognize the beaten and faded body of his old blue truck.

"Hey! My truck!"

Willy braked.

"What the hell! That's my truck!"

"You seem to be losing it a lot lately. And where did you leave the keys this time?"

Pete didn't answer him. It was an old dig. Everyone on Nashtoba always left their keys in their cars and their houses wide open, no matter what this new out-of-town police chief had to say on the subject. Pete jumped out of the Scout and peered into his truck. Yes, the keys were still in it. He obediently removed them, stuffed them into his jeans pocket, and followed Willy up the steps of the hotel porch.

"Ooooooooooooh!" A rocket sailed out over the harbor and the watchers on the dock all crooned after it. Pete didn't even turn around.

Willy collected Paula Steigler's room number at the desk, and they went up the stairs to the second floor.

They heard them from halfway down the hall. Or rather they heard Connie.

"You're goddamned right you are! You're one goddamned piece of work! And to think I was scared to *death* of you, you stupid—"

Pete and the chief looked at each other. Willy broke into a jog and rapped sharply on the wooden door. "Police!"

Connie didn't so much as take a breath. ". . . cow! I'll give you one minute, do you hear me? *One minute!*"

Willy battered on the door again. "Police!"

A white-faced Paula Steigler opened the door, but it didn't stop Connie.

"I said one minute!" She advanced on Paula Steigler. Pete

looked at her feet and noticed yet another of his possessions that had strayed.

Paula was back against the wall.

"You stinking, lousy, putrid—"

"Whoa," said Willy. He put a large but gentle hand on Connie's arm.

She shook it off, not so gently.

"Whoa!" said Willy again, but it seemed to Pete that he was talking to himself now. He looked . . . surprised.

"Pulverizing the garden! *Torching* the garden! *Knocking me out!* Say it! *Say* it! *You knocked me out!*"

Paula Steigler looked first at Willy and then at Pete.

"Hey, Connie," said Willy. "Back off, huh?"

Connie turned away for a second, but Paula Steigler didn't look like she was counting on the police chief to win out. She stayed up against the wall, and in a second Connie was two inches in front of her again with her finger in her face.

"Say it!"

"Yes," squeaked Paula. "Yes."

"You coshed me!"

"I co-coshed—"

"You torched the place!"

Paula nodded, fast.

Connie's hands reached to the general vicinity of Paula's shoulders, or possibly her neck. "You're under *arrest!*"

"*You're* under arrest," said Willy. "I mean it, Connie— you back off or you're under arrest."

Connie looked from the chief to Pete, her eyes green fire.

"Now," said the chief. "Paula Steigler. You're under arrest. You have the right to remain silent—"

"Oh, really? Tell *her* that!"

All of a sudden Pete was distracted from Connie and Paula by something his eye had caught sight of on Paula's bureau. The keys to the Bates house. It explained how Paula Steigler had gotten into the house, but it didn't explain everything.

Pete crossed over to the bureau and picked them up. "Where did you get these?"

Paula didn't have to answer him, of course, but Connie must have killed whatever resistance she had left. "Off the dash of your truck. That day at my aunts' house. When you walked around back with—" Paula Steigler looked with loathing at Connie, unable to say her name.

Those were the last words she spoke.

The chief led her out the door.

Pete drove Connie home.

"Nice shoes," he said as they pulled out of the parking lot.

Connie looked down at her feet. "I nearly fell down the goddamned stairs."

Out on the main road Pete shifted into fourth and that seemed to remind Connie of something else.

"I took your truck."

"I noticed."

"It was just that when Rita told me about the dark woman in the purple Saab I knew it was Paula and . . . It was the weirdest thing. I was so *scared* of her all that time. I just felt like she was in the right, you know? I felt I had no business with her aunt's house. I felt like a . . . like a *thief!* I couldn't look her in the eye. I felt like she had a right to the house, like she had a *right* to hate me. It was what I *deserved,* to have her hate me. I had no right to get mad. I didn't have a leg to stand on with her. Then the minute she hurt me . . . I mean she actually tried to *hurt* me! The minute she did that something snapped. *Nobody* has the right to do that! *Nobody.* And just like that I wasn't scared, I was furious! The *nerve* of her, you know?"

"Yes," said Pete, and he *did* know, now. But he wanted to go back to something Connie had said at the start, something that he thought would end up being important. "You said you knew it was Paula. You saw her? You remember her hitting you on the head?"

Connie stalled for a minute, fussing with Pete's shoes. "No, not exactly. I mean I *know* it was Paula Steigler. I mean *now* we know it was, don't we? She *confessed* right in front of the cops, didn't she?"

"I'm not sure confessions extracted under threats of violence are admissible in a court of law."

Connie snorted. Still, she seemed worried. "And these are only her minor crimes—assault and battery, arson, vandalism. What about killing Clara? She's not going to confess to *that*. We've got to have proof."

Hardy Rogers had so consumed Pete's thoughts of late that he had almost forgotten Paula Steigler had once been first in line for the crime of killing Clara. He debated whether to open the discussion of Hardy Rogers at this point. He looked sideways at Connie. She was gingerly feeling the back of her head, which had been shaved so that two remaining wings of soft gold hair on either side made her look like a cocker spaniel. She also looked white and tired, still a mere shadow of her former self, despite her recent outburst in the Whiteaker Hotel. *"God,* my head hurts," she said.

Pete decided to skip any talk of Hardy for now. "Willy made impressions of the tire marks in the garden," he said instead. "He's got them going over the basement and the house for other trace evidence right now. He has the croquet mallet. They might salvage some evidence off that."

Connie whipped around in the seat. *"What* croquet mallet?"

"The one Paula hit you with."

"A *croquet* mallet! That stupid bitch used my head for a croquet ball?"

Connie was off again.

Pete tried, but he couldn't help it. He listened to Connie's creative description for a good thirty seconds in silence, but then he burst out laughing. The laughing only served to redirect Connie's fury onto *his* head, but Pete didn't even care. He kept right on grinning.

Connie was back.

Chapter

23

The firecrackers were going right through Connie's skull. Every time one exploded she cringed in her seat. Pete looked sideways at her. He wormed his wallet out of his back pocket and pulled out the piece of paper with one hand.

"I'll stop and get this prescription."

"*What* prescription?" Connie grabbed the paper. Codeine. "I don't need it. I'd rather go to bed." Her little jaunt to the Whiteaker had taken its toll on her head, her feet, her mind.

Pete took the turn for Factotum.

Connie sat up. "Where are you going?"

"Home."

Home.

"You might not remember what Hardy said. You can't stay alone. Somebody has to make sure you wake up in the night."

"I can set my alarm."

"And who's going to know if you don't hear it?"

It was a good point. And since Pete didn't seem too bent out of shape by the whole arrangement, who was Connie to argue? *I'm taking care of her.* She leaned back against the seat and let him. It felt good.

But the holes that remained in her recall of the period immediately before and after her accident troubled her. If she hadn't remembered that Hardy didn't wanted her to stay alone, what *else* hadn't she remembered? Maybe she'd better find out.

"What else did Hardy say?"

Pete rattled off the rest of his instructions—staying off her feet, not eating much, no driving. Connie didn't much like it, but she was feeling so rotten she was starting to see the wisdom of his words. And who was she to argue with Hardy Rogers? "I guess he knows what he's doing," she said.

"Maybe," Pete answered.

Connie looked at him in surprise. "What do you mean, 'maybe'?"

"Nothing."

"What do you mean, 'nothing'?"

"Oh, nothing."

By then they were home. Pete hustled Connie past an extremely agitated Rita and into the bedroom. Connie didn't argue about it since right then it was exactly where she wanted to be, especially when the alternative was facing an irate Rita Peck. Pete helped her out of his sneakers, then she unceremoniously abandoned her shorts and climbed between the sheets. Pete returned with some ginger ale and saltines, then disappeared to calm Rita down.

Connie expected to be asleep before the door was shut, but instead she lay there with her eyes wide open, listening to Rita's rising voice and Pete's perfect complement of lower decibels.

Connie drank the ginger ale, ate the crackers, and looked around. Almost the first thing she saw was Annabel Bates's custard cup full of paper clips and rubber bands and bits of string sitting on Pete's bureau. What in the world was he doing with that? Connie couldn't stop looking at it. Suddenly she wanted it. She was coherent enough to sense the irony of it—here she was casting away a whole house full of more valuable things and ready to fight with Pete over a custard cup! But that cup *was* Annabel. Connie could look at that cup and see Annabel, untying a string instead of cutting it, carefully winding it around two fingers, tucking it in among her other treasured finds. And why was *Pete* saving it? Maybe they were more one of a kind than they knew.

The door finally cracked open. Pete peeked in. There were plenty of things Connie couldn't remember, but she could remember *something*.

"Hardy Rogers." she said. "What about Hardy Rogers?"

"I'll tell you tomorrow. Go to sleep. You have to wake up in an hour, you know."

Connie sat up. "I want to know what's got you so bent out of shape about Hardy Rogers."

"Oh, nothing," said Pete, but he stepped into the room.

"What? Come on."

"It's nothing," he said again as he sat down on the bed.

"What about Hardy?"

"Well . . ."

Pete began. Once he started he didn't seem able to stop. His hand, tense and corded, gripped the sheet between them. The gold hairs on the back of his hand glinted in the light. Connie slid her own hand under his. She could feel the calluses on his palm, three small ones, one big one on the palm just below his ring finger, the finger where his wedding ring used to be.

Pete had stopped talking. "Well?"

"I don't know," said Connie. "I just don't know. Doesn't it follow that *anyone* could have done what you accuse Hardy of doing? Couldn't anyone have found Annabel, gone in to Clara, given her the extra pills? Hardy didn't bring them with him. The pills were right there in the medicine cabinet all along. If Clara wanted to go, she could have told anyone who stumbled by to get the pills."

"But would Clara, or anyone without a medical background, know how *many* would kill her? Or *if* they would kill her? And would that person leave Annabel lying on the porch that way? The doctor would be more familiar with dead people. He'd know who was past help. He wouldn't worry so much about leaving her there."

"I don't know." Connie squeezed her eyes tight shut. She did it because she was afraid she was going to cry, but Pete must have thought she did it because of pain. He untangled his fingers from hers. "I'm going to pick up that prescription. The pharmacy closes soon."

He stood up, he turned off the light, and he left. Connie lay awake in the dark and waited for him to come home.

Pete had a lot on his mind. For one thing, he had the fate of the island's only doctor in his hands. For another, he had his ex-wife in his bed. Pete took his time at the pharmacy, striking up a conversation with the pharmacist, Arlene Beale.

"I'm glad you're open, Arlene, it being a holiday and all."

Arlene peered over the chest-high counter, behind which, according to the sounds, she was alternately shuffling papers and rattling pills. "Seven days a week. Fifty-two weeks a year. When you're the only pharmacy on an island with a causeway built back in the year dot as the only escape, you stay open. That's my philosophy, at least. Not these new chains, though! Closed Sundays, closed holidays, open at ten, sell a few hair dryers, leave at five. That's not what I call a pharmacy, that's what I call a department store!"

"Lucky for us you—"

Arlene stopped shuffling. She leaned her forearms on the counter so she could point emphatically at Pete during a key phrase. Her short curls quivered as she got wound up. "And computers! You think these fancy pharmacies have better records than I do? Do you?"

"No," said Pete. "I—"

"They don't. It's all right here." Arlene hefted a thick ledger book. "And it'll still be right here when the power goes out and the machine goes off-line and the fool behind the counter punches the wrong key and erases it all. Right here."

Pete looked at the thick book. It reminded him of something Hardy Rogers had said. *These twenty-two pills are such a certainty in your mind?* True, there were Dotty's notes, but if Hardy wanted more proof, Pete would give him more proof.

"I wonder if you could look something up for me," he said.

Pete asked her to confirm the date Clara's digoxin had last been filled and the number of pills in the prescription. Arlene shot Pete a funny look, but she seemed thrilled to have her record-keeping system put to the test. She thumbed through the ledger.

Pete was half right.

Or half wrong.

Dotty Parsons had told Pete that the prescription had been filled two weeks before Clara died, which would have been the end of May. The prescription was filled for fifty pills. Clara took one digoxin pill a day, and Dotty had expected to find thirty-six pills remaining. There had been fourteen remaining, twenty-two unaccounted for. But according to Arlene, the prescription hadn't been filled at the *end* of May, but at the *beginning*, leaving just over three weeks of digoxin pills taken by Clara, one at a time, that Dotty hadn't accounted for.

There were no missing digoxin pills at all.

"Funny," said Arlene Beale, as she shut up the book and handed over Connie's pills. "You're not the first person to ask me about Clara's pills. Hardy Rogers called to check. I think he just wanted to make sure Clara'd been taking them right—that he, or Clara, hadn't loused it up somehow. I told him, I keep track of these things. If fifty pills are supposed to last fifty days and they don't, I get on the phone and find out why. You think some chain more interested in selling hair dryers does any checking up like that?"

Pete thanked Arlene and left, his mind racing with the

various problems associated with rediscovering twenty-two previously missing pills.

The closer he got to home, however, the more the various problems associated with this new-old roommate of his pushed the matter of twenty-two digoxin pills straight out of his head.

Connie had a few problems of her own, the most pressing of which was the matter of her sanity. The problem wasn't that she couldn't remember *anything*. The problem was that she remembered some things but a few key details were left out. For example, she dozed off and woke up with full recognition of her current surroundings. The little detail she left out for a while was that two years ago she'd left here with another man.

That Connie didn't live here anymore.

That only *Pete* did.

And whoever was rustling around in the hall.

Connie got out of bed and crept to the window. Pete's truck was still gone. There was no car in sight. So who the hell was rummaging around out there? She pulled on her shorts and crept into the kitchen. She skated into the hall and peered around the dining room door.

The bandages on her feet muffled the sound of her steps and whoever it was didn't hear her coming.

"Hey!" she hollered.

He heard *that*. He whipped around. His baby-fine, long red hair followed right behind him. In his arms he held a cardboard carton that Connie happened to know was full of Pete's canceled checks.

"What are you doing with Pete's checks?"

The young man's face evidenced a moment's confusion. Was that what made him look so young? Or was it that body—a body that looked more resistant to croquet mallets and glass?

As Connie watched him the confusion left his face and it was replaced with that look of conviction only people under twenty-one possess.

Yes, he was young.

Connie pointed at the carton with a confidence born of age, experience, and control of the only way out—the door. "Put it down."

He did. Sort of. He heaved the carton at the window and threw his body through after it.

Yes, he did better with glass than Connie did, but Connie's handicapped brain wasn't done for yet. She saw him land and turn left, toward the beach. Connie went the other way, out the porch, and to the right. She was closer to the corner and got there first, despite feet stiff with tape and gauze, but he got there soon after; Connie could hear him pounding toward her over the grass.

What the hell. Her head couldn't hurt much worse than it did already.

As he came around the corner she threw herself into him right at the knees and brought him crashing to the ground.

Chapter

24

Pete pushed open his kitchen door expecting to find it dark and quiet and Connie sound asleep. Instead, she was sitting at his kitchen table across from the redheaded track star. Connie held a wet compress to her bloody knee, and the redhead leaned over his knees hiccuping painfully, struggling to breathe.

Connie pointed at the redhead. "Got the wind knocked out of him."

The redhead pointed at Connie.

Connie grinned. "Yeah. By me."

"What—"

"I don't know what yet. Right now I'm just letting him breathe. I caught him trying to steal a carton of your old checks."

The redhead shook his head furiously, still gulping. "Didn't . . . steal—"

Pete looked at Connie. "You—"

"Clipped him. Right at the knees. *Jesus,* does my head hurt."

"Here." Pete handed her the container of pills. He took his time getting her the glass of water so he could have a minute to think. The redhead. *His* redhead. Here.

Connie took a codeine. Pete took her compress, washed it out in the sink, and knelt in front of her to finish cleaning her knee. Every now and then he looked up at Connie. She was still grinning. At the redhead.

The hiccuping stopped. The redhead couldn't help it. He grinned back. He *was* a good-looking kid, but still—

"So who—" began Pete.

"Yeah!" finished Connie. "Who *are* you?"

The boy was breathing better now. "Alfred Dixon."

Pete looked quickly at Connie, but she didn't seem to remember where they'd heard that first name before. "What were you doing at the Bates house? And at Connie's? And what are you doing here? Why do you want my *checks?*"

Alfred Dixon half rose and Pete transferred his weight to the balls of feet, but Alfred didn't go anywhere. He sat back down. "I wasn't stealing your checks."

"Want a ginger ale?" asked Connie.

Pete wasn't so sure he wanted to be that hospitable until he knew what this kid was up to, but Alfred Dixon's eyes had lightened at the suggestion and Connie was pushing Pete away so she could stand up. Pete pushed her back down.

He got Alfred the ginger ale.

Alfred gulped it like a six-year-old.

"So talk," said Pete. Pete may not have crashed through a window and been knocked to the ground and cut his feet, but he was tired, and he was not quite so taken with the humor of the whole thing as Connie. "Why? Why did you break into two houses and rip them apart at the seams? Why'd you take my checks?"

"I told you, I didn't *take* your checks! I didn't know what was in the box! I was looking for something!"

"What?" said Pete, just as Connie said, "Why?"

207

The redhead looked at Connie.

"Because of my grandfather."

"Alfred Edison Standish?" said Pete.

Four eyes, Alfred's and Connie's, widened at him.

"Did you know him?" Alfred Dixon asked.

Pete shook his head. "I do know that he married Annabel Bates."

"How? How do you know that?"

"We found their marriage license."

Alfred Dixon's hands were balled up and white. His face was beet red. "You found the license? You found it? Where?"

"In the dump," said Connie. "But that's not the point. We want to know what the hell you're doing here."

Alfred shoved a hand into his jeans pocket and pulled out a wrinkled envelope. He handed it to Connie. It was addressed to Alfred E. Standish, in Monroeville, Maine, in Annabel's hand. "Annabel married my grandfather. A month later she left. My grandfather never saw her again."

Connie's fingers froze on the letter in her hand. She looked at Pete, and looked away again. Pete took the letter from her, the letter Annabel *hadn't* thrown out with the trash. He opened it, Connie stood up, and side by side they began to read.

The letter was dated April of this year.

"Dear Alfred, it began.

"I imagine your surprise at receiving this letter from me after all these years.

"As I write this to you I hold our marriage license in my hand. I am sure this document can no longer hold any meaning for you, and I am equally sure that you will hold no objection to the dismantling of the legal bond it represents. It is in the hopes of achieving this end that I am writing to you today. I wish to marry again. I hope and believe that the intervening years have sufficiently dulled the pain I most certainly caused you, that this letter finds you well, and that

you will look with favor on my request. Sincerely, Annabel (Standish) Bates."

Connie sat back down.

Pete pulled out a chair and sat beside her.

After an awkward interval, Connie spoke. "Why didn't they get divorced before now? If she left him, he could have divorced *her*. Why didn't he?"

"My grandfather said that at first he figured she'd come back. Then, when she didn't . . . when he found out she died . . ." Alfred looked down at his hands. "I love my grandfather very much. He . . . it's special with him and me. He knew he could trust me. He knew he could trust me to . . . to help."

"Help what?" asked Pete.

"My grandmother would have been upset. My mother, too. He didn't want them to know."

"To know what?" asked Connie, but that was because she still wasn't thinking quite straight. Pete knew.

"After Annabel left my grandfather—"

"Why?" Connie leaned toward Alfred. "Why did she leave? Did your grandfather tell you?"

"He never knew. Her family didn't like him—he thought that might have been part of it. They didn't tell their parents when they eloped. A month later Annabel left. Just ran away. It nearly killed my grandfather. It would have killed *me*, too."

"For Chrissake," began Connie, but something stopped her.

Pete cleared his throat. "How did your grandfather know Annabel had died?"

"He had an obituary from a local paper. I think someone must have sent it to him, someone he knew with connections to this island. He knew both Annabel and her sister had died. That's when he called me and asked me to come."

"*Why?*" Connie asked again, but Pete knew that, too.

Alfred sank back into his chair and shook his head. "To

find the license. But I *couldn't* find it. Then I checked and found out you inherited." Alfred glanced across the table at Connie. "I thought maybe you brought things to your place. I found out where that was." The self-satisfied smirk of a private-eye-in-the-making flashed across Alfred's face. "I kind of staked out the Bates house. I parked at the town beach. Nobody even noticed. Then I walked down the beach to the house and hid in the woods. That's how I saw that other woman start the fire. I was going to put it out. I would have put it out myself, but then you came along." He nodded at Connie. "You went in and didn't come out."

"Wait a minute," said Connie, but Alfred didn't wait.

"I saw you around the house a lot. And I saw *you.*" This time he nodded at Pete. "I recognized you from the day you chased me. I thought maybe *you* took it out, so I found out where you lived, too. That's why I came here tonight. Your truck was gone. I thought no one was home. If you took it from the Bates house and—"

"The *license?*" said Connie. "*Why?*"

"His grandfather and Annabel never got divorced," said Pete.

"Why *not?*" Connie asked again.

"At first my grandfather kept thinking she'd come back. Then, when he finally gave up on her returning, he just didn't think of divorce because there was no reason to. He had no plans to remarry. Then, after a while, it began to seem to him like he'd never really been married at all. It was so short. A month, that's all. He didn't mean to do something wrong—he didn't mean to—he just didn't think it made any difference. Who was to know? When he met my grandmother he married her without giving it a second thought. He still doesn't see much wrong with it, and he wouldn't have worried about it if he hadn't gotten that letter from Annabel. She had the marriage license. She wanted a divorce. He didn't know how he could divorce someone he'd pretended he was never married to in the first place. He didn't want my grandmother to know. He didn't know what to do. He did nothing for so long that she died, and then he was *really* in trouble."

"Wait a minute," said Connie. "If she were dead, they wouldn't be married anymore, anyway, right?"

"But neither was my grandmother."

"What?"

"My grandfather was already married to Annabel when he married my grandmother, so that marriage was never legal. My mother was illegitimate. He knew they'd be upset if it came out."

"If it came out? How the hell would it ever come out if Annabel were dead?" asked Connie.

"Annabel had the license," said Alfred. "My grandfather was afraid that with both sisters dead, someone would go through their things and find the license. They'd come looking for my grandfather. Wouldn't he be legal next of kin? He didn't want my grandmother to know."

Finally Connie got it. "So if somebody found the license they'd find your grandfather, and your grandmother would have found out she was never married to him at all."

"It's just what happened, wasn't it? You went through her things and found her license?"

"With variations," said Pete.

"With detours," said Connie.

"Through the dump," said Pete. "And we never would have looked for anything in the dump if you hadn't ripped apart the house that way. Annabel had thrown it out. No one would have found that license if you'd stayed in Maine where you belonged." But Pete didn't say it with any bite. He was starting to like Alfred a little by now.

"I'm sorry about the houses. I didn't break anything except your window. I just wanted to—"

Connie leaned forward. "You don't like Annabel, do you, Alfred? I could tell by what you did to her house. And I can hear it in your voice. Was it because she left him? Was it because she left your grandfather?"

Alfred puzzled over that for a second, looking down at his

hands. "No," he said finally. "Who knows what went wrong, what made her leave. I think the reason I don't like Annabel is because my grandfather loved her best. Better than my grandmother. That's what I heard in *his* voice. Even after all this time."

Connie looked at Alfred for what seemed like a long time. Then she snuck a look at Pete. She started to look away, but Pete caught her eye and held on to it.

Finally Connie stood up and hobbled out of the room. When she came back she had Annabel's marriage license in her hand. "Everything the sisters had was left to me," she said. "Pending a small legal battle with a great-niece. But I guess this doesn't belong to either me *or* the niece. I think this belongs to your grandfather, don't you?" She held the marriage license out to Alfred. "And I hope to God you never do anything else this dumb."

"You're not—"

"Pressing charges? No. At least, not for the Bates house and not for my apartment. As you said, nothing was really damaged. You'll have to talk to *him* about this little scene right here." Connie nodded at Pete.

"I'll pay for the window," said Alfred. "My grandfather gave me lots of money for gas and food and—"

"You'll *fix* the window," said Pete.

Alfred jumped up, ready to start on the window.

Pete grabbed his elbow. "Not now. I have one more question."

Alfred's Adam's apple bobbed nervously up and down.

"What's your time in the four-forty?"

Alfred told him.

It had been Pete's time in the 200.

Once.

Pete sat on the edge of the bed, listening as Connie talked. At the rate she was going, waking her up every hour was going to be a moot point.

"Annabel," said Connie. "I can't believe it. I wonder what

happened. I wonder what went wrong. She always seemed so levelheaded, so sensible, so—"

"Maybe she was," said Pete. "Maybe he beat her up or something. But even if he didn't—*whatever* it was—don't you remember that last letter we found in the dump? Annabel forgave *herself.* That's what's important."

Connie rolled sideways under the covers and looked at Pete for a long time. "You're pretty levelheaded these days yourself."

Pete yawned—he couldn't help it—but it only seemed to wake Connie up.

"I wonder what finally made her throw that marriage license out."

"Alfred didn't answer her letter. Maybe she planned to do what Alfred Standish had done. Throw out the license, ignore the marriage, get married again. To Otto Snow."

"Annabel, a bigamist. You just never know, do you? And this thing about Hardy Rogers. He gave Clara the extra pills. He moved Annabel. All those questions we had are answered."

Connie seemed to feel okay with that particular set of answers, and Pete didn't feel like bringing up the subject of the recovered pills just then. Hardy's supposed actions seemed to make Connie finally believe what he had said all along—that Clara hadn't suffered. It seemed to relax Connie. It was either that or the pain pill. In five minutes she was out.

Pete set the alarm for one hour and clicked off the light, but he didn't go anywhere. He stretched out alongside Connie. There wasn't anyplace else to go unless he wanted to spend two hours clearing Factotum junk off the hideaway bed, and besides, this was *his* bed. Once upon a time this had even been his wife. Pete bunched his pillow up under his head, all set to do some serious thinking.

"Hey," said Connie, "wake up."

Pete jumped up. The radio alarm was playing "Moonlight Cocktail." Pete had been dancing to it in his sleep.

"I woke up," said Connie. "I need a witness."

"Woke up?" Pete was in a time warp. He didn't know what Connie was talking about.

"I'm lucid, too. Ask me anything. How many fingers I have. How many peas in a pod. Who was the fortieth president. Who *should* have been the fortieth president."

Pete didn't ask anything. He was too busy trying to figure out why Connie was in his bed asking him about peas.

"Pete?" Connie clicked on the light.

One look at Connie's head and it all came crashing back. He sat up.

"I've been thinking," said Connie. "I don't think Hardy did a thing to Clara."

"Me either," said Pete.

"So what *do* you think?"

Pete pulled Connie's hair away and looked at her blood-soaked bandage. "I think in the morning we'd better get that dressing changed. Tackling Alfred Dixon didn't do it much good." He reset the alarm and turned out the light. He started to get up, but Connie grabbed hold of him.

"Don't go."

Pete took off his sneakers and his jeans and slid under the covers. He sort of noncommittally rolled toward the edge, but Connie pulled her body up against him, knees tucked into the backs of his and one arm tight around his chest, a nine-year habit that divorce hadn't erased. It felt so good it seemed like pain. Long after Pete thought she was asleep she spoke again.

"Pete?"

"What?"

"I like it here."

Pete didn't answer.

He lay awake between alarms the rest of the night trying to figure out why not.

Connie woke to a kiss on the forehead and a breakfast tray. Juice, coffee, Wheaties, and bananas. And a head like a hangover. She had the feeling the head was because she'd lain awake all night agonizing over things said and unsaid, not because of any croquet mallet.

"So!" said Pete. He was pretty damned cheerful. It didn't help. "Dotty Parsons is coming in a half hour to change that bandage. Eat up."

Connie wasn't hungry.

When Dotty Parsons arrived she observed the nearly untouched tray in her most professional manner, and Connie could almost see the notes as they were logged: "Appetite poor."

"So!" said Dotty brightly. She and Pete should have gotten together—one of them could have saved a word. The nurse opened her bag and got to work.

"Here," said Pete. "Let me help you." He picked up her bag and walked behind her to the table.

"Oh, that's all right, Pete. I can manage." Dotty Parsons joined Pete at the table. She extracted the usual gauze and tape and scissors and approached Connie again. "Now let's see what we have here." She moved Connie's head to the side to examine the wound at the back, but not before Connie got a good look at Pete, pawing through Dotty's bag.

Pete watched until Dotty Parsons finished bandaging Connie's wound. She returned the tape, scissors, and gauze to her bag. Pete picked it up for her and carried it out.

"What a shame," said Dotty as they paused next to her little Volkswagen. "What a shame for Connie to have to go through all this. Things have been hard enough, haven't they?"

"Yes, they have," said Pete. He leaned inside the car and placed Dotty's bag on the backseat.

"I really do hate to see someone suffer so *needlessly.*"

Pete straightened up. "I know you do." He watched Dotty closely as he opened his hand in front of her. "Yours?"

The small glass vial of injectible digoxin glistened in the sun.

Dotty Parsons blinked. She reached out for the vial, but Pete's hand closed over it.

"You took that from my bag. Why, Pete?"

"There were no missing digoxin pills. I checked with the pharmacy. Clara's prescription was filled weeks before you said it was."

Now it was Dotty Parsons's turn to watch Pete closely. "That's odd. My records are usually quite good."

"I'm sure they are. But you didn't want this digoxin to be the *only* choice, did you? You wanted twenty-two pills unaccounted for just in case the police got into it, just in case they got too close. You wanted enough pills missing so that anyone would be suspect, anyone who happened to walk up onto that porch and find Annabel dead. You were willing to do it, but you didn't want to go to jail for it, did you?"

Dotty Parsons made her first, and only, attempt at looking blank. It didn't work. "I don't know what you're talking about."

"Of course, what were the odds of the police getting into it? Not good. Why would they even care? Two deaths by natural causes. If you'd remembered to roll Annabel back over, if Paula Steigler hadn't tried to scare Connie off, if some kid hadn't burgled the house, they never would have given Clara's death a second thought."

Dotty Parsons didn't speak.

"I thought it was Hardy, you know. He never denied it. Was that because he knew it was you? Did you tell him? Did he guess? Was he trying to protect you?"

Dotty drew herself up into one stiff and solid cylinder of white. "I don't know what you're talking—"

"Yes, you do." Pete said it with sadness. He didn't know why he was badgering Dotty Parsons. He didn't know why he so badly needed to know. Or did he? Yes, he did. Because what if it wasn't Dotty? What if it *was* Paula Steigler, or Otto Snow, or one of the Coles? He started again. "I have to know if you did this, Dotty. I just have to know what it . . . what it wasn't. If it wasn't you, if it was . . . someone else, it makes a *difference*. Do you see?"

Dotty Parsons's eyes seemed to open a little wider. She

looked at Pete so intently that he could see her eyes flitting back and forth between each of his, as if she couldn't trust what she saw in just one.

Pete opened his hand and looked at the digoxin.

Dotty looked, too. "That doesn't mean anything, you know, Pete. This isn't the only vial of digoxin around."

"I know that."

"You know a lot, Pete. You make up a good story. I wonder if I could make up a good one, too."

"I'm sure you could."

"Say it begins with a nurse making a call. A professional call on a patient. Say there's a woman dead on the porch. Say this someone conducts a thorough examination of this dead woman and concludes that she really is dead—too long dead for there to be any point in any additional measures being taken. Say also this dead woman is the sole caregiver of an ill person, ill both physically and, of late, mentally as well. Say this professional person had seen much evidence of this invalid's growing anxiety over her own failing mental and physical state. Say this professional person reports to this invalid that her caregiver is dead. Say this professional person is asked to do a great favor for this invalid. Say this invalid has asked this favor before. Do you think it might be possible that this favor, which had been refused in the past, could be granted in clear conscience now?"

"I don't know," said Pete.

"Even if the invalid has asked *many times* to be 'let go?' Even if this professional person's one meaningful argument against—that the caregiver herself *needed* this invalid— even if that one meaningful argument is no longer there?"

"I don't know," Pete repeated. "No one can know. No one can judge someone else's decision to—"

"No," said Dotty Parsons. "No one can. And still, once in a while, someone must."

Pete looked at Dotty Parsons. She was asking Pete to make a decision that was almost as hard as the one Clara had made, as hard as the one Dotty had made. Was Pete

Chapter

25

It was Sunday. It was the sixth of July. A certain odd sort of peace had settled over the island, that peace that comes to a New England summer place two days after the Fourth of July. The summer was finally really here. Nobody had to get *ready* for it anymore. Connie and Pete sat on the back stone step in the sun and talked about the Bates sisters. Again.

"Dotty Parsons," said Connie. "I can't quite believe it. She always seemed like the type to go strictly by the book, you know?"

Pete shrugged. He was beginning to wonder about this fabled book. He was beginning to doubt there *was* one. "I don't know what I'm supposed to do. I suppose I could tell Willy and let him worry about it."

"You could."

Pete looked sideways at Connie and winced. A half hour before she had stood in front of Pete's mirror and hacked off most of the rest of her hair with his scissors.

"I want it to grow in even," she'd said.

Pete just wanted it to grow in. Even under his baseball cap it looked like a goat had grazed there.

"But I don't suppose Willy would figure you'd done him any favors," Connie went on.

"No, I don't suppose he would."

"And Willy's an officer of the law. It might be harder for him to turn his back."

"True."

"So maybe you should wait a bit. Nobody says you have to decide things right now, right?"

"Right."

But there *were* some things that did have to be decided right now, and those things weren't any easier. Pete cleared his throat.

"Connie."

Connie swiveled around.

"Last night you said something about liking it here. What does that mean, you like it here?"

Connie's chin rose, but her eyes remained dark shadows under the cap.

"Last winter you said you wanted me back."

Pete cleared his throat again. "I did. I do. But why do you want to do it now? Because you've been beat up? Because it's been kind of nice, me taking care of you, you letting me do it?"

Connie stood up, but not too steadily. "What the *hell* are you trying to say to me, Pete?"

"I'm just trying to figure out if this is the best time for you to be making a decision like this. If this is the best time for us to make it. If you come back, I have to be sure *why* you're coming back. *You* have to be sure. It can't be just because you *like* it here or because at the moment I'm your easy way out."

Connie took six quick paces away from Pete. She stopped and whirled around. "You're kicking me out. That's what you're saying, isn't it? You're kicking me out?"

Pete didn't answer.

Connie turned her back on him, facing the marsh and the still water beyond. She seemed to stay that way, not speaking, for a long time. "I don't mind telling you, this getting kicked out hurts," she said at last.

"I know. I know that."

"Did it hurt this much when I left you?"

"More."

"You're not just getting even?"

"No. I don't think so. No."

"And I suppose I'm fired, too?"

"I can't fire you—you quit, remember?"

Connie laughed, but not as if anything were very funny. Pete patted the stone beside him.

Connie sat back down. "I guess this is just another example of all the rest of it," she said finally. "About everything you've told me about Otto and Warren and Simon and Ella. It's occurred to me there aren't any ogres here. Not even old Alfred or young Alfred. Not Hardy. *Or* Dotty. And not Annabel."

"Or you."

Connie looked at Pete for so long that her eyeballs must have burned from not blinking. *"Or* me. Or you either, even if you are kicking me out. That's what I mean. No matter how mad you want to get, there's no one to get mad *at*. No matter how hard you look, there just aren't any monsters under the bed this time."

"Not even Paula Steigler?"

Connie seemed to think about that for a minute.

"Okay," she said finally. "I guess there is one *snake.*"

221

Chapter

26

Otto Snow was attacking his hedge again. Pete got out of the truck and smoothed out the stained letters Annabel had begun to Alfred Standish.

Pete explained about the letter Alfred Dixon had shown Pete and Connie, and then he showed Alfred the others.

Otto read the letters several times.

"She threw these out, Otto. Along with her marriage license."

"Threw them out?"

"It's just my opinion, of course, but it sounds to me like Annabel ended up pretty comfortable with her decision in the end. She threw the marriage license out. If you ask me, I think she figured out what was important in the end."

"What was that?"

"You, Otto."

Otto looked at the letters one more time.

"Me?"

"You."

Otto handed Pete the letters.

"You can keep them if you want."

Otto shook his head. The motion dislodged a few tears, but they were different tears this time. "Me," he said again.

Pete left Otto alone with his hedge.

What was left of it, anyway.

Hardy Rogers was just getting into his car when Pete pulled in.

"House call?" asked Pete, looking at the battered satchel the doctor held in his hand.

Hardy hefted the bag. "Hospital. Nothing in here but a mess of pens. To use on all those forms. Used to be delivering the baby was all we had to worry about. Medicine's changed a lot since I brought *you* into the world."

Pete squirmed. It wasn't like Hardy to bring up something as embarrassing as Pete's birth. "I won't hold you up. I just wanted to tell you—" Pete stopped. What *did* he want to tell him? That he knew? That he knew Hardy knew? What was the point? "I just wanted to tell you I talked to Dotty Parsons."

Hardy folded himself into the car, slammed the door, fussed with the seat belt, and finally rolled the window down, but only halfway. "Well, Pete? You talked to Dotty. Spit it out. What's on your mind? There's always *something* on it, isn't there? You do love to unload yourself, don't you? Now me, I've found sometimes things sit a little better *on* my mind than off."

"You trust yourself that much? You never doubt your own judgment?"

"I trust myself *and* I doubt my judgment. But I don't spend my life second-guessing myself, and I don't see much point in passing the buck."

No, thought Pete, not to me, anyway. But in a way Pete had *stolen* the buck. And where could *he* pass it?

Hardy peered up at Pete. "Now if you're through not saying whatever it is you came here to not say I suggest you back up and let me get on with my job."

Pete backed up. Hardy settled his hands in the ten and two position on the wheel, a position that made his shoulder bones protrude through his coat. The bones looked frail, not the kind of bones that could carry around a whole lot of weight.

"Take care," said Pete.

Hardy looked up, surprised.

"I mean . . . good luck. I hope this baby's less trouble than I was."

Hardy did some more peering before he spoke. "It was trouble well spent," he said finally, and he backed out of the drive, alone.

There was one more stop Pete wanted to make. *Needed* to make. His old Jeep truck rattled and bumped into Sarah Abrew's drive. Sarah was outside in her gardening clothes, an old denim skirt, white blouse, Keds from before they were in again, large-brimmed straw hat, cotton flowered gloves. She was in her gardening pose, bending over straight from the waist, legs stiff, one arm looped through a flat basket, the other scratching up the earth with a clawed tool. It made Pete's back ache just to look at her. When she heard Pete's truck she straightened up without much bother and walked to meet him.

"See?" She pointed toward a fringe of gray along the outer edge of her small strip of garden. "Connie brought them. From Clara's garden. Heather. I always loved Clara's heather."

"Nice," said Pete.

They stood side by side with Sarah's hand on Pete's arm, looking at the heather.

"I miss them," said Sarah. "Clara. Annabel."

"Me too."

"But I can't seem to feel too sorry for them. In the old days Annabel's heart would have quit long ago. We didn't have all these pills back then. These last years of Annabel's were an extra bonus. A gift. Then, when she went, she went—just like that. Not like Clara. Clara was ready to go a long time ago, Pete. She told me often enough. I can't feel sorry she finally got her wish."

Was this all Pete needed? A disinterested third party corroborating what Dotty Parsons had said—that Clara was ready to go?

"Now me," Sarah went on. "I'm not the least little bit afraid of being dead. It's just how I'm going to get there that occasionally troubles my mind. Not that there's any point worrying about it. Sooner or later I'll be dead, either way."

"Sarah." All of a sudden Pete couldn't take this anymore. He didn't want to talk about dying. He didn't want to talk about *Sarah* dying.

Sarah peered up at Pete from under her straw brim and gave his arm a tweak before she looped hers through it and steered them for the door. "But don't get me wrong, young man. *I'm* not ready to go—not by a long shot! Now are you going to read me that paper or not? We've got town meeting next month. I want to cast an intelligent vote. And don't tell me again how you think the town should purchase that empty old swamp!"

"It's not an old swamp, Sarah. It—"

"Swamp," said Sarah.

They went inside, arm in arm, still arguing about the swamp.

Chapter

27

They were back at Lupo's. The police chief was feeling gabby, which was just fine with Pete. The longer Willy talked, the longer Pete could just sit and listen. He still didn't know what he wanted to say.

"Of course, Steigler reneged on the confession that your wife extracted. But we found enough evidence around the Bates place to make the charges stick."

"You're sure?"

"Sure I'm sure. Those were her tire tracks in the garden. Two of her prints were salvaged off the croquet mallet, along with enough traces of Connie's blood and hair."

Pete made up his mind. He had to at least test the water. "So two of our little mysteries are solved. Paula Steigler. The redhead."

"Yeah, two," said Willy, but he didn't sound too worked up about it.

Pete decided that was a good sign. He stuck in another toe. "And there never really was another mystery, anyway. At least not officially."

"Right."

So was that it? Was it going to be as easy as that?

No, it wasn't.

"The only thing that concerns me at all is Paula Steigler. I hate like hell to hit her with these lesser charges while she gets away with something big."

Pete gave that some thought. "But even if she did do something to Clara, it didn't work. She didn't know about the will. She's not going to get the house or land. Connie *is.*"

The chief waved his hand. "So Steigler doesn't gain. But there's more to it than that if she committed murder."

Pete twisted his beer mug around a few times and then looked up at Willy. "I think I could ease your mind on that point."

Willy squinted at Pete. For a minute Pete suspected Willy wasn't going to ask. One look at his working jaw muscles and Pete knew it was a struggle, but finally Willy said it.

"How so?"

And now it came down to Pete. Should he pass the buck or not? What, after all, did Pete owe the town nurse? But somehow all Pete could picture was Dotty Parsons standing in his driveway looking at the vial of digoxin as he held it in his hand. Dotty had made a difficult decision, but all *she* had gotten out of it was a lot of sweat. She'd continue to sweat, too. What if Ella Cole really had seen someone at the Bates house? What if she'd seen Dotty? What if Hardy Rogers decided to confront the nurse about the falsified notes?

Pete drained his beer and looked his friend in the eye. "What happened to Clara happened with only Clara's interests in mind. No one else's."

And now the buck was Willy's. If he asked for more, would Pete give it?

Willy sat still for a long time, but finally he tipped his mug to Pete, drained it, and left the bar.

Pete heaved a sigh that almost blew his own empty mug off the table. Then he did something he rarely did.

Alone in the booth, he signaled the waitress for one more beer.

Chapter

28

It was the end of August. On Nashtoba the August days were as steamy as a kettle of clams, but by late afternoon people would be shutting their windows, and by nighttime the wool blankets would come out. This knowledge of the late-day drop in temperature didn't seem to help anybody much around noon, however. On the bench in front of Beston's porch Bert Barker fanned himself with the sports page, Evan Spender popped open his third Coke, and Ed Healey swiped at the sheen of sweat that coated every exposed yard of his flesh.

"So Steigler's not contesting the will," said Ed Healey. "I knew it, of course. What with the charges against her, it was a sure bet Connie'd get the Bates place after all."

"You should see what Connie's done already," said Evan. "She's painted the trim, Pete's helping with the roof."

"Convenient location," said Ed.

going to let this go? If he did, was Dotty Parsons going to charge around puncturing people with her syringe, an Angel of Death run amok? The tiny nurse stood up in front of Pete straight and strong and apparently clear-conscienced, but as Pete looked behind the outer ramparts he saw the greater humbleness within. He also saw the fear. Whatever Pete did or didn't do right now, Dotty would always know that he knew, that at any given moment he *could* turn her in. Checks and balances.

And besides, what could Pete do, even if he wanted to? One legitimate vial of digoxin wasn't much in the way of proof.

Pete opened his hand on the vial.

Dotty Parsons took it.

"What's a convenient location?" snapped Bert. He always got cross in the heat.

"The Bates house. Convenient location, just down the beach from Factotum that way."

"She's still working at Factotum? I heard she quit."

"Pete hired her back. Again. But that wasn't what I meant. Not exactly."

"Then what the Christ *did* you mean, Evan? Spit it out!"

Evan elected not to spit anything, but Ed Healey gave a knowing chuckle.

Bert got even crosser. "Oh, what do you old nincompoops know anyway?"

Suddenly Ed Healey heaved his several bellies more tightly on top of each other and peered into the street. "Well, well, well. Speak of the devil!"

Evan and Bert looked. Connie and Pete were just walking out of the Garret Gold antique shop carrying a matching pair of brass table lamps.

"Oh, give it up," said Bert. "Those two are worse than Otto Snow! By the time they get married again they'll be so old they'll die on their honeymoon! In their sleep!"

"I should be so lucky," said Ed.

"I'll say amen to that," said Evan.